Patrick Doherty

Principal English Writings of the Late Rev. P.J. Doherty

Prefaced by a sketch of his life

Patrick Doherty

Principal English Writings of the Late Rev. P.J. Doherty
Prefaced by a sketch of his life

ISBN/EAN: 9783337097318

Printed in Europe, USA, Canada, Australia, Japan

Cover: Foto ©Raphael Reischuk / pixelio.de

More available books at **www.hansebooks.com**

PRINCIPAL ENGLISH WRITINGS

OF THE LATE

REV. P. J. DOHERTY

Patrick John

PREFACED

BY

A SKETCH OF HIS LIFE

" Dilectus Deo et hominibus."

ERIN GO BRAGH

QUEBEC

PRINTED BY L. H. HUOT

Proprietor of "Le Canadien."

1873.

PREFACE.

IMMEDIATELY after Father Doherty's death we published his principal French writings. To-day we are happy to complete our task by giving to the public his English productions. Although Mr. Doherty wrote these pages not dreaming that they would ever be published, yet we believe they are well worthy of perusal, and that they reveal a superior mind and distinguished literary talent. We will say no more here, leaving to the public to appreciate their merits.

At the beginning of this volume will be found the short biographical sketch which preceded his French writings.

L. H. P.

BIOGRAPHICAL SKETCH

OF THE

LATE REV. P. J. DOHERTY. [1]

Consummatus in brevi explevit tempora multa.

Being made perfect, in a short space he fulfilled a long time.

(WISDOM, iv., 13.)

THESE words of Holy Writ meet with their happiest application in the young priest whose recent loss the entire country bitterly deplores. Mr. Doherty lived but a short time, scarcely thirty years from the cradle to the grave ; but in that brief space he managed to group the works and labours of a long and eventful life. If we are to judge the man, the Christian, the priest, not by the number of days which God allots to him, but by the happy use of the talents and powers with which God has enriched him, we may with certainty say that in truth Mr. Doherty is one of those who have lived long in but little time.

[1] This biographical sketch has been translated from the French of the Rev. L. H. Pâquet, professor, Laval University.

Mr. Doherty was born at Quebec on the 2nd of June, 1838. His father, Patrick Doherty, and his mother, Bridget Byrne, had both emigrated from Ireland, bringing with them, as their only treasure, the most unsullied reputation and that unwavering attachment to the Catholic faith which characterizes the noble children of Green Erin.

At the baptismal font he received the traditional name of Patrick. Rejoicing in the birth of this son that she had so often asked from the Lord, his mother desired thenceforward to devote him to the Priesthood, hoping that God would realize the desire of her heart, and would give to her child the precious grace of vocation. That maternal vow, inspired by grace and gratitude, soon began to be realized. Little Patrick had scarcely begun to prattle when he already used to declare, with that childish guilelessness free from all doubt, that he wished to be a priest. Doubtless this was the mother's vow finding an echo on the lips of the child as yet unable to grasp its meaning or its bearing. This believing woman did not fail to see, in the innocent trait we have cited, a presage that made her happy. Her joy was at its height, and her maternal heart dilated with content and happiness, when the child, interrupting the recital of his alphabet upon his mother's knees, used to suddenly turn towards her and say : " Mamma, I assure you that I shall be a " priest, and that I shall preach to you a sermon for " your salvation."

*
* *

Thus it was from the lips of his mother that he received the first rudiments of instruction, and drank in sentiments of the most tender devotion, especially towards the Blessed Virgin. Excellent school, best of all schools, that of a truly Christian mother. Never did he forget the lessons he received then. What the heart helps us to learn is not easily forgotten.

The youthful Patrick, like other children of his age, had, however, to be sent to a public school. Preference was given to that of an excellent Irish Catholic, Mr. Kennedy. This good man's science was, perhaps, a little limited ; but his faith was boundless; and that was, after all, the most important point.

The progress of Patrick, under his new master, was very rapid. He had hardly been three years taking lessons from Mr. Kennedy when the latter said to him, one day : " My dear friend, you must change " your school, because I have now taught you all " that I know."

Patrick bade adieu to the good Mr. Kennedy to enter the school of the Brothers of the Christian Doctrine. Those excellent masters, as modest as they are devoted, prepared him for his first communion. It is impossible to describe the angelic piety with which Patrick, at the age of ten, accomplished that act, so touching,—that act; the most important, perhaps, in the life of a Christian. He was already the model of all his little comrades ; and every one admired the candour of his features, the sweetness of his countenance, the grace of his manners, and the piquant vivacity of his mind. The priests who then ministered in St. Patrick's Church, and the Rev. Mr. McMahon, of illustrious memory, in particular, had not failed to take special notice of the pretty child with the winning ways who took such interest and pleasure in the things of the sanctuary. " What a pity," they used to say to each other, " that so rare a subject should not be placed in the " Seminary ; he would, without doubt, make a " remarkable priest."

Nothing, however, as yet, induced them to urge

the matter. Moreover, the time that Patrick spent at the Brothers' school was not thrown away. There, under the vigilant eye of his masters, germinated in his heart those happy sentiments that his good mother had sown in it at the outset, and which she continued to cultivate in the intervals left to her dear Patrick between school-hours.

Mr. Doherty never forgot the two or three years he passed at the Brothers' school. Nothing could equal the respect he preserved, through life, for those early instructors of his youth. He had for them a sort of veneration; and we heard him describe, quite recently, the lively and salutary impression made upon his mind by those simple and devoted men. "I did not understand all of them," he used to say, amiably; "I did not understand a "word of French; but even when they prayed in "French, I shared, in listening to them, the live- "liest emotions."

Nevertheless, the time had come for him to make a new change in his life. His talents, his application to study, had advanced him rapidly in his classes; and Patrick, for his age, had an amount of instruction sufficient to permit him to embrace the career of trade.

He experienced for a moment the temptation of following that career. Singularly enough, his mother, who had hitherto dreamt of nothing but the Priesthood for her child, appeared to enter into the new views of Patrick, and had even procured him a situation in a commercial house.

But this temptation—for it was one—was soon dissipated. God had special views upon young Patrick: He permitted, in time, a happy intervention, which recalled the son and the mother to their original idea. One of the priests of St. Patrick's

Church, more and more impressed with the dispo-
sitions and qualities of the child, soon induced Mrs.
Doherty to consent that the boy should be placed
as an extern scholar in the Seminary of Quebec.

From the time of his entrance there was not
a moment's hesitation in his mind. He was determined to consecrate himself to God, and he applied
himself more and more to conform his life and
conduct to the sublime calling he wished to
embrace.

He remained as an extern during the entire
course of his studies. During four months only, at
the close of his latter year of philosophy, he
desired to experience the life of an intern, persuaded to adopt that course by M. L. J. Casault, who,
looking upon Mr. Doherty as a future professor of
the Seminary, wished to see him better enabled to
master the rules and inner customs of the house.

His scholastic life may be summed up in a few
words : " He was a perfect pupil." Piety, obedience,
steady application, regularity in the fulfilment of
his duties, brilliancy of talent, amiable modesty,
which enhances two-fold its value and its merits,—
all these qualities were combined in young Patrick
to make of him a model scholar.

Success could not fail to smile on him. He did
not, however, remain content with the ordinary
triumphs that a merely laborious student is sure to
carry off at the close of the scholastic year. His
conduct, ever exemplary, free from every trace of
stiffness or ostentation, procured for him, while he
was yet in *Cinquième*, a medal of honor,—an extra-
ordinary reward for any scholar,— a 'distinction
almost unheard of for an extern. We remember
with what grace and ease he received from the
hands of the Superior that flattering mark of high
distinction from his master. No doubt he was
happy. What would not be his mother's joy on

seeing her dear Patrick thus decorated ? We can, nevertheless, state that his legitimate happiness was not greater than that of his fellow-students.

In fact, he had already gained the affection of all those with whom he had come in contact. Already he had begun to exert over their hearts that gift of fascination which he possessed in so eminent a degree, which later made him, to use the consecrated formula, the friend and favourite of every one. Sincerely beloved by all his fellow-disciples, he was not satisfied with edifying them by his conduct; but he even knew, in their intimate gatherings, how to amuse them in a thousand charming ways, ever new, ever witty.

A character so richly endowed is rarely met with : and we doubt if there could have been found in a youth of his age a finer assemblage of qualities equally solid and amiable.

*
* *

His great talent for writing revealed itself in the first years of his course of studies. He was only in *Troisième* and *Seconde* as yet, when his literary efforts were crowned with remarkable success. In *Rhétorique*, he was thoroughly familiar with the French language ; and we find in the *Abeille*, a little journal edited and printed by the scholars, some of the most charming pieces, where force and wit vie with the most polished elegance.

During his two years of Philosophy he continued to write in the *Abeille*, and was one of its most brilliant editors.

The sojourn and the amusements at the *Petit-Cap de St. Joachim* inspired some of his most delightful productions: one cannot read them without admiring the exhaustless resources of his imagination. It is impossible to find anything prettier or more sparkling.

We shall not undertake to appreciate his writings: we prefer leaving to the reader the pleasure of judging for himself the marvellous facility, the flexibility of expression, the refinement of style, and lastly, and above all, the piquant originality with which he had learned to wield the French tongue.

And yet, strange to say, Patrick did not know one word of that language when, for the first time, he came, a timid and guileless child, to take his seat *en Septième!* Is this not something marvellous, indeed?

It was thus in French that he shivered his first lance as a writer. He did not, however, forget his mother-tongue: the writings he has left in English, and which date chiefly from the last two years of his life, are in no degree inferior to those which French literature owes to him. His letters from Rome, at the time of the Council, his itinerary, will be read with pleasure by any one who can relish the beauties of the language of Shakspeare.

* *

We mentioned, a moment ago, the *Petit-Cap de St. Joachim.* This name sounded very sweetly in the ears of Mr. Doherty. While a very young scholar he began to pass his vacations there : every year, faithful to his love for that little earthly paradise, which nature seems to have created specially for the school-boy in his holidays, our amiable Patrick was the first to arrive. We shall not relate—we never could relate—the thousand and one amusements which he contrived to create there ; all the agreeable tricks he used to devise ; the life and animation that his inventive mind, his endless gaiety, scattered around. As scholar, seminarist, or priest, Mr. Doherty has been, during I cannot say how many vacations, the life and soul of St. Joachim.

The echoes of *Petit-Cap* will long repeat the name
of him who had succeeded, by his never-failing wit,
in rendering the stay at St. Joachim (the dearest
and most popular spot that one could imagine) a
source of the happiest reminiscences.

*
* *

We are far from having exhausted the narrative
of his school-life. We must, nevertheless, pause
here, and follow him in a new phase of his life.
His vocation for the ecclesiastical state, as we have
already seen, was not of recent date, since, while
he was yet on his mother's knees, the idea rose in-
stinctively in his soul, and revealed itself in his first
youthful sallies. He was invested with the *soutane*
in September, 1861, and was immediately appointed
Maître de Salle in the Junior Division, and Professor
of *Sixième.* His first year at the Grand Seminary
was marked by a very serious malady, which brought
him to the verge of the grave, and dealt to his
delicate constitution a fatal blow, from which he
never completely recovered.

After a year's professorship in *Sixième* he was
appointed to teach English in the various classes, an
office that he held during the whole of his sojourn
in the Seminary.

Never did professor excel him in the art of
securing the affection of his pupils. When he was
Maître de Salle, he frequently spent the evening-
recreation at the foot of the *Tribune des Exercices*,
surrounded by a large number of students, narrating
a thousand little stories, which he contrived to em-
bellish and give fresh interest to by episodes invented
on the spur of the moment, and delivered with
inimitable grace. The children took such a lively
interest in these entertainments, that they never
hesitated to sacrifice their most cherished games in
order to listen to the stories of Mr. Doherty.

The year 1864, which was his third year in the *Grand Séminaire*, deserves special mention. Those who, like ourselves, have been in a position to know his scrupulous regularity, his spirit of self-sacrifice and abnegation, will not be surprised to learn that he believed himself called to the religious state. While yet a scholar he had thought of becoming a Jesuit, and spoke of his intention to some of his friends. From the time of his entrance in the Grand Seminary he had been leisurely maturing that idea of his youth. After having prayed, consulted, and obtained the prayers of others, he made up his mind, made generously to God the sacrifice of his liberty, of his friends, his family, and, with one vigorous stroke, shattered the thousand ties that had bound him so strongly to his birth-place. We were more pained than surprised at receiving in Rome a letter in which he informed us of this important decision : « When you shall have received « this letter,» he wrote us, « I shall be a novice with « the Jesuits, with the grace of God, on the 18th July. « Congratulate me, my dear friends, on having been « the object of such kindness from the Lord; for « you know it is a great grace to be called to a re- « ligious life.» And after having commended him- self to our prayers, he bade us adieu before des- cending, with a joyful heart, into that tomb of the noviciate where the young man, singled out by God, must renounce his own will, that he may give him- self up entirely to that of his Divine Master. God was satisfied with the sacrifice. One thing only was wanting in his vocation, an essential thing in the severe life of a Jesuit: it was health.

Four days after his entry in the noviciate he was, as he himself wrote to us, " on his pallet, at- tacked with pleurisy." He was, therefore, compelled to return to the *Grand Séminaire*—not that he re- nounced his cherished idea of becoming a Jesuit, but hoping that time would bring him the necessary strength to follow what he always believed to be his vocation.

Having never gained sufficient health to resume the noviciate thus prematurely interrupted, he had, at least, the consolation of having done all in his power to accomplish the will of God : no doubt he has also, in the eyes of Heaven, the merit of a twofold sacrifice.

Mr. Doherty entered Holy Orders shortly after his return from the noviciate, and added to his baptismal name that of *Joseph*, wishing to ally his devotion for that great saint with that which he ever entertained for the Blessed Virgin.

Ordained Priest on the 11th March, 1865, he celebrated his first Mass in the church of the Ursuline nuns, where, some time previously, as a Deacon, he had delivered his first sermon.

From that epoch dates for Mr. Doherty that active life, that useful and brilliant ministry, which is known to every one, of which all remember the chief acts ; and which was marked, for the few years of his sacerdotal career, by many and signal services to religion.

We have already mentioned the happy character with which Providence had endowed him : he united the finest qualities of the heart and of the intellect. His amiability, the affability of his manners, were equalled only by that Irish wit, so quick, so original, that every one admired, and of which the source appeared inexhaustible. We shall not dwell at greater length on the beauty of his character : suffice it to state what all repeat—he was a charming and unique type of grace and refinement.

Those happy qualities, joined to his talent for writing and speaking, enabled him, even from the beginning of his career, to render to this city and to the Diocese valuable services. Some there were who, through sympathy, perhaps, for his feeble health, thought that he did not sufficiently spare his strength. True, with his indefatigable zeal, he was prodigal of his health. But how can we charge that to him as a crime? That defect, if such it be, is an almost necessary accompaniment of the very finest qualities,—charity, which leads to help others,—the ardent love of God's works, which does not sufficiently weigh the requirements of a frail constitution.

Mr. Doherty, while continuing to teach English in the Seminary, devoted himself to preaching, and won in that ministry the most brilliant success. While yet but Deacon, he desired to inaugurate his pulpit career by the evangelization of the lowly : he preached and conducted alone the services of an entire month of Mary for the *employés* of the Seminary. Those good folks have not forgotten that beautiful act of benevolent charity : they manifested it to him at the time, and they still retain all their gratitude towards him.

He did not, perhaps, possess all the qualities which go to make the transcendent orator : he was certainly deficient in that exuberance of physical strength, more necessary than is generally considered to give to the mind all the spring it feels inert within itself. He supplied the want of such a strength by the resources of his imagination, by the marvellous facility of his diction, and especially by an exhaustless fund of sweet unction, which he owed to his admirable piety and the most tender love for the Blessed Virgin.

It would be absolutely impossible to state the number of sermons, instructions, and homilies that he preached in all the churches of Quebec, and in a great many of the country parishes, both in French and in English. Naturally, even passionately fond of preaching; having the greatest facility in preparation; speaking without the slightest effort, save that of physical strength, which he despised, he was just the man to be invited to preach everywhere, at any moment; and he was too good to refuse.

He preached at St. Patrick's Church a whole Advent and an entire Lent, besides a great many detached sermons, all of which were listened to with admiration by the Irish population. He further gave at the St. Patrick's Institute, of which he was for some time President, many lectures on various subjects, both literary and religious. He ever succeeded, thanks to the immense resources of his mind, in deeply interesting the numerous audiences that always drew after him; and on one or two occasions, amongst others, when it became necessary to defend the Irish race from the unjust attacks of a minister from Montreal, Mr. Irvine, the Hall of the Institute was found too small for the number of those who desired to hear him, and the vast proportions of the Music Hall had to be secured for the occasion.

*
* *

The St. Patrick's Institute did not fail to acknowledge Mr. Doherty's important services on many occasions. Indeed, the special meeting which took place immediately after his death, the resolutions of condolance voted there, the presence of all the members in a body at his funeral, attest how proud were the Irish population to possess within their ranks a young Priest so distinguished as Mr. Doherty.

It is a remarkable fact that he was equally familiar with the French and English languages, either in writing or in speaking. We were even inclined to think that he had a more profound knowledge of the language in which he had pursued his classic studies ; but those who have perused his English writings affirm that the language of Shakspeare had no more secrets for him than that of Bossuet.

He often wrote, as it is well known, to refute error or to combat the calumnies spread in certain journals by prejudiced or ignorant minds. His polemics were always refined, polished, and ever supported by the best argumentation. In order to convey as exact an idea as possible of the labours which occupied Mr. Doherty during the first years of his sacerdotal life, we should mention here several conversions to the Catholic Church, which are due to his skill and to his zeal. One can easily understand the joy he felt on bringing back to the fold those poor strayed sheep. " I think, " he wrote, in May, 1865, upon the conversion of an important personage, who had even been a Minister of the "High Church," " I really believe there is nothing so consoling, so touching, as to behold the abjuration of a Protestant. Let us beseech God to increase the number of those happy returns. " Assuredly, he is now receiving from those whom he recalled to the true faith that powerful aid of prayer which he then invoked for them.

The year 1869 found Mr. Doherty much enfeebled in health. It was evident that his office of Professor, combined with the outside labors which his ardour led him to undertake, was becoming too fatiguing for the delicacy of his constitution. He resolved, but not without grief, to bid adieu to the Seminary, and to devote himself entirely to the sacerdotal functions, of which he had hitherto shared the labours, more through zeal than as a duty.

But, before taking a new position, he wished to visit Europe and the Holy Land. Such had long been his favourite dream. At last he had the happiness to visit Ireland, the land of his fathers ; to assist at the opening of the great Council ; to receive the benediction of the immortal Pontiff ; to embrace with love that sacred soil sprinkled with the blood of Jesus Christ. He performed the voyage as a man of mind and sentiment, not satisfied with the barren admiration that leaves no lasting trace behind it, but seeking to store up for his soul, of a Christian and a Priest, a treasure of precious reminiscences, from which he might continually derive the sweetest and most pious emotions.

Hereafter, doubtless, some one shall publish the narrative of his journey and the letters that he wrote from Rome and from Jerusalem to his sister(¹) and to some friends. We have been happy enough to peruse several of those pages impressed with faith and admirable piety ; of those magnificent descriptions, in which are spread out before you all the wealth of his splendid imagination and all the endless resources of his mind.

We would have wished to reproduce some of those pages ; but, unfortunately for French readers, all that he wrote during his journey is in the English language.

Of his stay at Rome we need mention one incident only : it was the close friendship he formed with the Canadian Zouaves. Those brave and noble youths were not long in discovering in Mr. Doherty one of those minds ever ready to please, with whom social relations are so agreeable.

He obtained among them, and throughout the

(¹) Sister St. Christine, a nun in the Ursuline Convent.

whole battalion, an immense popularity. As is well
known, he returned from Rome in company with
the first detachment of our courageous defenders of
the Pope, and was appointed their chaplain during
the voyage. His name has ever remained an order
of the day with those heroic crusaders of New
France.

*
* *

On his return from Rome, in the spring of 1870,
Mr. Doherty was sent as vicar to St. Catherine's. It
was thought, no doubt, that a sojourn in the country
would be favourable to the recovery of his
health, already endangered. The hope was vain : at
the end of ten months, after having won at St.
Catherine's, as he had done wherever else he had
gone, universal esteem and affection, he returned to
Quebec, to assume, at St. Roch's and the Marine
Hospital, the post left vacant by the death of the
lamented Mr. Joseph Catellier.

He had hardly been installed in his new office
when he was compelled to leave it. It was for him
a new and very painful sacrifice ; but his health
required it. His friends prevailed on him to seek in
the climate of Georgia, U. S., the recovery of his
strength, which was becoming more and more
exhausted. He was absent three months ; and when
he returned, although he was not cured, there was,
nevertheless, a most happy change in his condition.

He was not allowed, however, to again fill the
office of Chaplain to the Marine Hospital ; but he
courageously resumed his former position as vicar
at St. Roch's.

It is there. in that good and religious parish of St.
Roch's, under care the most attentive and the most
likely to restore his health, had such been the will
of God, that Mr. Doherty passed the last year of a
career full of labor and of good works. His friends,
his colleagues, the excellent pastor, who ever

shewed him the most charitable, the most fatherly
attention,—all desired to see him more careful of his
health, more sparing of his strength. But how
could so intense an ardour be moderated? How arrest
and keep in repose that devouring activity which
God had given him, and which he had devoted to
the service of religion? To prevent him from working, to have restrained him from exercising that
ministry unto souls, would have been to render
him unhappy, and, perhaps, to have hastened the
moment of his death. It was better, while regu-
lating his zeal by friendly counsel, to leave it its
necessary scope.

His sojourn at the Parish of St. Roch's had not
been long, scarcely a year since his trip to the South.
Nevertheless, in that short space of time he often
preached, and always with that talent of persuading
and of going straight to the heart which ever distinguished his sermons. During the last Lent, notwithstanding his assiduity at the confessional, he
found time to give to the members of the St. Vincent
de Paul Society a series of conferences, in which
he narrated with graphic clearness the principal inci-
dents of his journey to Rome and to the Holy Land.
He was preparing to preach in the congregation of St.
Roch's for the solemn occasion of the 80th anniversary of the birth of Pius IX., when he felt the
shock of the disease that ended his days.

The entire population of St. Roch's were deeply
attached to him, and loved him sincerely. One could
never be tired of admiring in him that sweet
charity that is ever seeking to console the sorrows
of others,—that indefatigable zeal that never had
any other care than to do good to souls,—that tender and confiding piety which edifies men and
leads them to love God.

We have already briefly mentioned the worship
he had vowed to the Blessed Virgin. It had been

his favourite devotion from the earliest years of his infancy ; and as he advanced in life his love for the Mother of God became more and more lively. His eloquence was admirable whenever he preached upon this subject, so dear to his heart. Whenever he had a grace to obtain, it was to Mary that he addressed himself,—to Mary, in whom he had placed all his confidence, and whose devoted and grateful child he shewed himself during his whole lifetime.

Indeed, it was during the beautiful month of Mary, in fulfilment of the desire he had expressed, that the Blessed Virgin came to withdraw from the world him who loved her tenderly, and who so often, in the pulpit and in the confessional, had excited in the hearts of others the love of that Mother of Mercy. Mr. Doherty was stricken in the very midst of the exercise of the most sacred and the most consoling ministry.

On the evening before Ascension-day, after having heard confessions until a very late hour, he felt the first inroads of the cruel malady that snatched him from the affections of us all.

He literally passed from the confessional to his death-bed. A stronger constitution, a state of health less shaken than his, might have had a chance of escaping the danger.

As to him, already so weak, he was overpowered at once ; and he could not survive the first complication.

He died on the 20th of May, at about midnight, after having been fortified with the last rites of our Holy Religion.

We shall say but little of his obsequies, which attracted to the vast church of St. Roch the most numerous and most fervent concourse it were possible to witness. It can be said that the entire city took part in that demonstration of mourning. Catholics of both origins, mingling their ranks, their

regrets, and their tears, wished to testify, by their
presence, the profound esteem, the sincere affection,
that for many years they had bestowed on this
young Priest, so good and so amiable.

The clergy, in great numbers, after having assisted at the solemn service chanted in the church
of St. Roch, accompanied as far as the Ursuline
Chapel the mortal remains of Mr. Doherty. There,
in peace, his body reposes, under the pious care of
his beloved sister and the good Religious Ladies,
who had always rightly esteemed him ; while his
soul enjoys already, we are confident, the reward
of the Just.

.·.

Our task is ended. May this feeble token of friendship contribute to preserve intact and vivid the
remembrance of the young Priest, whose loss so
painfully affects both religion and our country.

We shall now let him speak for himself,—him
who knew so well how to speak whenever he tried
to enliven or to agreeably amuse, but especially to
instruct and edify ; and we wish for the reader the
same pleasure that we experienced in perusing once
more these pages, sometimes grave, though oftener
gay and lightsome, but always amiable and witty, in
which Mr. Doherty reveals himself with all the
qualities he possessed.

LETTERS

WRITTEN BY THE REV. P. J. DOHERTY DURING HIS TRAVELS

IN EUROPE AND THE HOLY LAND.

DERRY, *October* 12th, 1869.

DEAR ST. C., (¹)

The first great episode is over. The ocean is crossed, and we (²) now sit snugly ensconced in Mrs. Foy's front parlor in Foyle street, Derry-down-Derry. I will give you a rough sketch of our perils by land and sea.

SATURDAY, 3rd *October.*—We left the wharf at 10 A.M., and drifted lazily down the river till about 2 P.M., when the tender brought us the Montreal passengers. Then to the right-about, and we were off at the rate of 13 knots an hour. I felt at first rather lonesome at leaving behind so many kind and loving hearts; but a good dinner set us all in good humour; and after enjoying until night-fall the beautiful panorama the St. Lawrence unfolds in succession, we retired for the night.

SUNDAY. — Arose after six. Morning devotions. Breakfasted at 8½. Weather very rainy, but cleared up about noon. As we passed the several little churches on either side of the river, we united in intention with the devout worshippers who enjoyed the privilege of attending at Holy Mass. Once or twice we caught the sound of the prayer-

(¹) Father Doherty's sister, who is a nun in the Ursuline Convent, Quebec.

(²) Father Doherty had two or three *confrères* as his travelling companions.

bells, and they seemed to tell us, in their own way, of the beautiful link which binds all Christians in the communion of faith and merits. We acknowledged joyfully the dogma, and blessed God for so bounteous a privilege.

At 4 P.M. we stopped at Father Point to send the pilot on shore with the mail-bags, and then the last connection was broken off with America. We must now make the trip whole and entire, save in case of shipwreck. We witnessed, after tea, a glorious sunset: such gold-tipped clouds, such lightly-shifted scenery, such gorgeous heavens! Truly then might we say: " The Heavens are telling the glories of God! "

When darkness set in around us, we sat for a long time at the stern contemplating the phosphorescence that followed in the wake of our ship. A thousand bright sparks, like glow-worms, leap forth at every minute from the boiling surge, and are drowned in the waters, to be immediately succeeded by as many more.

MONDAY.—A little child was buried this morning : it died last night. The burial was not very solemn, as far as ceremonies were concerned; still, there was something impressive in the scene. Poor little thing! just eight months old, and already cast away into that dark rolling flood, there to be for long ages in silent expectancy !

TUESDAY.—The only land in sight is *Belle-Isle*. The fog is very dense, so that we wade cautiously through it all day. At 7 P.M. we arrive at the outermost point, called the *Pointe d'Amour*. We gaze with somewhat of affection on this last stretch of land ; and a feeling of awe creeps over us as we launch at last fully into the dark, dismal, night-covered ocean, so mighty, so trackless, so like eternity, if anything here below can be compared to it.

WEDNESDAY.—Here my manuscript fails until Saturday. The vessel, which had been gliding so gently until now through the waters, began to roll and lurch from side to side. Now, it is all very well to be rocked in infancy ; but manhood cannot stand it, nor womanhood either.

My dear C., if you have a spite against any one, just let me tell you how to punish him. Just get a big cradle, and rock him in it. If he does not cry out for mercy in a precious short time, his heart (not to speak of his stomach) must be less sensible than mine.

Ugh! when I think of it! And how it changed people's manners, too! Staid, sober old fellows, that used to pace the deck with a solemn measure-tread, might now be seen rushing, from time to time, with most indecorous velocity, to the ship's side ; and there they would remain for ten minutes at a time, jerking their bodies, and gazing intently and stupidly into the sea.

Two persons conversing would suddenly turn from one another, and set to......well!—I will not say *what* ; but they would both shew unmistakeable signs of utter disgust ; yet, you would see them the next day as great friends as ever.

And so on until Saturday morning, when every one seemed a little refreshed, and perhaps accustomed to the ship's motion.

Still, I must say that we had a beautiful passage throughout, as far as Sunday, when it began to rain and blow in right good earnest. The winds whistled ; the vessel creaked ; the waves boiled and lashed, until Monday, at 6 o'clock, when we got to the lee of Tory Island, off the north coast of Ireland ; and the rest of the passage was calm enough, though rather tedious, as we did not reach Derry until four o'clock this morning, Tuesday, the 12th October.

We were unfortunate enough to arrive in the

2

. dark, so that we could not enjoy the sight of the north-western coast of Ireland.

Derry, which we have just visited, is a handsome little town of 22,000 inhabitants. Thirty years ago the Catholics were very few in number; now they number 13,000. We visited the Christian Brothers' school, built on the precise spot where St. Columba passed his youth. There are many historic souvenirs connected with Derry. Prominent among them is the great siege, when the Protestant sustainers of William beat back the Jacobites. Two monuments commemorate " the glorious, pious, and immortal memory. "

***

PARIS, Hallow-Eve, 31st Oct., 1869.

My dear St. C.,

......I have seen a great deal of country since last I wrote—Ireland, England, Belgium, Germany, and France ; and my candid, honest opinion of the whole is, that there is no place like home. In fact, whether from fatigue or constant change or cold (for it is very cold here, and has been for the last week), I often found myself wishing that I was once more at home, passing one of those pleasant Sunday evenings such as we used to pass all together last winter. However, let us hope that they will return again—at least for most of us. I always pray, in those beautiful churches we visit, for the whole family and my kind friends, that God may bless and preserve them, and may give me the happiness of returning soon and safely among them once more.

But there is no use in pining; and, indeed, I fear you will think that I have done nothing else than weep and lament for home since I left. It is true that I often think of home, and in dreams I have been back with you—I do not know how often; still,

we have had a great deal of enjoyment, and have
seen many, many strange sights, capable of pro-
ducing lasting impressions and of giving much mo-
mentary pleasure. In this letter I will tell you
about my travels through Ireland only.

DERRY.—I told you in my last that I had landed safe
in Londonderry. It is a beautiful little city, clean
and orderly, and the Catholics are in a majority,
though it is considered the bulwark of Orangeism.
We saw the place where St. Columbkille passed his
youth at his father's castle : it is now occupied by
the Christian Brothers. A beautiful Catholic cathedral is being built a little outside of the city.

From Derry we went down the river Foyle, through
Londonderry, and into the county Tyrone, and
stopped at a handsome little town called Omagh, a
little south of Lough Neagh, celebrated by Moore.
The scenery is delightful all along, and, indeed, all
through Ireland. The grass is certainly greener
than in Canada ; its mountains undulate most gracefully into lovely valleys ; even in the desolation of
the vast bogs there is something sweet and touching. On the hill-tops you see handsome ruins of
old castles and abbeys ; and here and there are the
" round-towers of other days," standing out like
lone sentinels on the mountains.

OMAGH has a population of 13,000, mostly Catholic ;
a handsome church, some fine public buildings,
and a large convent. But it is painful to notice how
fierce party-spirit is everywhere. Protestants and
Catholics are at daggers drawn ; and on the fences,
walls, and sides of houses, you see, written in chalk,
epithets and phrases offensive to one or the other.
Poor Ireland !—it is a pity that her fruitful soil
bears such unhappy fruits of discord.

ARMAGH.—From the county Tyrone we went by
Portadown to the county Armagh, in the midst of
which lies, on four hills, the city of Armagh, an

Irish compound, meaning "The hills of the willows." It was here, as you know, that St. Patrick established his primatial residence ; and, oh ! what a thrill runs through the soul as you catch from the entrance of the town the first sight of the blessed' spot ! But, alas ! though the church he built is still there on its primitive foundation, it is not the church that Patrick adorned by his virtues. It now belongs to the Anglicans, and they have removed many tokens of ancient piety. The cross of stone which he raised in the centre of the town is now lying in a dilapidated condition, near the west end of the cathedral, with the chair from which he taught. I kissed both reverently. On a hill opposite is a very grand Catholic church, in the Gothic style ; it was begun forty years ago by Bishop Crawly, and is now nearly completed.

From Armagh we proceeded down the eastern coast of Ireland, through Dundalk and Drogheda, at the mouth of the river Boyne. The river is famous in history : it has at Drogheda a splendid bridge, nearly as handsome as the great Menai bridge which I saw in Wales some time later.

At about 10 P.M. we reached DUBLIN. I will not attempt to describe Dublin. It would take a whole letter to do it justice. We visited all its beauties : the Four Courts, the Bank, formerly the Parliament, its many churches, Phœnix-park, and Glasnevin cemetery. It is in Glasnevin that O'Connell is buried. A round-tower marks the spot; underneath is a crypt containing his body. I touched his coffin, and brought away a branch of holly that lay on it, after breathing a prayer for the repose of his soul, and for the success of the great cause in the furtherance of which he spent his life.

My companions left me in Dublin. They went on to London, and I continued my journey toward the south of Ireland. I took my ticket from Dub-

lin to Nenagh, a town in Tipperary ; and after passing through Kildare and the King's county, I found
myself among the hills and dales of the most Irish
county of the land.

NESAGH is a very pretty little market-town, of
about 10.000 inhabitants ; and, as I have said, it
lies in the very heart of Tipperary. I was very
much pleased to find here the real genuine Irishman, with all his characteristics, outward and in-
ward. The men—at least the farmers—all wear the
corduroy knee-breeches and swallow-tailed coat
with bright buttons. The dress shews off to great
advantage their fine athletic limbs. The women are
enveloped in the blue cloak with a large hood,
under which you can distinguish a clean white
border of a cap.

Every one appears in good humour : gay laugh-
ter and jokes ring around you on all sides Here
you see the far-famed low back car, drawn by an ass
or a jennet. By the way, there is an immense number of asses in Tipperary ; but, not like in many
other places, they are all quadrupeds. Here, too, you
can see the jaunting-car,—not the jaunting-car of
Dublin, but the *rale* thing, in all its primitive simplicity. There are bell-men, too, in Nenagh ; and I
stopped to listen to one of them, who was giving, in a
sing-song tone, the faithful description of a runaway
dog, *who had been lost or stolen*, with *liver-coloured
hair and a stand-up tail*, and promised a large reward
to the finder.

There was also a ballad-singer under the window
towards night. He sang through hi nose, like a
Yankee pedlar : « *All of a handsome maiden, who
sthrolled down by the purlin' sthrame.* » You cannot
imagine how interesting I found all these things :
they brought me back to the *Traits and Stories* by
Carleton.

I hired a jaunting-car, and rode out among the

mountains, about six Irish miles, to Killeen. I have rarely met such beautiful scenery ; but, in general, the condition of the people is not to be envied, owing to the bad system of the land-tenure. They dare not make any improvements on their farms, for, if they did, the rent would be raised. A gentleman in Nenagh told me that one of the farmers, whose daughter, a fine little girl of 12 years, desired to be sent to the convent, dared not send her ; for, if the landlord thought he was able to educate his daughter, he would make him pay more for the farm he holds. This abominable landlord-right, it is to be hoped, will soon be done away with ; and then the South will be able to compete advantageously with the North.

I next went to LIMERICK. The cathedral, 900 years old, is now in the hands of the Anglicans. I saw the famous *Treaty-stone*. I crossed the Shannon, and examined the fortress, which still bears the marks of some hard fighting.

CORK.—Sweet Cork ! It may not be so large as Dublin, but it certainly is handsomer : its streets are wider than those of the capital, and many of its buildings are fresher and better proportioned. And then there is the river Lee !

" Oh ! the bells of Shandon,
They sound so grand on
The pleasant waters of the river Lee !"

I have seen the Hudson and the Saguenay, the St. Lawrence and the Rhine ; but the river Lee surpasses them all. I drove up the banks of the river as far as Blackrock convent, which is just by the castle, and in sight of the ruins of the castle of O'Connor ; and no one could wish to see anything grander. I saw Blarney-castle, in Sleepy Hollow, a fine old ruin ; but let me be distinctly understood when I say that I *did not* kiss the Blarney-stone.

From Cork I hurried off to WATERFORD ; and, oh!

how shall I describe what I saw there ? How shall I
tell half the kindness, the true Irish hospitality I
met with in the Ursuline Convent of St. Mary? It is
quite a princely building, about two miles out of
town. The interior is beautifully fitted up, and the
new buildings will be really magnificent. But
neither the tall waving trees, nor the rich gardens,
nor the heavenly chapels, nor the beautiful classes,
are anything when compared to the golden hearts
that are shut up in this sweet secluded spot. .... But
I must stop here ; else I would be tempted to write
volumes on all I heard and saw, not to speak of the
classes, in which I had the pleasure of meeting the
pupils. I have often heard of Irish thrushes ; but I
can safely say that no thrush ever sang half so
sweetly as these young Irish ladies.

And now for Kilkenny! It is a charming town,
with a great noble castle. I did not stay long in it,
but started off, through the Queen's county, for
Dublin, and thence for England, passing through
Wales.

———

Lyon, 15 Novembre 1869.

Ma chère Ste. C., ([1])

Je t'ai déjà donné un récit assez sommaire de
mon voyage en Irlande, jusqu'à mon retour à Dublin ; c'est donc là que je veux commencer aujour-
d'hui, après t'avoir dit où je suis et en quelle com-
pagnie je me trouve.

Comme tu peux le voir au haut de la page, nous
sommes dans la bonne ville de Lyon, dans le sud-
est de la France. Cette magnifique cité est remar-
quable, à mon sens, non par la largeur de ses belles
rues, ou l'étendue de ses squares, ou, comme on les

([1]) The few following pages are written in French in the
original manuscript ; we reproduce them as they are.

appelle ici, de ses *Cours ;* non par ses riches manufactures de soieries, dont la renommée est euro-
péenne ; mais par un titre de gloire bien plus haut
que tous ces avantages matériels, bien plus vrai,
bien plus durable que tous ces succès commerciaux.
C'est du sein de Lyon, protégé par Notre-Dame de
Fourvières, que s'est élevée, pour se répandre en-
suite sur toute la terre, la belle œuvre de la Propa-
gation de la Foi !

Et cette œuvre lui vient non pas de quelques-uns
de ces hommes, dont les statues ornent les places pu-
bliques et dont le marbre et le granit conservent les
traits ; mais, comme tu le sais, d'une pauvre petite servante, humble et inconnue. Ah ! chère C., je me
suis dit ici avec plus de conviction que jamais : Le
monde connaît peu ses véritables intérêts ; il erre au
sujet même de ce qu'il a le plus à cœur ! Qu'a-t-il
fait pour toi ce grand Louis XIV, si ce n'est prépa-
rer une révolution qui a failli te broyer sous ses
coups ! Qu'a fait pour toi ce Napoléon, dont l'ambition enlevait tes enfants pour les faire mitrailler sur
le champ de bataille ! Cependant, ce sont là les hé-
ros que tu honores. Mais la pauvre servante qui
attire sur toi tant de bénédictions ; mais cette jeune
fille qui a fait inscrire ton nom dans les annales de
l'Eglise de Dieu ?...... O ingratitude ! O aveugle-
ment !

J'ai parlé tout-à-l'heure de Notre-Dame de Fourvières, la patronne de Lyon. Tu n'es pas sans avoir
entendu parler de ce célèbre sanctuaire, de tous les
miracles qui s'y sont opérés. Eh bien ! Je l'ai vu
ce lieu béni, je m'y suis agenouillé au pied de la
statue antique que la piété des fidèles a si richement
ornée, et j'ai fait brûler un cierge à la chapelle ar-
dente en l'honneur de l'Immaculée Conception de
notre mère à toi à moi et du monde entier.

Lyon est bâti sur les deux rives de la Saône et
du Rhône qui s'unissent à l'extrémité sud de la

ville ; et la vallée des deux fleuves est juste assez
étendue pour qu'on ait pu y asseoir une ville de
120,000 habitants. A chaque côté s'élèvent des
montagnes, et celle qui se trouve à l'ouest prend la
forme d'une falaise très abrupte et haute d'environ
400 pieds. Or, c'est sur la crête de cette montagne
et tout près du bord que s'élève la petite chapelle de
Notre-Dame. Le dôme allongé qui couronne l'é-
glise est surmonté d'une belle statue dorée de la
Ste. Vierge, haute de 18 pieds, et d'un beau travail.
L'intérieur est littéralement couvert d'*ex voto*, fruit
de la reconnaissance pour des faveurs reçues. Tu
vois, chère C., que la bonne Marie est aimée ici
comme chez nous ; et ici comme chez nous et ailleurs on a raison, car elle est bonne partout.

Mais je m'aperçois que je m'attarde trop sur ce
sujet ; j'oublie que je dois te parler de l'Irlande.

J'arrivai à Dublin, du sud de l'Irlande, un mardi
soir ; et comme je voulais à tout prix rencontrer
mes compagnons de voyage en Angleterre, je réso-
lus de prendre le bateau pour Liverpool le soir
même. J'appelai donc un *jaunting-car*, ce qui n'est
ni plus ni moins qu'une voiture ordinaire *tournée à
l'envers*. En effet, l'intérieur de ce char est à l'exté-
rieur, ce qui fait que vous êtes assis à angle droit
avec la route que vous parcourez. Quoiqu'il en soit
et remettant à plus tard une description fidèle de ce
nouvel instrument de supplice, j'engageai donc une
de ces voitures, et donnai ordre au cocher de me
conduire en toute hâte à la gare du chemin de fer
de l'Est. Nous voilà donc à rouler *presto* sur le
pavé glissant de *Eccles-street*. Tout-à-coup le cheval fait un faux pas et va culbuter ; le cocher par-
vient à le retenir dans sa chûte, mais il le fait dévier
de sa route ; le cheval mal affermi sur ses pieds se
dirige vers le trottoir et vient heurter avec violence
un poteau au gaz. Bang ! Pan ! un choc violent,
une secousse terrible, un bruit de tonnerre, et tout

est arrêté. Où suis-je ?...... En voyant dévier le
cheval je prévis que quelque chose de fâcheux pou-
vait arriver, et je sautai lestement sur le haut de la
voiture. Un instant après, le choc avait lieu, em-
portait le siége que je venais de quitter et jetait mon
bagage dans la rue. Si j'étais resté sur le siége,
j'aurais eu pour le moins une jambe broyée. Tu
vois quels périls environnent les voyageurs.

L'accident que je viens de raconter nous retarda
un bon quart d'heure, car le pauvre cheval en était
presque mort. J'arrivai en conséquence trop tard
pour prendre le convoi, et je dus rester à Dublin
jusqu'au lendemain.

A cinq heures, le lendemain, je me faisais éveiller
afin de prendre le train de 5½ h. pour Queenstown.
J'ai vu cette fameuse baie de Dublin qu'on m'avait
vantée au Canada ; et vraiment elle est d'une beau-
té à ravir. Mais j'avais peu d'envie de l'admirer
longtemps, car le temps était très-mauvais, un fort
vent soufflait de l'Angleterre et nous apportait un
froid qui ressemblait à celui du mois de décembre
là-bas au Canada. Et encore était-ce là son moindre
défaut : car il avait soulevé la colère des flots, et
nous eûmes une véritable tempète durant les six
heures de traversée entre Queenstown et Holyhead,
distance de 64 miles.

WALES.—We landed at Holyhead at about 12
o'clock, and, after partaking of a hasty dinner, I
took the train for London. Our journey lay through
Wales, which I crossed from end to end. It is a
most romantic country The gentry of England
come here to pass the bathing-season, and have
built on the cliffs neat country-seats. The mountains were all covered with snow ; there was ice on
the lakes, and the people generally were clad in
their winter garments. We stopped for a time at
Bangor, so famous in the ecclesiastical record of
England's early days of Christianity. You may have

read, in Bede's history, of the Monks of Bangor. They were an obstinate set of men who opposed St. Austin, and clung with all the tenacity of Britons to their ancient customs.

I saw the ruins of Cærnarvon castle. King Edward's son was born here, and received the title of Prince of Wales, which has ever since distinguished the eldest son of England's monarch. You have heard of the famous Menai bridge which connects Anglesea with North Wales, the largest suspension-bridge in the world, and one of its wonders. I saw it in all its beauty, amid the wild scenery of its surroundings. We next came to Shrewsbury : its mountains are very grand, and in some places resemble the Alps on a small scale.

We next arrived at CHESTER, an old, dilapidated town, full of the ruins of ancient monasteries and convents. But the matin, chimes, nor vesper-bells are no longer heard. The old monks lie buried in the crypts ; and above them, in the cloisters, resound the noise and bustle of commerce. From Chester the road lies south-east to London, passing through well-tilled fields and noble parks, with neat little brick towns here and there. And at last we were in the great metropolis of the commercial world.

LONDON.—Fancy one single city having as many inhabitants as all Canada !—upwards of 3,000,000 people agglomerated in one great, heaving, noisy city !—streets that extend miles and miles, lighted with gas ; shops with every article of use or luxury ; buyers and sellers, wine-merchants, clothing-stores, cutlery, silverware, hair-dressers, tailors, shoe-makers ; men howling out, at the top of their voices, the merits of their merchandize ; women begging of you to buy wares ; little boys screeching out the name of their newspapers ; omnibuses, cabbies, police-men, soldiers ; crowds here and there and every-where, jostling, jolting, laughing, talking. Good

God !—what a hubbub ! I thought Chicago a noisy
city, and was glad to get out of it ; but it is as the
silent desert compared to London.

I visited all the principal and most interesting
things in London ; and of them I will give you, at a
later period, a true and faithful description.(¹)

From London, where I rejoined my companions,
we went to Canterbury, where St. Augustin established his Primatial See. The church is still
standing ; but, like in Armagh, it has changed hands.
It was in this church that St. Thomas-à-Becket was
murdered. Here, also, St. Augustin baptised the
Queen of Kent, Bertha.

Dover resembles Quebec to a certain extent. Its
fine chalk cliffs have a fine effect by moonlight ; and
from the heights we distinguished the coast of
France.

BELGIUM.—We sailed from Dover to Ostend, a sea-
port town in Belgium ; and on the passage across
I really, for a time, gave myself up for lost. We had
a very heavy sea and a raging tempest. I got very
sick, and was lying in the cabin when a tremendous
wave struck the vessel. The engine broke, and the
water came pouring in. You may imagine that we
all rushed on deck, and found everything in confusion. The pumps were working fast and strong ;
the ship was rolling fearfully, and the sea breaking
over her. The boats were loosened in case of need, and
everything prepared for the worst. I knelt down
in the water, and offered up my life to God, the

(¹) No doubt it was the intention of Mr. Doherty to complete
his notes at some future time ; but the rapidity of his travelling and the delicate state of his health did not allow him to do
it. All this first part of his relation is very brief and rather in-
complete : we give it, however, such as it is ; and we have only
to regret that sickness and premature death prevented Father
Doherty from adding to his written relation the thousand
interesting details which his friends so often heard from his
lips.

Master of all. I need not tell you how vividly the remembrance of friends and relations rushed across my mind at that moment, and how miserable all the pleasures of the world appeared in the face of eternity. Would you believe it?—the only thing that seemed worthy of a thought, at that supreme moment, was a small alms I had given to a poor woman during the day. The panic lasted about half an hour, when the engine was made all right, and the vessel continued her journey. Still, we all kept wishing for land, and were very glad to arrive, though cold and wet, at 3 o'clock in the morning, after a perilous voyage of nearly 7 hours.

We had to pass through the custom-house ordeal at Ostend ; but the Belgian officials are extremely polite and liberal. Indeed, the « whole affair » in Belgium is on liberal principles, if principles can in reality be called *liberal*. I do not think so ; for, in itself, a principle is the most exclusive thing in the world ; and, in practice, it is, I believe, pretty clear that those who advocate *liberty*, or *liberality*, as they call it, are, in general, found to possess very little of either the one or the other. Thus, the constitution of Belgium admits of everything and every one : you may do and say as you like ; you may publicly reverence God or blaspheme Him, as you wish ; you may hold and propound any doctrine you please, from the wildest atheism to the purest ascetism. The king reigns by the will of the people, and, consequently, only does what the people wish. All this looks very nice on paper, but, in the execution of its ordinances, has done very little toward the furtherance of happiness in the kingdom. There was less beggary and more order in former times ; for, when a people is left entirely free, they become a great wild urchin, uneducated and wicked ; and wickedness engenders misery.

But I am standing here philosophising in the cold,

while I should be looking after my ticket for
Bruges. We all look mighty blue, and have still
two long hours to wait for the 7-o'clock train. The
town is plunged in profound sleep, save and except
a few coffee-houses, called *estaminets*, of a very doubtful character, whence the sounds of drunken
carousing mounts into the pure morning-air with
the fumes of bad tobacco and worse whisky. At
6 o'clock the stillness is broken by the tolling of
the *Angelus*. We recite the beautiful prayer all
together; and it reminds us of our home beyond
the waters, and of our true home in heaven.

There is a stir in the streets; the shadows of
night fade away; the train arrives from the interior;
now there is a bustle of passengers and baggage.
We buy our tickets, stow away our portmanteaus,
get into a *coupé*, and are whirled away, at the rate of
30 miles an hour, towards Bruges.

Belgium is a very level country, and well cultivated; but the lack of hills and mountains makes
it at least monotonous in the extreme. Two hours
bring us to Bruges; and here begin our troubles.
We are surrounded by beggars and *portefaix*. Men,
clad in white shirts and wooden shoes, call themselves *commissionnaires*, and beg of us to allow them
to carry our baggage to any house we will please
to mention. We have great difficulty in shaking
them off, and proceed on foot to a hotel, opposite
the station, called the *Singe d'Or*. Here our first
thought is for a good sleep. We are shewn to our
respective rooms, and are soon wrapt in a refreshing
slumber that lasts until mid-day.

The population of Bruges is about 30,000. The
people speak French and a most abominable con-
catenation of unearthy sounds called Flemish. Lord
deliver me from ever learning such a language!
The working-class wear *blouses*, blue or white, and
great wooden shoes, like canoes. The women have

large blue cloaks, such as I saw in Tipperary ; a great many go bareheaded.

We visited a couple of churches, for which visit we had to pay dear; for here the churches are closed from 12 o'clock A.M. till 3 P.M. ; and you are totally left to the tender mercies of the old *Sacristain* if you wish to penetrate into them at this time. They contained nothing very remarkable, except the paintings, which are, indeed, very remarkable for the corpulency and round Dutch build of the saints and angels. There is, however, one very handsome work in St. Michael's church : it is a Madonna with raised weeping eyes. The tears are done to life: you would imagine, on a near approach, that they were drops of water which had just fallen or been placed on the *tableau.* There is a high Gothic tower with a beautiful chime of bells ; but we did not ascend it, for we wished to catch the 4-o'clock train for Brussels. The most remarkable feature of our visit to Bruges was, undoubtedly, our wars with the officious guides. As a rule, we never had less than three at a time offering to conduct us anywhere and everywhere. We abused them; called them illnames ; told them they should be working to gain an honest living, instead of thus idling about the streets, &c., &c. But all was of no use ; they *would* follow us ; they *would* persist in shewing us what we could plainly see ourselves, until at last we had to threaten personal violence. My immense size and warlike demeanour had a salutary effect on their nerves ; so they beat a hasty retreat.

From Bruges we took tickets direct for Brussels, the capital of Belgium, at which we arrived, passing by Ghent, at 6 o'clock in the evening. The next morning we were up early, and went to hear mass in a fine old Gothic church belonging to a community of nuns, whose name I forget. As we were leaving the church we were accosted by a gentleman who called himself *Monsieur Colas*. He said that he presumed we were strangers, and knew we were Catholics by the fact of our assisting at mass. We told him we were priests from Canada; and he thereupon informed us that he was president of the St. Vincent of Paul's Society, and would be happy to be of service, if we wished it, in shewing us over the city. We accepted, with thanks, and found him extremely well-informed and very polite.

We first visited the market-place in front of the City-Hall. The building is pure Gothic, and dates. from the sixteenth century. The three other sides of the square are bordered by houses bearing the marks of the ancient guilds; these are equally of the middle-ages. In those days of simple faith no one was ashamed of his profession. Religion had taught each one that the will of God had placed him in the position he held; and he was not only content, but happy, in the exercise of the duties it imposed upon him. The shoemaker was satisfied with making shoes; the cutler with making knives; the tailor with *suiting* his customers. In their honest pride, the different members of the various guilds or trades adorned their houses with symbolic marks of their profession, that their children, after them, might remember how their fathers gained their livelihood by honest industry.

And not only did this bring happiness to the individuals, but it reflected and secured happiness to society. There was no false ambition no—constant striving to attain the first rank in the community : hence those great upheavings of society were then unknown. This idea was carried out in every sphere. The farmer's wife did not dress like the knight's daughter ; yet, though she was not decked out in silks and fine cloth, she was just as much respected. But those days have gone by : since other teachers than the Church hold the ear of the people, they have been taught other doctrines ; the ideas of classification have been voted *old* and out of fashion ; they have been called the *sovereign people.* Every man is equal, say the demagogues; every man has a right to aspire to the highest position. Thus, drawing false conclusions from a trueism, they corrupted the minds of the masses, inspired them with unlawful ambition, enkindled in every breast the lust of power, and sowed the seeds of those fierce revolutions that have swept through nations like dread hurricanes, unseating authority, and engendering poverty, misery, and crime.

We then visited the cathedral church of St. Gudule. It is a magnificent Gothic structure, and, standing on the face of a hill, it towers over the greater part of the city. The two most remarkable features, apart from the triumphs of architecture, which it contains, are the pulpit and the holy chapel. The pulpit, in blackened oak, is quite an object of curiosity. A large palm-tree, about 40 feet high, holds the body, or box, where the preacher stands, and around which are carved representations of the seven deadly sins. Below are life-size statues of Adam and Eve, in the attitude of repentance. A large serpent is entwined all round the tree ; its head reaches the top, where it is crushed by the Blessed Virgin. This, with the figure of Death, which is the fruit of sin, completes the whole work, and gives the full history of the original fall, its consequences, and the final triumph of grace.

The royal palace is very handsome ; but, at this moment, it is the abode of mourning. The king has recently lost his only son and heir, a child of nine years of age. Poor parents!—they may, one day, rejoice for what now causes them so much grief! In front of the palace is the square, a vast public promenade, overshadowed by stately oaks. The. statue of Godefroi de Bouillon stands at the principal entrance ; for, as you know, this is the native place.of the noble crusader, whose example has been followed by the Belgian Zouaves.

The streets in the new part of the town are wide and clean. The jewellers' shops are filled with exquisitely—carved objects, in gold and silver. The flower-market is tasteful and brilliant. The street called «La rue de la Reine» is covered in, from end to end, with a glass roof. Of course, the Brussels carpets and laces abound everywhere. We bade adieu to Mr. Colas, and returned to the hotel, well satisfied with our promenade.

We next took tickets for Louvain, the seat of the celebrated University, and arrived there at two o'clock in the evening. The cathedral is an old Gothic building, with some pretensions to grandeur. But the gables and contreforts are too numerous, while its crumbling walls detract from its beauty. The sight of an abandoned ruin is pleasant : there is something suggestive in the ivy-crowned walls and maimed turrets ; but a church still open to service should, I think, be kept fresh and repaired ; otherwise, it seems a silent reproach to the faithful who worship in it. The University is the chief attraction of the city. We had not, however, time to visit its different departments, as they are scattered, here and there, in different quarters of the town. The library is valuable, and contains 200,000 volumes,—at least the guardian said so, and I thought it just as well to believe him as to take the trouble to count them. It was here we first heard of the celebrated Troppman murder, and we saw the photographs of the victims and their assassin.

PRUSSIA.—We next partook of a frugal dinner at the hotel, and set out for Aix-la-Chapelle, the city of Charlemagne. On our arrival we were introduced to the Prussian officials, with whom we performed pantomime, not being conversant with

each other's language. It became an understood
thing between us, however, that we were not
contraband, and were in quest of a good hotel.
So they allowed us to pass, and we reached
" L'Eléphant d'Or " at 6½ o'clock P.M., and were
shewn to our rooms. After a copious supper in German, we set about taking notes of the day's travel.
We were all of one opinion concerning the flatness of
the country and the high state of cultivation of the
fields and meadows. We had admired the shepherds
and their dogs attending their flocks, and the neat
little villages scattered here and there. There are
no fences in Germany, and, indeed, no visible
boundary-lines between the properties of different
people ; but I suppose that the Germans, who
are a very profound people, have found some
metaphysical method of making things all right.
You and I, dear C., have often heard of what is
called *« Des chicanes d'Allemands »* which intends to
insinuate that the Germans are prone to quarrel
about matters of the slightest importance ; but the
good-nature and liberality I noticed everywhere
leads me to believe that the *dicton* is at fault, or
conveys an idea totally different from the popular
acceptation.

Every third person wears an uniform of some
sort or other ; and, indeed, everything is carried out
in the most uniform manner. In Prussia, all is on
the clock-work system : the railroad-agents, at least,
and the conductors, are, I am sure, every one of
them, wound up with a key ; and as for the
soldiers, they certainly are on wires. The care that
is taken of passengers, and the supervision that is
exercised over them, would be very consoling if it
were not, at times, vexatious. If you smoke in the
cars, you must put the ashes of your cigar into a
little tin-box ; if you expectorate, you are required
to do so in a certain place. You must not move

from your seat until the conductor opens the door; and, during the transit, he thrusts his head into the *coupé* every five minutes—to see, I suppose, if you are not standing on your head or chewing gum.

The next morning we all went to church in Sunday rigging. We had our *testimonials* with us, so that the priests made not the least difficulty about our saying mass. I celebrated the Holy Mysteries in the Jesuits' church, and afterwards attended Grand Mass in the Cathedral. The bishop had already left for Rome; but the Chapter of Canons carried on the ceremonies with almost episcopal dignity and *éclat*. A man, dressed in flaming red from top to toe, preceded the celebrant; then came two yeomen in cocked hats; then followed two deacons, two sub-deacons, a host of minor servants, and, finally, the canon who said mass. The ceremonies were very imposing. We were introduced into the sanctuary, though we did not wear the ecclesiastical dress; so that we enjoyed a full sight of all that was going on. Although my voice is far from being good, dear C., as you know yourself, and often remarked, yet I joined in the chant of the *Kyrie*, the *Gloria*, and especially the *Credo*,—not exactly with the purpose of swelling the chorus, but to give vent to my feelings. My heart was full. I had come from the distant shores of America, and was now in the midst of Germany. I did not understand a word of the language of the country : the customs and manners of those around me were new; they had other thoughts than I on many subjects, and other aspirations; and, notwithstanding, as soon as they joined in prayer, we were brothers ; our faith, hope and love became mingled and united ; we were no longer strangers, but members of the one fold, participating in the same sacraments, acknowledging the same Head. Never did the beautiful unity of Holy Mother-Church strike me more forcibly. Never did

I join in the recitation of tho *Credo* with more joy and thanksgiving.

The church is very old. It was begun by Charlemagne in the eighth century. His tomb is here, and also many relics of the great emperor. We saw his skull, enclosed in a golden bust. The treasury is exceedingly rich. I bought a little book describing all it contains; and as I bring it home, I refrain from giving any account of it here. The choir has been lately restored, and is very handsome. The windows (there are four, besides the chancel) are sixty feet high ; the stained glass is a work of great merit. The two subjects I admired the most were tho « Assumption of the Blessed-Virgin » and the « Proclamation of the Dogma of the Immaculate Conception. » The figures are all life-size : the portrait of the Pope is perfect.

After dinner we went to visit the city : it is small and irregular. The shops were all open, though the piety of the people, their attendance at mass, and their respectful demeanour, had edified us. The population amounts to 60,000, almost all Catholics. Apart from the churches and the town-hall, there are no great objects of interest. So we made but a short stay, and started for Cologne, on the Rhine.

We arrived in the middle of a shower of rain, and were conveyed from the railroad-station to the « Hôtel du Dôme,» about three minutes' walk from the great cathedral, the vast proportions of which seemed to acquire more than usual grandeur, seen through the mist that surrounded them. I need not give you a description of this « work of ages.» It is the most perfect specimen of Gothic architecture in the world. It is 511 feet long by 230 wide. The towers on the front are not yet finished ; when they will have been completed, the top of the edifice will be 500 feet above the level of the square. To me the Gothic style has ever seemed best adapted to churches. It sprang from Christian art; it symbolizes Christian ascetism; its slight vaults bear aloft the voice of prayer; its slight airy colonnettes shoot up heavenward, like ejaculatory aspirations of the heart; it makes of the temple a house of prayer. But there is something specially overawing in viewing this, the triumph of art, filled on a Sunday evening, as twilight descends, by thousands of pious Christians, kneeling in prayer before the Blessed Sacrament. A solemn benediction was being given as we entered: the voices of little children mingled with a powerful but sweet-toned organ, singing the Litanies of the Blessed Virgin. Then the *Tantum Ergo* was taken up by the whole multitude; the incense rose in curling wreaths; the little bell tinkled; and, as I bowed to the ground in unison with all, I thanked God that I again found the same faith and worship as in very-far-off home. There are four naves and a middle aisle in the church. The chapel of the three wise kings of the East is to the right. Tradition says that they lie buried beneath a handsome altar near the choir.

Many of the streets of Cologne are so narrow that two persons can hardly pass abreast; but others are wide and spacious. There is, as in Brussels, a handsome street vaulted in with glass.

We visited a church dedicated to St. Ursula and the 11,000 virgins: it is old, but is being repaired.

Several churches were filled with little children attending mass, under the supervision of their masters; they sang sweet little German hymns with a very pleasing effect. Altogether there is a quaint mediæval air about the city and its inhabitants, very much in harmony with their great cathedral.

We were here first introduced to a complication of coinage, which I defy any traveller to make head or tail of. We had silver *grotchen* and another kind of *grotchen;* we had *kreutzers* and *thalers,* and *florins* worth 2s. 1d. and *florins* worth 2s. 8d., and a host of other little coins, all pronounced with the most forcible guttural sounds. Indeed, the only thing you have to do is to give a couple of sovereigns to the person you deal with, and trust to his honesty for the right change. I think that this was one of our chief reasons, for beating a hasty retreat from the city, to which must be added the desire of becoming acquainted with the glorious scenery of the Rhine. I will not, however, undertake a description of the day's travel along the banks of the beautiful river from Cologne to Mayence ; for I bought you a book with photographic views and a full account of the names of the different fortresses and towns that border it.

We made two stoppages, so as to enjoy the scenery and visit the principal towns. At Bingen, where the mountains begin to recede from the river-side, I remembered the lay of the Irish poetess, which I had so much admired last winter in our readings at the Institute. The scenery is enchanting. The river makes a grand curve, forming a sort of basin, closed in, on each side, by a lovely green valley, on which repose gracefully neat little villages. In the distance are the vine-clad mountains, topped with old castle-ruins that date from the times of Roman power.

The two chief towns are Coblentz and Mayence. Coblentz is built, like Quebec, at the junction of two rivers. The blue Moselle here joins the green waters of the Rhine, and you can distinguish the point of union by a reddish streak near the mouth of the former. A bridge of boats brings you to the foot of a frowning citadel.

Mayence is one of the great fortress-towns of Prussia. It is a sort of perpetual challenge to France not to cross the Rhine. The town is swarming with soldiers, great, stout, thick-built men, that look as if they could fight and had fought well. The cathedral is not handsome, though the hotel-keeper assured us that it was one of the finest in Germany. The only thing I found worth remarking was a statue of Guttenberg, the inventor of the art of printing. We were in his native city—at least they told us so. From my hotel-window I had a splendid view of the Rhine. There was a great deal of bustling and commerce going on in the streets and away across the bridge that opens the route from Mayence to Frankfort. The market was full of grapes, so tempting in their luscious ripeness that I bought a whole armful of them from a little German woman in a white cap. I handed over the equivalent of sixpence in silver, and she gave me so much change in small coin that I thought she was paying me for buying them from her. Money is so subdivided here, that the unity might be classed amongst what our professor of mathematics used to call *les infiniment petits.*

The weather was cold and rainy ; so we sacrificed our desire of seeing the citadel, with its Roman antiquities, to that of going further south in search of heat. Accordingly, we set out for Strasbourg, the frontier-town of France in this locality, and arrived there late in the evening, having bidden adieu to Germany and its gutturals. I cannot say much on the country, for we did not stay long enough to form an intelligent opinion of the people. But one thing became evident, from the little intercourse I had with those who spoke French : this was an intense and undisguised hatred for France and the French people. They appear eager for a war, and boast roundly that the event of the struggle would be a complete establishment of the superiority of the Prussian over the French soldier.

FRANCE.

We were, of course, in raptures at finding ourselves once more in a country where we could make
ourselves understood without having recourse to
an interpreter. It is a great bore not to be able
to speak the language of the people among whom
you are travelling : you immediately become, as it
were, deaf and dumb ; you cannot glean any infor-
mation concerning the country or its inhabitants
from your fellow-travellers ; and if you question the
agents about the starting of the trains, the names
and qualities of the hotels, &c., your only answer is
a shrug of the shoulders or a sort of disdainful
silence.

Strasbourg has a strong French garrison, and has
a number of iron foundries. The people are very
proud of their splendid cathedral and the great
astronomical clock it contains—one of the wonders
of the world.

I mounted to the very top of the steeple to get a
view of the country around about, and was rewarded
for my pains by being nearly frozen to death and
blinded by a furious snow-storm. I will not describe the clock nor the church, for I bought a little
brochure which gives you a full account of both. I
did this everywhere I could, dear C., both for your
sake and mine ; for it saved me the trouble of
writing, and it assures you a more complete description of the places. I may remark, however, that
the clock of Strasbourg is a thing which must be
seen to form an idea of its wonderful perfection.

Next day we started for Nancy ; and here our
caravan divided, two of our fellow-travellers having
gone direct to Paris, whilst I and Dr. B. took tickets
for Metz, *en route* for the Duchy of Luxembourg.
There are formidable fortifications all round Metz ;

3

indeed, it is quite a triumph of military genius, and it would be hard to conceive how the largest besieging army could penetrate into the place. The population is about 40,000. We suffered much from the cold, for there was ice in our basins in the morning, and my poor nose was as blue as a blue-bag when I came down to breakfast. By good chance, the hotel-keeper was most polite : he introduced us to his family, and made us as comfortable as could be expected. He treated us to five or six sorts of wine, among which was a glass of the veritable *Chartreuse*. We saw the town from end to end ; but, apart from the fortifications, the esplanades, and some iron foundries, there is nothing remarkable.

We then started for Luxembourg, passing through the Ardennes, and catching, now and then, a sight of the Meuse as it meanders through the valleys. We passed the plains of Fontenoy, so famous by the brilliant victory gained by the Irish brigade, in the service of Louis XV., over the allied troops of Germany and England. At two o'clock we entered the Duchy of Luxembourg, now under the protectorate of the King of Hanover. The fortress, once impregnable, has 'fallen before the exigencies of the jealous politicians of Europe : it is now almost completely dismantled. But Luxembourg belongs neither to France nor to Prussia. It is a miniature free State, and its miniature sovereign is as proud of his position as was imperial Cæsar in times gone by. The miniature army, composed of 250 men, have as proud a step and as fierce moustaches as the Roman legions in the days of Augustus ; and the miniature parliament discusses the interests of state with as much vehemence and acrimony as if the fate of Europe depended on their vote. The local papers were most amusing, from the fierce invectives they indulged in : one mildly styled the other a *traitor to his country;* the other retorted by reminding his adversary that he was the *corrupted* slave of power. When we left, the quarrel was undecided ; but we, nevertheless, took tickets for Metz, where we passed another night with our kind host and his family.

From Metz we went to Rheims, and put up at the hotel in which the father and mother of Jeanne d'Arc resided during the coronation of King Charles. Rheims is the head-quarters of Champagne, and, in honour of the event, we presented ourselves with a bottle of real *Champagne,*—no New-York adulteration, but the real *Simon-pur.* It is delicious, and only costs five francs a bottle. The cathedral of Rheims is one of the most splendid Gothic buildings of France. Many kings have been crowned at the high-altar; the last was Charles X.; the first, as you remember, was Clovis, who was baptised by St. Rémi. I saw the tomb and relics of the good saint. There are also in the treasury of the church many precious souvenirs of olden times.

The Archbishop's palace, with its suite of royal apartments, is decidedly grand. The public squares and promenades of the city are large and well kept. The population amounts to more than 200,000.

At last we were on the direct line of the great capital of the world, as the Parisians call their city. Paris, with its wonders, was within a half-day's journey ; and it was not without some degree of emotion that we stepped from the *coupé* as the train stopped underneath the beautiful station of the western district of the imperial city. We drove to the hotel of «Bon Lafontaine,» and there found our two companions, who had arrived the previous day.

Our first visit, next morning, was to the church of «Notre-Dame-des-Victoires,» where we said Mass, in thanksgiving for this part of our journey, so happily accomplished. (¹)

(¹) There is nothing more in Mr. Doherty's manuscript con-

ROME, 24th *November*, 1869.

My dear friend,

We arrived in Rome last night, eight of us—five priests, two doctors, and a bishop. We had been together all through Upper Italy and the South of France.

I had a moonlight trip on a gondola in the salt-water streets of Venice. It is something that cannot be described. For my part, I do not think anything can be more beautiful.

We came here from the far-famed shrine of Loreto. I said Mass there in honor of the Blessed Virgin. I stood in the very room where «The Angel of the Lord declared unto Mary,» - where the little Jesus lived and grew up in grace and virtue—where He *obeyed* Mary and Joseph. Oh! the thrill that those old blackened walls send through you, as you stand in their midst! They are covered outside with the richest marbles, and gold and silver lamps and ornaments are in abundance.

The plains of Castelfidardo are quite close—say a couple of miles distant. We visited them, walked over them, saw the trees with the marks of the bullets, prayed over the tombs of the fallen braves; and then we left for Ancona, where Lamoricière made his last stand.

But what caused me the greatest plaesure was the sight of the «Rock of Spoleto,» where Major O'Reilly

cerning Paris and the other parts of France which he visited. Want of time and fatigue from rapid travelling prevented him then from noting down his impressions of the French people and their country. He travelled also throughout Northern Italy, and arrived in Rome on the 23rd November, whence he wrote to a friend the annexed letter. On the 30th of the same month he went to Naples, where he spent a few days before the opening of the Council. From Naples he addressed to the friend just mentioned a very witty letter, which we are glad to be able to reproduce.

and his Irish brigade stopped the whole Sardinian army, and surrendered only when resistance was useless. The citadel they defended is there still. I pictured to myself—as I stood close by the scene—ten years ago. I fancied I heard the rattle of musketry, the booming of cannon, and the tramp of soldiery. I then listened, and heard, above the hoarse voice of war, ringing from out the blaze of battle, that wild clear Irish cheer. that has so often resounded on the battle-plains of Europe and America. All is silent now and peaceful. But the living wrong remains, and will remain as long as the fair fields and fertile hills of this lovely country are in the hands of the robber-king.

———

NAPLES, 30*th November*, 1869.

My dear friend,

I am in a sort of *doldrum*. I arrived at Naples this evening,—and what do you think ?· You might be hanged for guessing, and never make it out. The whole town was illuminated !···Chinese and Venetian lamp-burners at every corner,—music playing,—crowded thoroughfares,—in a word, the greatest sight you ever saw, even in Connaught. You know how naturally timid and retiring I am in my disposition ; you may, therefore, fancy how confused I felt at so flattering a reception. Of course they told me at the hotel that the rejoicings were for the birth of the young prince of Naples. But I know better. The Piedmontese government probably got news of my coming, and hence all the hubbub. It is very annoying, I assure you ; still, one must put up with it. If the government *will* be foolish, and if the people *will* burn gas and olive-oil, how can I help it ? The only thing that surprises me is, how did they get wind of my coming ? I suppose it is a trick of yours, or some of St. C.'s doings. I wish to goodness you could keep your tongues to yourselves;

you would save me a deal of unnecessary blushing, and the government a great deal of lamp-oil.

But, rationally speaking, I have just witnessed a most splendid illumination. You can have no idea of what taste those Italians can display. A splendid street, about as wide as Crown-street, in St. Roch's, with six-story houses on each side, two miles long (not the houses, but the street), and as straight as the last broom-handle that your wife broke on your back (I hope), was brilliantly lit up from end to end. Gas-burners, shaped into all kinds of forms ; lamps of every color, simulating roses, lilies, snow-balls, etc., etc., etc., festooning the houses ; thousands of ill and well-dressed people in the highest glee,—and all this on a dark night, contrasting with the dark pall overhead ; the glorious bay of Naples, in the fore-ground, dotted with the glimmering lights hung from the masts; and, towering above all, the great volcano, with its lurid volume of fire jutting straight up, like the warning-voice of Death, mingling with the shouts of pleasure—or, if you wish, like an expiring candle in a black-tin candlestick ;—this is what I have just seen.

To-morrow myself and two French priests proceed to visit the ruins of Pompeii and ascend the burning crater of the volcano.

We left Rome this morning. I have not yet obtained an audience. I expect to see His Holiness with our dear archbishop, whom may God bless and preserve. I saw Pius the IXth on Sunday, in St. Peter's. It was like a glimpse of heaven. He was carrying the Blessed Sacrament. Oh ! such a crush of people ! I thought, at one time, that I was going to be turned into a six-inch-thick plant. As for my hat...... well...... I will not say it was made as flat as a pancake, for I often ate pancakes a good deal thicker. However, it may be a consolation for you to know that I was instrumental in flattening a

few of my neighbours'. One fat old monk will bear
my impress, I think, to the day of his death. I was
actually ground into him. And such groans!—good
gracious!
    I visited the Catacombs the day before yesterday.
It is a solemn sight, and a fit pendant to the visit
paid to the Coliseum. The ruins of the Coliseum
recall the heroic struggles of the Martyrs of Christ;
its sands were reddened by their glorious blood;
but, when the wild beasts had torn them, in their
rage, amid the infuriated shouts of 100,000 spectators, the huge mob retired, satiated with blood, and
then the mangled remains were stealthily gathered
by some pious friends, and borne away to this
silent abode. Here, in the under-ground chapels,
the funeral-rites were perfomed, and they were
laid in the crypts that border the alley. Oh! how
glad, how proud I was to be able to gaze on the
unmistakeable proof of the love and reverence those
first Christians had for our Blessed Mother! I
prayed before her sweet image, in the Catacombs
underneath St. Clement's church, and kissed it with
something like awe; for it is a witness to the fact
that the devotion to Mary is now only what it was
1,600 years ago.

Rome, *7th December*, 1869.

My dear St. C.,
    To-morrow is the day of days. Before the sun
sinks again to rest, the Great Council will have
opened, and Pius IX. will have achieved, in face of
the most desperate opposition, the greatest triumph
of his glorious reign! There are upwards of seven
hundred Bishops, Archbishops, and Patriarchs, in
the Eternal City at present; and no end of Priests,
Monks, and strangers. I have just returned from
seeing the preparatory illumination in the city;
and, as I may not have much time at my disposal

to-morrow, I will begin my letter to-night, that it may be ready for this week's post.

I went to the Vatican this evening, and had the happiness of getting a good view of the Holy Father. There were about 7000 persons in the inner court of the Palace as he left for his evening drive, on his way to the church of the Holy Apostles ; and you may be sure that we cheered him lustily. In fact, I was quite uproarious on the head of it ; but no one took any notice of me, for wherever he appears there is the wildest enthusiasm.

I did not go as far as the church ; but those who assisted. at the benediction say that they never witnessed such an ovation. About 20,000 men, women, and children awaited his arrival in and around the church, and cheered him repeatedly. The dear, loving, good old man ! If you only could see him, not as his portraits paint him,—for they do not render him justice,—but *as he is !* Such sweetness !—such serene majesty ! And, oh ! to see how lovingly he blesses the kneeling multitudes, as he passes by !

After the crowd had departed I wandered into St. Peter's, to see the great Council-Head. It occupies one of the lateral chapels of the church, on the right side, directly opposite the tomb of the Apostles SS. Peter and Paul. There are eight or nine tiers of seats on each side, covered with green cloth interwoven with handsome flowers in gold. At the upper end is the throne of the Pontiff,—a massive raised seat of purple and gold. In the middle of the room, on the floor of the chapels, are seats for short - hand writers. Three - beautiful paintings represent three great councils : one above the throne—the council of Jerusalem ; the other on the right side—the council of Ephesus ; the third, opposite—the council of Trent. The whole offers a magnificent *coup-d'œil*, and is worthy, to some extent, of the great assembly. I must not forget the galleries, above, for diplomatists, ambassadors, and royal personages. The walls are richly inlaid with the purest of Italian marble.

As it was getting late, I started for home, crossing down the great *piazza*, with its fountains and obelisk, and through the street that leads to the bridge of St. Angelo. The Papal colours are flying from the battlements. There are crowds on either side of the bridge; a soldier tells me that the people are waiting for the return of the Pope, so I decided to wait there, too.

I accordingly sat down on a stone-bench, near an angle of the bridge ; and there, unnoticed and uncared for, I began taking notes of the busy and varied scene that swept by like some beautiful panorama. I was in the Eternal City, on the very bridge where thousands—nay, millions—of pilgrims had come before me to worship at the tomb of the Apostles ! Here was the city older than Christianity, mighty before the cross was raised for salvation ; the city whence the legions of Rome went forth to conquer the world—where the consuls, the dictators and pagan emperors made laws for the universe ! Rome, where the barbarians smote' the colosses of earthly power, and did the work of Providence, without even thinking that they were its instruments ! But all these had passed away ; and if the greatness of Rome had been based on the might of one or the other, it would long since have sunk into oblivion, like so many other empire-cities. Yet, Rome is not a desert ; Rome is peopled with the nations of the world ; Rome is still mighty. And why ? Because the hand of God upheld it ; because His vicar is here ; because it is sanctified by the presense of him with whom Christ promised to remain for ever.

All these thoughts, and many others, passed

through my mind as I sat all alone in the growing
twilight, looking at the thousands that passed and
repassed unceasingly! And, oh! such a varied
spectacle! —cardinals' carriages with their richly-
caparisoned horses ; dragoons with their brass-
helmets and clanking swords ; Spanish priests with
their great turned-up hats, like canoes ; French
priests with their little capes and *rabats ;* Eastern
priests from Turkey, Greece, and China, with flowng.
beards and Turkish bonnets ; theological students,
some in white, others in red, others in blue, others
in black soutanes ; smart little zouaves with a sort
of half-run ; Roman peasants with high-crowned
hats and immense cloaks, looking, for all the world,
like brigands. Here come a *garde noble*, with a gold-
embroidered uniform ; and now a long-eared donkey
tied to a small cart, carrying—I do not know how
—nine persons. Next is an Armenian abbot with a
very tall cap and turned-up toes to his boots ; and
then two poor musicians, called *Pifferori*, the sound
of whose bag-pipes and clarionet is the nearest thing
in the world to a cross between a pig's squeal and
a turkey's gobble. The people are talking French,
'English, Italian, Spanish, German, Portuguese,
Greek and Arab (oh! how filthy these Arabs are !) ;
in a word, every known tongue in the universe.

And I am witnessing all this, listening to all this,
enjoying it all, seated on the brink of old Father
Tiber !...... The evening is delightfully refreshing ;
the weather is beautiful, like an evening toward
the end of August or the beginning of September
in Canada. The grass is quite green on the borders
of the river and on the castle-moat. Flowers are
growing in bloom in the little garden-plots here
and there. All the windows are open. Every one
is dressed in summer-attire. Oranges and lemons
are ripening on the branches, whilst you are

digging one another out of the snows up yonder towards the far-north-west.

But I can not sit here all night. I am getting hungry, and the shades are thickening; so, without waiting for the return of the Pope, I am off, down the street called *Monseratto*, to my boarding-house, right opposite the palace of the king of Naples, and in view of the chapel where St. Jérome and St. Philip Néri passed part of their lives, next door to where St. Bridget lived in an ecstasy, and within two minutes' walk of the *Campo di fiori*, where Cæsar fell assassinated on the Ides of March.

The Romans have been invited by the authorities to illuminate their houses for to-morrow evening; but they will not wait for to-morrow. The city is just beginning to be illuminated, with that taste so proverbial with the Italians; and, as I enter my room, I hear the cannon of the Castle booming in the distance, to announce the first Vespers of the holy feast of the Immaculate Conception. Good night!

9th December.—I had a presentiment of future delay when I began my letter, and I was right, for it is now Thursday evening; the great feast is over, and, between one thing and another, I have not been able to continue my letter since.

I left you on Tuesday night, when all was expectancy for the morrow. As usual, the great question was: Will it be fine? Unfortunately, it was not fine. The day broke amid a storm of pelting rain, and such rain as is only known in Italy. You have nothing like it in Canada. It beats down your umbrella; it gets in through the seams of your coat, and then right through your pores, and into your very bones. The chief want you feel, after having been out in a storm here, is to be well rung out, shook, and hung up on a clothes-line to dry, and then be ironed to take out the "creases."

Therefore, as I was saying, when I awoke in the morning, the rain was battering away at the window-panes, as if impatient to *duck* me; the sky was of a heavy leaden hue, and the spouts were almost choking. I got a first wetting on going out to say mass; and before I got time to dry, I had to start again for St. Peter's, as the ceremony was announced for 8½ A.M.

A zouave, who was on patrol that night, told me, since, that there were people on the church-steps from 12 *o'clock* P.M. The carriages began to arrive at 4 o'clock in the morning. When I left my boarding-house, the crowds that were wending their way to the church were something like the general judgment, both for numbers and variety. All you could see, as you approached, was an immense sea of umbrellas of every hue, from the elegant brown silk to the light blue cotton. I arrived at 8 o'clock. The zouaves, with their guns and bayonets, formed a double line for the procession to pass through, in the middle of the church, leaving an open space of about twenty feet or more. The rest was the disputed right of every individual, as *he* or *she* might happen to conquer it. On entering, I gave up all hopes of being able to see anything; for the ranks were six or eight deep behind the soldiers, and as closely packed as any jury that ever sat at the Irish assizes. Suddenly, there was a commotion behind me, as I stood on my tip-toes, and I heard an authoritative voice ordering place to be made for a bishop who had arrived late, like myself, but who had a better right than I had to pierce the crowd and get to his place.

Now, thought I to myself, here is a chance quite providential for *you*, Patrick, agrah! The crowd swayed a little for the bishop (a fine fat man—God bless him!)—and before his secretary could follow, I had my elbow, planted into the poor man's ribs, and was making my way between the both. As he was very fat, I had little trouble in following him ; and the people, taken by surprise, or thinking I was a grand-vicar, let me pass up to the third rank. But here they perceived the trick, and maybe I had not to pay for it ! There was a general cry of indignation around me, and especially behind me ; in fact, they were so *riled* that the poor secretary *lost his passage*, and was thrust back. If it would have been possible to get me out, I would not have been long there either. But I was so completely jammed up that they had to leave me where I was. One little Italian, with bushy whiskers, gave me a *prod* with his elbow in the breast that left his mark; but I returned it with such vehemence, on the side of his head, that he will have a headache for all next week. Do not be scandalized at this. It was every one for himself on that day. We all spoke so loudly and so angrily, that the soldiers ordered silence. And so, there I was in the third rank, while others who had been in the church since six o'clock were far behind me. But I was destined to still further happiness. The crowd pushed so much that the front line broke the picket, upon which the said unfortunate front rank was ordered behind by an open passage, and we came up directly behind the zouaves ; and this is how I came to have a splendid view of the entire procession. It is calculated that there were not less than 80,000 persons in church, and some say that there were 100,000. I cannot say who is right, but I know that all the place was as full as it could be.

The procession was announced for $8\frac{1}{2}$ A.M., but we had to wait for full three-quarters of an hour before there were any signs of its approaching. There were a few false alarms, and every one used to stretch his neck and say : " *Here they come !* " Then, after a few moments, it would be found out that it was only some official running along the open space, on some errand or other. At last the canons of St. Peter's, in short white surplices, the thurifers and cross-bearers, moved up, and placed themselves with the choir-boys, in a line along the sides. A short time after, the Empress of Austria passed down, with a brilliant suite ; then the dukes, duchesses, generals, and a number of distinguished persons,—so we knew that the time was coming for the sight.

At last the great doors of the church were thrown open, and we heard the singers of the Sixtine Chapel chanting the *Veni Creator*. All was commotion. There was a rush to the front ; but the little zouaves held the line bravely, and kept the people back. Soon the great golden cross was seen in the doorway, over the heads of all ; the voices of the singers became more distinct, and the bishops began to pass before my eyes. All was a dead silence then ; every one was intent on seeing as much as he could. But, oh! such a brilliant spectacle ! No pagan emperor, in the height of his power, ever dreamt of anything half so brilliant or imposing. There they were, the real masters of the world,—the pastors of the flock that extends over the whole world,—the fathers whose voice had been heard in every coun-try,—the representatives of that authority before which kings quail and nations are silent,—the bishops of the Church-militant of Jesus Christ, who had come in love and reverence from far-off lands, at the call of that glorious old monarch who fills with such dignity the chair of Peter. Yes ! there they were, from every land—our own dear bishops of Canada ; bishops from South America ; from every part of Europe, except barbarous Russia ; from the East, in all the brilliancy of Oriental gold and jewels, swarthy and tanned, with venerable flowing beards ; from Africa, and Asia, and Oceanica,—all assembled, all robed, all marching past in

solemn slow procession, in the grandest temple that
the world knows ! The Bishops came first, then the
Archbishops, then the Patriarchs, then the Cardinals,
then the Roman Senate ; and last of all, full of regal
dignity, his countenance lit up with heavenly joy,
the greatest man in the world, a saint among saints,
a king amongst kings, PIUS THE NINTH ! He was
surrounded by his household-troops, and followed
by ambassadors from different nations. Oh ! it was
a royal sight !

They all marched up to the tomb of the Apostles,
where they prostrated themselves for a moment
before the Blessed Sacrament, four by four; and
then, turning to the right, they entered the Council-
Hall, and took their allotted seats.

High-mass was celebrated and a sermon preached.
All the bishops then came to pay homage to the
Supreme Pontiff. The decree for the opening of the
Council was read and acquiesced in, and *Pius IX.
declared the Council opened.* So much for the malice
of the Pope's enemies. « Blessed are the weak, »
says the Bible, « for they shall possess the land.» Pius
the IXth had not the earthly power of many kings
of the earth ; his armies and fleets did not cover
land and sea ; he was despoiled of his possessions ;
he was even laughed at and pointed out with scorn
for not joining in the movement which false ideas
termed *progress.* Yet, to-day, while kings are trem-
bling in their palaces, whilst thrones are tottering,
he whose confidence was in God alone sits enthron-
ed amongst the rulers of men's conduct and belief,
surrounded by the love of all, and stronger to-day,
more glorious, than all his enemies together! Rome
is wild with joy. Notwithstanding the bad weather,
the city was again illuminated in the evening; bands
of music and of singers might be heard everywhere ;
and everywhere the name and fame of the Pope was
blended with the sounds of joy and exultation.

Rome, 12*th December*, 1869.

My dear St. C.,

I had an audience from Pius the IX. ! ! !—not alone, of course ; for this happiness I must wait longer. But at last I saw him, stood close to him, heard him speak, got his blessing, *wept with him.* You must know that it is very hard to get an audience just now, for there are so many strangers in Rome ; and, besides, the varied wants in connexion with the Council take up a good deal of the Pope's time. . You may think how busy he is when you learn that half the bishops have not yet had private interviews. Our own dear old Archbishop has not even got his answer to his request ; so you see I was beforehand.

Yesterday, then, the news spread that the French priests (from France) were to be admitted into the presence of the Pope ; but as there had already been false reports, it was not generally believed. However, on Saturday the report became a certainty, and the French priests were in high exultation. There are about 200 of them in Rome, all distinguishable by the *rabat ;* and as I wear the *rabat*, too, I am often taken for a French priest, save and except my *beaver-hat*, which makes me look as strange in Rome almost as if I wore my night-cap in the streets of Quebec.

To prevent a crush, it was ordered that all priests should present a letter from their bishop, certifying that they were employed in France. But we (the priests of Canada) thought we would strain a point in the matter, and risk a presentation without the *pass.* We had nothing to lose in the event of our not succeeding, and everything to gain if we were accepted. We accordingly explained, at the door, in a very humble manner, our position, and begged admittance. The good-natured old man who " pre-

sided at the door," as we say in the Institute, let us
pass ; and we were ushered in through two, suites
of apartments, and took our place round a handsome
throne erected at the end of a long *salle*, all glittering with gold and purple tapistry, and enriched
with valuable paintings. We had to wait for about
an hour, for the Pope was, at the time, giving an
audience to the Italian priests. At last, a prelate
came to announce the arrival of. his Holiness and
proclaim silence. Soon after, Pius the IX. entered
the door, and immediately there was a shout of joy :
Vive Pie IX.! Vive notre Pontife-Roi!

The good old man smiled benignly, and ascended the throne. When the first noise had
subsided he stretched out his arms : " My dear children, » said he, «*you are the voices,*»—making a very
happy allusion to our enthusiastic cries,— «*you
« are the voices crying in the desert;* and the desert
« is the world with its aridity for virtue, its
« want of fruitfulness in Christ. Like St. John the
« Baptist, your mission is to announce the Messiah,
« to prepare the world for his coming ; and, oh !
« fulfil that mission faithfully, for your reward will
« be the measure of your fidelity. Fulfil that mission
« in accordance with the Scripture—*opere at sermone ;*
« *by voice and example.* Example is a great thing in
« the world. If the priest is good and holy, the peo-
« ple will be good and holy. Keep, then, your hearts
« pure ; burn with love for God, and be active in His
« service. Do not neglect to preach the word of God ;
« nourish the souls of the faithful with pious and
« solid instructions.»

Such is the analysis of the discourse which our
Holy Father gave us. But I have deprived it of all
the brilliant ornaments, both of word and gesture,
which made it one of the most forcible and really
touching sermons I ever heard. You should have
seen that good father in the midst of his children,

like Jesus amongst his apostles, exhorting them to the service of God, winning their hearts by the eloquence of his gifted tongue. He said a good many witty things during the course of his speech, thus sweetly mingling the light and solid, and rendering the effect more durable. But when, towards the close of his speech, he bade us adieu, and requested us all to live and work in such a manner that we might all meet in Heaven, he became pathetic and sublime. He wept with tenderness; and I remarked that whenever he pronounced the holy name of God, he did so with profound recollection. We all wept with him, and knelt to receive his benediction. There were there many men who never met in the same room before, and who may never meet again; but we were all one family of brothers there; we all had one thought—a profound sentiment of reverence and love for our Holy Father, and a desire, strong and heartfelt, to obey his infallible command.

The Pope looks well and hearty, thank God! He was in excellent spirits; his face beamed with a heavenly smile. I wish you could see the large portrait of him in the University; it is the only really good one I have seen. He is of the middle height, slightly corpulent, and looks to be about 60 years old. His voice is sweet and full. He speaks French with a pretty strong Italian accent, but speaks it very correctly. His hair is of a silvery white, which gives him a very venerable aspect. It was said that if Garibaldi, Mazzini, or any of his enemies, could only hear him speak for five minutes, they would fall at his feet in contrition for their faults. I do not doubt it, for every one feels a subjugating charm in his presence.

I am about to start for the Holy Land. You remember that, for some years past, we have established the custom of meeting together, at midnight-mass, in presence of the little cradle of Bethlehem. This year, through God's grace, I shall, on Christmas, be on. the very. spot where Jesus was born. Oh ! I will pray for you, in this holy place, with more fervour than ever, as well as for my friends.

I saw the archbishop (') again on Saturday. I cannot tell you how kind he has invariably been since I am in Rome. He told me he thought I had a vocation for Rome, for he fancies I speak excellent Italian. The fact is, that I learned four or five words of that language while in Quebec ; and by twisting and turning them. in divers ways, I used to act as interpreter, on the way to Rome, for my companions. But, *a little learning is a dangerous thing.* I will, therefore, try and augment my small store if I remain any time in Rome.

ON THE ROAD TO JERUSALEM.

December 15th, 1869.—We left Rome this morning by rail, at a quarter past ten, *en route* for Jerusalem. Our caravan consists of four priests from Canada. We are now at Caserta, the head-quarters of a former dukedom, which has vanished amid the changes brought on by the late revolution. We are about an hour's ride from Naples, due south of Rome ; but, instead of continuing our journey towards that city, we shall, to-morrow morning, take a south-eastern route, striking directly through the Apennines, with the intention of reaching Brindisi by Friday, to catch the boat that leaves for Alexandria.

We are now staying at the hotel « Villa Réale." Our landlady is French ; and as, I presume, she has not for some time spoken her own language—all the inhabitants here being Italians—she makes up for lost time, and inundates us with the floods of her volubility. The « man of the house » tries, now and

(¹) Archbishop Baillargeon.

then, to get in a word sideways; but he is silently
admonished by a look from his better half, and
settles down into his native insignificance. He is
reduced to rub his hands and nod at us politely,
when he leaves the room or returns from an errand.

Caserta is a regularly-built little town of about
16,000 inhabitants. It looks almost deserted, as it
reposes quietly in the moon-shine. There was hardly any one to be met in the streets as we passed
through them, on an inspection-tour, after supper.
The Apennines surround us on all sides. The ducal
palace is a splendid residence. The front is about
300 feet long, and the architecture is tasteful and
simple. At each side of the principal building is a
long semi-circular wing, which runs out to the distance of 200 feet, thus forming a sort of three-sided
piazza. After a long ramble through the town in
the beautiful moon-light, we returned to our hotel.
A half-hour's pleasant chat on our « first day's adventures,» and then we retired to make our *notes*,
say our prayers, and go to bed.

16th December.—We were up at 5 in the morning,
exactly two hours before the sun. A hasty breakfast, a very sympathetic «good-bye» to mine host, a
short wait at the station after buying tickets for
Bari,—then, in comes the train, up get we, off goes
the whistle, and, through the bracing air of early
morning, we are borne along at the rapid rate of 30
miles an hour. Our speed soon slackens, however,
for we begin to ascend the Apennines, and in places
the grade is almost as sharp as part of the Alps.
As we rise above the surrounding country, the
prospect becomes grander and the view more enchanting. There is a purple haze spread over the
fields, through which we can distinguish the shepherds' cottages and luxuriant plantations of olive-
trees. Away to the right is the muddy Volturno,
making its way, as best it can, to the Mediterranean.

Little villages nestle here and there in the open plain, on the mountain-side. The crops are in full growth, though it is the 16th December ; the wheat is already about three inches high. And now the glorious sun peeps out from behind the mountain, gilding and beautifying every object, chasing into the very clouds the morning vapors, imparting its own warmth....But, hold ! I must not run away from my subject : I am only making notes.

At Meddoloni, half-way up the mountain, we find ourselves in the middle of a vast quarry, from which a number of women are extracting a greenish sort of earth. When it is exposed to the sun, it becomes hard enough to furnish material for building houses. It is strange to see how sturdily those low-sized, broad-shouldered females work and toil I see very few men among them. These are the real advocates of woman's rights. If the question were to come to a struggle, these *Donne* would do more to ensure an issue favourable to the cause than all the female spouters of New-York, and of the States generally. But—poor benighted creatures!—I fear very much they know little more about woman's rights than they do about the latest New-York fashions. But, no matter; there they are, working away like ants on a mole-hill ; and here are the mountains getting more and more beautiful, the air fresher at every moment, the olive-trees denser, the cactus wilder; and here we are rising, rising, rising, till at last we reach a vast plateau, from which the view is simply sublime. Volcanic cones, silent now, shoot up all around at our feet ; arched bridges of stone span ravines, the depths of which are impenetrable to the eye ; a murky mountain-torrent tears its way down the sides of the hills, now leaping into cascades, now widening into a miniature lake, but still ever pursuing its way, like a steady, persevering

man with one idea in his head, and fully bent on its
accomplishment.

We pass many stations with strong Italian names
and very poor accommodations for travellers. Happily we have provided for our wants at Caserta, and
we take a ten-o'clock lunch or second breakfast at
Solopaga, on cold meat, good bread, cheese, figs,
oranges, and capital wine.

The peasants all wear large, ample cloaks, high
pointed hats, and blue breeches and leggings. It is the
exact reality of the pictured brigands with whom you
may be familiar,—only *not so clean.* The hair is « in
flowing curls, » but quite uncombed ; the cloak is
loosely thrown over the shoulder, and hangs in
artistic drapery down the back ; but—Lord !—« it's
all full of patches, and where there's no patch
there's a gaping hole ; » the breeches (excuse me)
are of celestial blue, or once were ; but as they grew
old, they, too, had to be patched, and the new clap-
boarding has so many different colours that it is
hard to make out what really was the « primitive
dye. » However, you must not think that they cut a
ridiculous figure ; no ; but there is a sort of native
majesty, or, rather, innate grace, in those follows,
that makes them really handsome and picturesque
in the midst of their rags. I saw a fellow, at the
station of San Félice, whose habiliments seemed
almost antediluvian : it seemed as if the slightest
wind would shake them to pieces ; yet, he moved
with the step of an emperor, and his *tournure,* in its
tout-ensemble, would have graced the veriest dandy
of the Bois de Boulogne. Blumhart would have
taken him for a model.

At 11 o'clock A.M. we reached a miserable little
village called San Spirito. Owing to the inundations
of last year, the road is completely disconnected
between this place and Starza ; so we are obliged to
leave the train and continue our journey in large

ómnibuses, drawn by four, six, arid sometimes eigĥt horses, according to their bulk. There we were, then, on the grounds of regular Italian adventure ; in the midst of mountains as high and as bald as those I had seen in Tipperary; in the midst of the Apennines, surrounded by men wearing the cos- tumes of brigands, fierce, lawless-looking clowns, and in the classic «diligence »!—an exact copy—or, rather, original—of the pictures I had so often seen in connexion with stories of Italian brigands. But, alas! railroads and *gendarmes* have spoiled the romance of travelling !

Our baggage was taken from us and placed on the top of the vehicle ; but I held on like grim-death to a black portmanteau which contained the eatables. My three companions were placed in one omnibus, and, before I could ascend, a fourth per- son got up with them; so I was obliged to look out for another seat somewhere else. This raised a laugh against me, on the part of the venerable *con- frères ;* but I paid them back for it shortly after, for, at every turn of the road where I could catch sight of them from the window of my carriage, I used to flourish the bottle of wine and a huge sandwich, while they could feed on nothing but expectation and scenery. Revenge is sweet, especially when ac- companied by ham and washed down by *vino di vellrtri.*

The country, through which we ploughed our way in the mud for three hours, is a compound of deep grassy ravines and high mountains, and is torn up here and there by torrents. The people are working at the railroad, repairing the disasters of last year's inundations. The workers are, here as well as elsewhere, women and asses ; the men are to be met lounging lazily round the *trattorie*, or little inns, discussing politics and sour wine. The women, though busy at work, have not been entirely

forgetful of that great object in woman's life,
the *toilet!* Their dresses are neatly got up, and rejoice in the most trenching and brilliant variations.
« Roaring red and bright yellow» are the staple
colours. They are generally covered from top to
toe by a mantle of the fiercest scarlet, and the groups
that we descry sitting on the grass, on yonder hil-
lock, look like a bunch of bright poppies flourishing
in the sunshine. They all have brass ear-rings about
three inches long, which scarcely form any contrast
with their bronzed necks. All seem joyously happy.
We passed a troop of lancers on patrol in the mountains. Their nodding plumes and flashing lances
gave them a picturesque look as they stood out against
the clear horizon directly over our heads. At 1½
P.M., our carriage drew up at Storza, and we again
took the railroad. We now begin to descend an
inclined plane, and are evidently getting out of the
chain of the Apennines. Finally, at Bovino, the
mountains disappear, and we are issued into a vast
level country, very well cultivated ; and soon after
we descry, slightly to the east, the outskirts of
Foggia, a town of 40,000 inhabitants, where we shall
change cars and have an hour's wait. We shall,
therefore, be able to get a good dinner and have a
look at the place.

4½ P.M.—We are now starting for Bari, where we
sleep to-night. After a great deal of *research*, we
found a respectable hotel in one af the principal
streets of Foggia, and took dinner. The beefsteak
was as tough as tanned leather ; the soup *au vermi-
celle* and wine were, however, tolerable, and the
charge moderate. We rambled through the town
for half an hour or so. It is well built, regular and
clean. There is a very handsome public promenade
at one end of it. A double row of twelve Corinthian
pillars stand at the entrance. The walk is about a
mile long, and is terminated by a very pretty little

Grecian temple, something like the temple of Vesta in Rome. We met an Italian monk, who, on learning that we were priests, treated us with great kindness, and invited us to the monastery. We could not accept his invitation. He told us that the people were, in general, good and religious. The monks receive a salary from the government, in compensation for the properties that have been taken from them.

Our route to Bari lay through vast plains, on which fed, peacefully, countless flocks of sheep. Shortly after our departure, two Italian lawyers came into the *coupé*. They got into an argument, the one with the other, and we were treated to a regular scene from the « Plaideurs de Racine.» They argued, demonstrated, screamed, thundered, and gesticulated for three long hours, and with such apparent vehemence and animosity that I thought a duel would surely be the result. I, however, saw them shake hands warmly as they parted at the station.

Bari is a very handsome town. Our « patron d'hôtel» boasts that it is the second town in Italy for size, importance, and beauty. It has 50,000 inhabitants. We could not judge well whether his praises were merited or not, for we only saw it during a moonlight-walk in search of a cup of tea. I may add that my journey was bootless: in none of the hotels or *cafés* did they appear to have the slightest knowledge of the plant; and here I began to be convinced that I must give up, for a time, my favorite indulgence. I had to do so; for, with the exception of a « cup of hyson» at Mrs. Swan's house, in Corfu, I was destined to see tea no more till I returned to Rome. Here, as at Caserta, we were surprised to find the streets almost entirely deserted at 9 o'clock in the evening; and so much the more so, as in other towns of Italy (if I may be allowed to use an Irish

4

bull) night was generally the noisiest part of the
day. So much the better, perhaps.

17th -- *December* —We were up this morning at
a quarter to five, and at twenty minutes to six we
started for Brindisi. We had the whole *coupé* to
ourselves; so, as we were, all disposed to sleep, we
coiled ourselves up, each one in his own corner, and
were soon in the land of dreams. We thus jolted
through a troubled slumber until we woke to see
the first glimpse of the Adriatic sea, as it glanced
in the rising sun, like a sheet of gold, away eastward. We shook off our drowsiness; and after
admiring for a time the immense groves of olive
trees as they rushed past us on their twisted trunks,
the extensive brick-fields, the numerous flocks, &c.,
we all read our office, as a preparation for breakfast,
at Brindisi. At 9 o'clock exactly the train stopped, and
the guard cried out: " Brindisi! " We immediately
came out, and found ourselves in a handsome station,
apparently in the midst of the country. On inquiring
where we were, we were told that the town lay
about a quarter of an hour's drive from the station.
Thereupon we hired a rickety old carriage—the
only one on command,—and, packing ourselves into
it as well as possible, hurried off, at a lame trot
towards " L'hôtel du Grand Oriental. " The hills and
mounds that hide the view of the city, have an
ancient look; the farms and cottages seem covered
with the dust of ages; and, as if to keep up the
illusion, our old *vetturino* drove a horse whose great
age, however worthy of respect in itself, was a
great obstacle to our rapid progress. I thought he
would fall to pieces every time he made a feeble
attempt to kick, when the whip fell on his ancient
ribs.

 Brindisi is older than Christianity. Horace speaks
of it in one of his odes. Its streets are narrow and
winding, roughly paved, and bordered by one-story

stone houses with flat roofs. Our hotel is at the lower end of the town, facing the port. We found better fare here than anywhere else since we left Rome ; but if the steaks and butter were fresh, the bill was extremely *salty*, I assure you.

We had been told that a vessel would start from Brindisi, direct for Alexandria, on Friday ; but we now find that it is not the case. The Austrian vessel from Trieste, which goes to the above-mentioned place, will come into this port on Sunday, and leave on Monday evening, touching at Corfu. There is, however, at the whar, fan Italian steamer, which leaves for Corfu this evening ; we decidethat, since we must wait *somewhere* until Monday, it is better to remain at Corfu than in this dull little place. So, notwithstanding the efforts of the hotel-keeper to determine our stay, we take our cabins on board the *America ;* and after a rapid run through the town, we came on board, and at 2 o'clock P.M. sailed out of port into the calm blue waters of the Mediterranean. The weather is delightful, though, perhaps, a little too warm ; the sea is as smooth as a mirror; we enjoy a fine view of the coast of Italy as we run outside the mole that protects the harbour, and now we may consider our voyage as begun in reality.

4½ P.M.—I am now sitting all alone at the extreme front of the vessel; my companions are below finishing the office of to-morrow. Signor Ritano Florio is pacing the quarter-deck, humming an Italian song ; three Austrian sailors are conversing, in a guttural language, near the stairs that lead to the lower deck. We are now out in the open sea : there is no land in sight except a long narrow blue line due west ; it is all that remains of Italy. When shall I see it again ? Above the line of land, the horizon is painted with gold, purple, blue and red— a glorious shroud that the sun has left behind him.

To the south, a full round moon, as mild-looking and complacent as a German matron, rides in the yet unstarred heavens. The sea is still very calm. I hope I may avoid sea-sickness. They tell us that we shall reach Corfu by three o'clock to-morrow morning.

10½ P.M.—I am now just on the point of turning in for the night. We had a glorious evening on deck—a pleasant chat, a round of songs, and the *Ave Maris Stella*, with night-prayers, all together, under the steady gaze of a most brilliant moon. The ship goes on splendidly. The weather is very warm, as the month of June in Canada.

CORFU, *Saturday*, *18th December.*—We reached Corfu this morning early, but remained on board until 7½ A. M. From the deck of the ship the island seems to be almost a barren rock. The town rises in amphitheatre from the water's edge, and is crowned by a frowning fortress called *Castel Nuovo*. A peal of bells sends forth joyous sounds on the air: it appears that this is a great festival—St. Spiridion's day. A small boat is waiting for us, to convey us from the ship to the wharf. The quai is crowded with men, most of them *porteurs*, who make desperate efforts at seizing our baggage to carry it to the hotel. Most of them wear the Turkish costume—red shoes, pointed and turned up at the toe, white stockings (or, in some cases, none at all), large blue petticoat-trowsers, and a tight-fitting jacket, the whole surmounted by a small red cap with a black or blue tassel. They have mostly black flashing eyes and fierce moustaches, and are as brown as berries. We manage to shake them off, and, confiding our «goods and chattels» to a hotel-boy, who is in waiting, proceed along the filthy, uneven, up-hill streets, to « l'hôtel de l'Angleterre.»

Corfu is one of the Ionian islands, formerly under the protectorate of England, but now incorporated into the Greek empire of king George, whose capital is Athens. The island is of an irregular oblong form, its greatest length being about 26 miles. The town of Corfu is situated at the western extremity, and has a population of 25,000 souls—Greeks, Turks, Italians, Albanians, and a few English merchants.

The Greeks wear the national costume, somewhat similar to that of the Turks; the Albanians also wear a peculiar dress, which makes them look like a cross between a Scotch Highlander and a ballet-girl. The cap is high and pointed; the jacket is close-fitting; then comes a white petticoat, very full and nicely plaited, which reaches almost to the knee; the legs are encased in extremely tight skin-fitting pantaloons, finished off by a neat congress boot.

Corfu is the residence of the Catholic metropolitan of the islands. He has the title of archbishop. The city contains about 6,000 Catholics, whose wants are administered to by two priests. The Julian calendar, by express permission of Rome, is followed here; the Catholics are, therefore, 12 days in arrears of the rest of the church with regard to the celebration of the festivals: thus, Monday will be the 8th of December and the feast of the Immaculate Conception, while on our calendar it is the 20th.

The Greek schismatic priests number between 300 and 400 on the whole island. Most of them have a wife and family—(Lord help them!). As a general thing, they are poor and ignorant. I may as well remind you, here, that the Greek church proper is quite different from the Russo-Greek church, which is under the guidance of the Czar. The former is ruled by a council of 12 Patriarchs, who meet at Athens. The priests and bishops are, in a great measure, paid by the government.

Those schismatics do not, of course, believe in the universal supremacy of the Pope. They look on him

merely as a Patriarch whose jurisdiction is restricted
to Italy and its environs. They say mass, hear confessions, and recite the breviary. They also believe in
the Transubstantiation, in Purgatory, and in the
invocation of the saints. Their chief error lies in
their belief that the Holy Ghost does not proceed
from the Father and Son, but from the Father alone.
We had all those details, and many others extremely interesting, from the Rev.Canon Lightwood,
one of the canons of the Cathedral. He was formerly
chaplain to the English troops stationed here. We
went this evening to present our credentials and
obtain permission to say mass: we were very kindly
received, and we obtained all the necessary faculties.
Mr. Lightwood offered to accompany us to-morrow
evening on an excursion through the island.

I was very much amused this morning by the novel
method of the milkmen in disposing of their com-
modity. Out in Canada, the cows are milked in the
stable; the milK is then put into cans, and brought
round from house to house. But here, they have a
much easier way, and one that prevents any dishonest mixture of water in the lacteal produce. The
goats are driven along the streets, and are milked
according as the demand is made. A little girl runs
out of the house, pays her *deptak*, or copper, and
milks the full of her little vessel, just as unconcernedly as if she were opening the stop-cock of a barrel
of beer. The little goat, meanwhile, browzes on the
stray blades of grass near the sidewalks, as tran-
quilly as if it had nothing to do with the whole
affair.

This evening, at about 5 o'clock, there was a fear-
ful row under the windows of our hotel, and a
picket of soldiers with fixed bayonets captured three
very ugly specimens of human ruffianism. Somewhat later, we were serenaded by a band of itine-
rant troubadours,—an extremely harmonious and

pleasing way of asking alms. They went away
rejoicing.

I told you that, as we landed on the wharf this
morning, the bells were pealing out joyously to announce the Greek festival of *St. Spiridion.* His remains are contained in a beautiful marble tomb in
the church of St. Nicholas ; but, unfortunately,
the temple is in the hands of the schismatics, who
« do honor and reverence him » as their noblest patron and protector. After taking breakfast, we made
some necessary ameliorations in our toilet, and
wended our way to the church, where a great crowd
was already assembled ; and, entering the building,
we found them singing the *Kyrie eleison.* I thought
that it must be a Catholic church of the Greek rite,
and we all joined in with the devotion as piously
as possible. We venerated the relic of the saint,
knelt or stood with the congregation, signed ourselves with the sign of the cross, struck our breast ;
in a word, we must have been a subject of edifica-
tion to all around us ; and when, at the end of the
mass, the celebrant came out to destribute the
blessed bread, we went forward, kissed his hand,
and received our portion. All was well so far ; but
when, after the ceremony, we went to the sacristy
to shew our papers and ask permission to say mass
next day (Sunday), we were rather gruffly informed
that « they were *orthodox,* and had no communion
with the Latin Church.» I felt inclined to give a
long low whistle, and say, « Oh ! oh !» But I didn't ;
we merely « backed out, » and made ourselves scarce
in half a minute. We enjoyed a good laugh over the
adventure, and promised to be more cautious hereafter about joining in with strange devotions. It
was subsequent to this that we found out the Catholic church and became acquainted with Canon
Lightwood.

Sunday, 19th December.—I said mass this morning at eight o'clock in the cathedral ; I gave communion to *Karam*, Prince of Lebanon, who is at present staying in exile at Corfu. We afterwards assisted at Grand Mass, at which there was some very good singing and quite a large congregation. I was happy to notice much outward piety and recollection among the assembled faithful.

At two o'clock in the afternoon we hired a carriage, and, accompanied by Mr. Lightwood, set out on an excursion to *Gastouri*, at the further extremity of the island, and from which a magnificent view of all Corfu can be obtained.

We left the town, through a gate erected by the Venetians, and still bearing the arms of the proud Republic. Proceeding through a long level plain, through groves of olive, fig-trees, and cypresses, we arrived, after several hours' drive, at the foot of the high mountain on whose rocky sides is built the village of Gastouri.

Nous (¹) descendons ici de voiture et faisons une bonne partie de la montée à pied. L'air est chargé de parfums; sous nos pieds, à chaque instant, nous foulons des plantes odoriférantes. Les paysans, habillés à la Turque, conduisent çà et là leurs troupeaux, dont la laine est longue et soyeuse. A la porte des chaumières, basses et mal construites, nous voyons les femmes, la tête enveloppée d'un voile blanc. Elles portent leurs cheveux roulés en turban autour de la tête. Sur le plateau le plus élevé de Gastouri est construite la maison de campagne de je ne sais plus quel médecin de la ville, et c'est d'ici que l'on peut jouir du magnifique coup-d'œil de toute l'île. Au loin, vous voyez les montagnes de l'Albanie, couvertes de neige ; le lazaret et l'île de *Voglio di Vido* reposent dans l'onde tranquille de l'Adriatique; à vos pieds vous avez la ville

(¹) Two pages of the manuscript are in French.

avec son port plus vaste que celui de Naples; et, tout autour, dans les crevasses des montagnes, au sein des forêts, ou sur des plateaux isolés, apparaissent des villages coquets dont les blanches maisons contrastent avec le vert feuillage qui les entoure et les protège. Il y a 72 de ces petits hameaux, ayant chacun 3 ou 4 églises grecques.

Nous sommes revenus par l'esplanade, devant la ville. Il y avait une foule très-considérable qui écoutait silencieusement la musique d'une bande militaire. Rien de gai et pittoresque comme les mille couleurs des habillements : le jaune, le rouge, le vert pâle, le ciel bleu et le blanc tranchaient agréablement sur la pelouse verdoyante, et donnaient à ces groupes animés un aspect des plus ravissants. L'aimable chanoine a dîné avec nous à notre hôtel.

L'Eglise de Corfou est très-ancienne ; le Christianisme y a été prêché par *Jason* et *Sosipatres*, deux missionnaires envoyés ici par St. Paul. Leurs reliques sont encore ici, et, chose assez curieuse à constater, les catholiques, qui en sont les possesseurs, les prêtent quelquefois aux schismatiques pour leurs solennités religieuses. Il y a, du reste, assez souvent semblable échange fait de part et d'autre. Horace a composé une de ces odes ici à Corfou.

Après la chute des Romains et de l'Empire Grec, cette île a été conquise par les Turcs. Les chevaliers de Malte s'en sont emparés, puis les Turcs en sont devenus de nouveau les maîtres. Les Vénitiens l'ont enlevée aux Turcs ; mais ceux-ci l'ont reconquise pour la troisième fois, et l'ont gardée jusqu'à la révolution qui a assuré l'indépendance à la Grèce. Elle a formé pendant quelque temps une espèce d'état libre sous la protection de l'Angleterre ; enfin, il y a quelques années, elle est entrée avec les autres îles ioniennes dans le royaume grec dont elle forme encore partie aujourd'hui.

Monday, 20th December.—To-day, according to the

Julian calendar, is the 8th of December, and hence
the feast of the Immaculate Conception. I said mass
at 9 o'clock, and assisted at grand mass. In the afternoon we went to pay a visit to Prince Karam, who
resides in the hotel next to our own. After waiting
for some time, the Prince was announced, and we
were introduced to a fine, intellectual-looking man,
apparently about 40 years old. He received us in a
very cordial manner; cigarettes were handed round,
and coffee was afterwards served in true Oriental
style. Karam was, during the struggle between the
Maronites and the Druses, the terror of the Turks;
he resisted their forces for thirteen months, and
gained over them no fewer than seven battles. He
commanded in person, and was invariably to be
found, during action, in the hottest part of the fight.
He answered our numerous questions concerning
the strugg,le with readiness, and gave a very modest
account of his own doings. He is sincerely pious.
He speaks French very fluently. We were greatly
charmed with his frank and courteous demeanor.

Mr. Lightwood, who appeared determined to make
us enjoy our stay as much as possible, brought us,
in the evening, to the residence of Mr. Swan, an
Englishman who has been here with his family for
the last fifty years. We had tea and music—quite
an evening-party at home. Finally, at 9½ P.M., we
bade good-bye to our kind hosts, and returned to our
hotel to pack up and prepare to leave.

The steamer from Trieste was signalled at about
10 P.M., and she was to start at 3 o'clock in the
morning. We determined to go on board immediately. We paid our bills, came down to the wharf,
got into a little boat awaiting us, and were rowed
to the ship «Hungarian,» a fine screw-steamer of
the Lloyd line. Adieu, Corfu, and a kind remembrance for the Rev. Mr. Lightwood, whose genuine

hospitality and Christian kindness we shall not
easily forget.

Tuesday, 21st December.—We have now passed
our first day on the sky-blue waters of the Mediterranean. The sea is like the *Mare vitreum,* or *glassy
sea* of the Apocalypse; the heavens above us are
cloudless, and the sun fiercely hot. We have a
very havy cargo in the hold—thirty head of cattle,
which, as steerage passengers, remain on the lower
deck day and night : they appear to enjoy the trip
vastly, so far, but not half so much as a dozen
roosters that from their coops shout defiance to each
other all day long and a good part of the night.
Among the cabin passengers are two talkative old
Russian ladies, who are bound for Jerusalem; a
Scotch engineer going to Cairo; a Greek merchant
with a big paunch and enormous grey moustaches that he might tie behind his ears; a Yankee
from Philadelphia, who has been all round the
world; and ourselves. At 10 o'clock A.M. we passed
between Cephalonia to the west and Ithaca to the
east. The latter is the ancient kingdom of Ulysses,
rendered famous by Homer's poem. Here lived
Penelope. Both islands appear from this a low
chain of barren rocks, shooting up now and then
into an extinguished volcanic crater. Further on
we pass close by Zantha, and can distinguish north-
ward the entrance of the famous gulf of Lepanto ;
it forms the separation between the Morea and
Turkey in Europe. Several large vessels are in
view ; but, from want of wind, they do not appear
to be making much headway.

Wednesday, 22nd December.—This morning we ran
along the island of Candia at a splendid rate. Candia
was known, in ancient history, by the name of
Crete, and the Cretans were famed for their skill in
archery. The place was lately the scene of much
bloodshed. The inhabitants revolted against the

Turks, and were only subdued after a protracted
resistance. If I do not greatly mistake, St. Paul
passed some time here. The weather is extremely
sultry. We are now shaping our course almost
directly southward, and shall probably lose sight of
land before to-morrow. The sea is a little more agi-
tated than since we left; however, I think I am
getting used to the sea-faring life : I do not feel the
least symptom of sea-sickness, and enjoy a very good
appetite.

I am sitting all alone on the hurricane-deck.
Away to the north-west appears, sinking gradually
into the bosom of the ocean, the last faint outlines
of European land. All the rest around about is the
trackless deep. Due west is the full round globe of
the sun plunging down almost perpendicularly into
the waters. Just as he dips, a golden path of light
shoots across the whole way between the orb and
our ship; the sky is of a beautiful pale blue; but,
towards the horizon it takes a purple hue, and then
blushes into fierce red, which is gradually converted
into a bright flame-colour in the immediate vicinity
of the mighty disc. Nothing can render the exquisite beauty, both of colour and structure, of a burnished arch of clouds that appear to follow in the
wake of the sun, like a glorious shroud about to be
thrown over his grave. I had often read of a «sunset
at sea»; but the reality is beyond any description.
The ocean appears so round and flat, that it gives
one almost a liking for the primitive theories on the
form of our globe. Wordsworth, the English poet,
once gazed on such a scene ; and he thus beautifully
connects its pourtrayal with the praises of the
Immaculate Mother. Let me repeat the lines :

"Woman ! above all women glorified !
Our tainted nature's solitary boast !
Purer than foam on central ocean tos't ;
Fairer than Eastern skies at sunset strewn
With fancied roses."

How beautiful must she not, then, be ! and, oh !
how worthy of our love, since her beauty is only
the outward form of her goodness !......

The sun went down over Africa, which, though
now not very distant, is hidden from our view. It
has just sunk over the country of Syphax and Mas-
sinissa, of Cyprian and Augustin. It now streams
along the plains where once stood Carthage in its
glory,—where the Church once shone so bright till
it was extinguished in blood beneath the cruel onset
of the Vandals !

About nine o'clock the moon arose from out the
waters, and now rides serenely in the highest heavens. A furrow of silver light glances along the
tops of the tiny waves. Fond friends may gaze on
that self-same moon to-night, and fond hearts may
now be thinking of me, as I remember them. But,
oh ! how wide is the space that separates us ! No
matter ; we are all under the eye of the all-seeing
God ; His almighty arm is outstretched to over-
shadow and protect us, and, with His blessing, we
shall all meet again. Good night, dear sister ; and
may Heaven watch over thy repose.

Thursday, 23rd December. —No land in sight to-day;
but they tell us that we shall sight the land of Africa,
perhaps, before to-morrow morning. The day passed
pleasantly; but the sun was rather warm to render
the promenade on deck comfortable. I have just
closed my breviary, after reciting matins and lauds
for Christmas-eve. All is silent on board, for most of
the passengers have retired to bed, and others are
quietly reading. I am sitting at the long table in the
cabin, concluding the day's notes. The only noise I
can hear, apart from the dull monotonous noise of
the turning screw, is the rumbling of the waves that
beat against the sides of the vessel.

To-morrow, then, please God, we shall land in
Africa ! How little I thought, at this time last year,

that by next Christmas-eve I would be coasting along the Mediterranean, amidst scenes and weather so different from Canada! Yet, here I am, so very, very far from home, and so near that Jerusalem which our office commemorates so often in these holy times! "Oh! how I long to catch a sight of the city of Zion, the land of Promise, and kneel in prayer at our Lord's tomb!" We thought, when we left Rome, that we would have the happiness of passing Christmas-day either in Jerusalem or Bethlehem; but that is now impossible, If, however, all goes on as well as heretofore, we shall be there for the Epiphany. Up to the present time we have every reason to thank God, for they tell us on board that the weather is unusually fine for the season; and, so far, we have not had the slightest disappointment or accident to regret. It would be ingratitude not to attribute, under God, our good fortune to the prayers of those whose warm love and charity urge them to pray for us continually. We shall not forget them in the Holy Land.

AFRICA.

Friday, Christmas-eve.—Here I am, dear C., once more on *terra firma*, seated in my room at the "Hôtel Péninsulaire," in Alexandria." I got up very early this morning, for I desired very much to get the first glimpse of Africa as it rose out of the ocean. When I came on deck I was informed that we had come in sight of the light-house, off the harbour, during the night, but that we had "bet about," as the sailors say, till day-break, to wait for the pilot. Looking over the *lee-bow* (please note how nautical my language is getting), I perceived a very tall white house, with a red top, rising from a low ridge of sandy hills. The house was the *pharos*, or light-house,—no longer the once far-famed "Pharos of

Alexandria," one of the world's wonders in ancient
times,—but a common place affair, such as I had
often seen at home. The sandy hills were the first
peep of the *land of Cham*. Shortly after, the shore
extended; rocks appeared here and there at the surface of the water; then we began to descry quite a
forest of masts; next came heights crowned with
fortifications; and, at last, Alexandria revealed itself
to our view. At 6½ o'clock we took in the pilot from
his little boat in which he had come to meet us. He
was a swarthy Arab, short and thick-set, with grey
curling beard and whiskers. He wore a green turban,
a long, faded, blue, tight-fitting coat, a pair of red
turned-up shoes, *and nothing else*—at least, I think so,
for I could neither see breeches on his bare legs nor
shirt on his bare bosom. (P. S.—I afterward found
out that he had both those essentials of decency,
but in such a dilapidated condition that they might
be looked on as a «flimsy excuse.»)

Notwithstanding this penury of dress, he steered
us safely through the shoals and ships that crowded the port and its entrance ; and at 8 o'clock we
cast anchor in full view of the town, at about half
or perhaps a quarter of a mile from the landing-
place.

In about two minutes, we, and, indeed, all the
passengers, were surrounded by a horde of half-
naked Arab boatmen, who had clambered up the
sides of the ship, and who insisted, with shouts, vociferations, pleading and gesticulations, in every
tongue, known and unknown, on carrying us off, bags
and baggage, body and bones, into their respective
boats, and thence to the wharf, for any price we
wished to mention. Such a Babel of confusion,
and such a vagabond-looking set, I never before
had met, and hope never to meet again.

It was my good fortune to single out one more
respectable than the rest, and whom I afterward

found to be a good honest Maltese Catholic, who rendered us good service as a guide in the city. His name was Philip. I bargained with Philip, and for 8 francs he undertook to convey us to our hotel, which he did to our satisfaction.

So, here I am, after taking a good breakfast and performing some necessary obligations, sitting in a handsome room in a hotel opposite a large square called « La place des Consuls. » We cannot go out to visit yet, on account of the great heat; so I thought I might as well complete my notes from last evening.

Later in the day we set out, when the heat had somewhat abated, to seek for a Catholic church, so that we might have the consolation of saying mass on Christmas. We very luckily had not gone far up the street when we met a Capuchin monk with a great flowing beard. He turned out to be the chaplain of the English-speaking Catholics, a Prussian by birth, and exceedingly affable. He conducted us to the vicar-general (the bishop is at the Council); and our papers were examined and approved, so that we can celebrate the Holy Mysteries on to-morrow. The good Father promised to call on us during the course of the evening, or to-morrow, and we came back to our hotel.

Saturday, Christmas-Day.—A merry Christmas to you, dear C, and to all kind freinds across the waters! I said my three masses in St. Catherine's church this morning; and then, after grand mass, we hired a vehicle to go round the city and see the sights. Alexandria was founded by Alexander the Great, and since then has been subjected to a great many different masters; it is now, with the rest of Egypt, under the sway of Ismael Pacha, a sort of unruly vassal of the Sultan of Constantinople. It contains 200,000 inhabitants, formed of components more heterogeneous, I think, than any other city in the world, All the European nations have their representatives, either merchants or attached to the consulate. Would you believe it? I made the acquaintance of a fine little Irishwoman, named Mary Duggan, formely of Halifax,—previous to that, of Waterford, and now ultimately settled down to teach school to the *Nagurs* of Africa. And right glad she was to see me when she learned that I was an Irish priest. The poor Irish!—the same all over the world!—warm-hearted, generous, and with the same undying love for faith and country. She was delighted to hear that I had been to Waterford! she knew the present bishop, and also the Ursuline Convent of Mount St. Mary. She made me promise to go and see her on my return from Jerusalem.

My acquaintance with Mary was formed at the concert, from which I have just come. It was organized by Father Meinrich,—the Prussian Father of whom I spoke yesterday,—and was given by the «German Benevolent Society,» assisted by the band from the Christian Brothers" school. Father Meinrich had insisted on our coming; and it was very trying, I can assure you, for our feelings, to sit for three long hours, listening to German songs and speeches, in a densely-crowded house. We, however, applauded loudly like everybody else; and I ventured even to call for an *encore* to one of the songs, which got me in high popular favour. It was during an interlude that I heard a young woman (39 years old—she told me so after, when we had become confidential) speak English behind me. I asked her whether she was Irish, though I had already detected it from her fine Irish southern brogue. «I am, indeed,» she replied. «So am I,» said I. And so we got «a-talking,» and did not listen much to the performance afterwards. Poor Father Meinrich was astonished to see Mary and myself such great friends. «Where did you meet Father Doherty before, Mary?»

« Troth, Father, I never laid my eyes on him before
to-night, nor he on me. » « And how did you become
acquainted ? » « Oh ! » said she, « we Irish are like the
Bedouius; we'd know one another ten miles off, and
in the dark, too. » But I must come back to where I
left off.

Besides the Europeans who inhabit what is called
the « Quartier d'Europe, » there are Egyptians,
Coptes, Abyssinians, Turks, and Greeks. The Arabs,
too, are in great numbers, and inhabit the « Quartier
Arabe, » a filthy region with narrow winding streets,
bordered on each side by small shops called *bazaars*.

The European part of the town, which is farthest
removed from the present harbour, is very handsome. The streets are wide and clean, and are daily
watered, to lay the fine white dust, which, under the
slightest wind, rises in clouds, and is almost blind-
ing. The houses are, in several places, as fine
as any I have seen in the best European cities.
There are several large squares, having shady
walks, flower-beds, and fountains of water. But
when, turning from this quarter, you enter the
« Quartier Arabe, » you are introduced to sights,
scenes, and smells of a very different order.

Fancy a whole labyrinth of lanes running in
every direction, and crossing each other with most
inextricable confusion, covering an area of about a
mile deep by two miles long, and extending all along
what is called « Le port-neuf. » Most of the little one-
story houses are shops, the reunion of which is
called a *bazaar;* and the name is appropriate, for
the variety of the wares is quite astonishing. The
streets are, in many cases, only ten feet wide; in
the middle runs a filthy stream that carries away a
portion of the effluvia; the rest is eaten by hungry
dogs, or remains evaporating in the sun, emitting
odors that have not the slightest affinity with « the
essence of roses. » The crowd is so dense that you

can hardly pass; and the Arabs gesticulate so emphatically when speaking, and shout so loudly, that you would imagine they were all quarrelling. The little children are crawling about or sitting at the door-steps, many of them, as Byron would say, « in naked majesty. » The men have turbans of different colours, an open shirt, and a pair of wide trowsers reaching to the knee. The women are all closely veiled.

Your historical knowledge has already made known to you that Alexandria was famous, in former times, for its learning, as well as by its commerce and enterprise. Right opposite the city is a little island : it was here that the Bible was translated by the Seventy Interpreters into the Greek language. It was in Alexandria that learning principally flourished in the first ages of Christianity. Here the Gnostic heretics had their schools ; here the Arians persecuted the great St. Athanasius, who was bishop of Alexandria ; here lived Origenes and St. Cyril ; here was burned the great library by the Caliph Omar, in the seventh century ; here Pompey succumbed to the fatal graces of Cleopatra ; here, too, the same queen held enthralled by her beauty the triumvir Anthony ; and, in fine, it was near Alexandria that the famous Lord Nelson defeated the French fleet at Aboukir, and blasted the fruits of Napoleon's splendid victories in Egypt.

But all these souvenirs are now, perhaps, forgotten, or, at least, little thought of, amid the noise and bustle of modern industry. Alexandria, to-day, though still considerable, is greatly diminished from what it once was. Indeed, no traces of its former history remain, save the two monoliths called « Pompey's pillar » and « Cleopatra's needle, » which stand at opposite extremities of the city.

Christmas is now in the past, and we intend starting to-morrow for Port-Saïd, *en route* for Jaffa. Our

passports had been taken from us when we landed,
that they might be examined by the Turkish authorities; we got them back to-day at the office of the
British consul, whither they had been sent......

"We hired a vehicle after breakfast, to take us as
far as Pompey's pillar. We passed through the Arab
village, amid the mud-cabins and little, naked, children; then out of the city, through the Gabari gate,
and down towards the strand, to see the catacombs.
They are square caverns, dug in the rock along the
beach, for about a quarter of a mile; they did not
appear to me to be very interesting. The heat is so
great that I fear I shall be awfully tanned by the
sun. We passed a caravan of pilgrims on their way
to Mecca. It seems that we shall meet them often
now, for this is the season for this devotion. They
reminded me of a gipsy camp. They had pitched their
tents on a great pasture outside the city; and were
cooking some victuals to be eaten after sun-down.
The camels stood grazing near the tents. The men
and women were sitting in groups; engaged, I
suppose, in prayer. They had strings of beads in
their hands, and muttered as they passed them
through their fingers. I had already met many
Turks in the city thus «saying their beads», as they
went along the streets, or as they sat at their shop-
doors waiting for customers.

"The present month is their *Rhamadan*, or fasting-
time. It began on the 6th current, and will terminate
on the 6th of January. The faithful eat absolutely
nothing from sunrise to sundown; but they pay up
for lost time during the night. The law of Maho-
met allows them to eat as much as they like during
the night-time; and they are not slow, from all
accounts, in putting the privilege to good advantage.

"We next passed by a Turkish cemetery. The
tombs are flat slabs of stone, six feet long by four
feet wide, slightly raised from the ground, but

laying flat; at the head and foot is a long narrow stone surmonted by the crescent. It is forbidden for Christians to go through this holy ground; so we had to drive round the base of a hill, and on coming to a turn in the road we perceived Pompey's pillar on the summit.

I here transcribe *verbatim* from my note-book. *26th December.*—I am now leaning against the base of Pompey's pillar, a splendid monolith of pink granite, 114 feet high. It is of the Corinthian order, and its proportions are exquisitely beautiful. Its position sets it off to much advantage, being on the summit of a hill which slopes down from it on all sides. Beneath me, looking westward, is the Turkish grave-yard, with its white stones glancing in the sun. Beyond is a fine grove of trees, and still further rises the splendid palace built by Ibrahim Pacha, the late Khedive of Egypt. Southward I see the glittering waters of the Mediterranean, and to the east I can descry the minarets of Alexandria. As I write, I am surrounded by a whole troop of little half-naked Arab urchins, clamouring for *backshiche*, and offering all sorts of objects for sale.

We then drove along the canal of the Nile for half an hour, amid most enchanting scenery. The road was shaded by tall over-branching trees, and bordered by handsome country-seats, chiefly belonging to the merchants of the city. There are orange groves with the most tempting golden fruits, acacias, fig-trees, and a host of most beautiful flower-plots. It is a little paradise. We then visited the palace of Ishmael Pacha, the present governor, who resides generally at Cairo, and drove home through the European quarter, just in time for six-o'clock dinner.

27th December.—I said mass this morning in honour of the Holy Family, to whose native country we are travelling. The cathedral is dedicated to St. Catherine, the patroness of all the eastern churches. It is a very fine building ; over the front altar is a very handsome picture of the saint confuting the pagan philosophers : it is a gift from the Empress of Austria. The Capuchin monks, who attend the church, have a convent close by ; they are kind and pious. On the other side the Christian Brothers have a large school, attended by 600 children. The Jubilee is now going on, and is preached in French and Italian alternately by the friars. There is also a nunnery, but I had not time to visit it. The Greek schismatics are very numerous here, too ; their church of St. Nicholas is clumsily built, but very large. There are Armenians (Catholics), who also follow the Greek rite ; they are presided over by a Patriarch, now in Rome.

I noticed a singular phenomenon here. Among the inhabitants of the city are a number of Nubians, as black as the...... I was going to say as the devil,—but let us say the ace of spades,—and just as ugly. Now, above all others,—just imagine ! they must needs dress from top to toe in the purest of white ! The great wenches, with lips as red as cherries and as large as plum-puddings, flaunt a white muslin veil over a loose white dress ; and the darkies, with their great rolling whites of eyes, have white turbans and white shirts. What's this for ?—can you tell ? Is it misplaced beauty or love of contrast ? *Chi lo sa ?* I told you that the Arab and Turkish women are veiled. A piece of bamboo descends across the middle of the forehead to the top of the nose ; there it meets a cross-bar, and from this hangs a triangular black piece of cloth, which covers the face to the chin when the wind does not blow it aside. The chin is tattooed with blue ink, and the nails on each hand are besmeared with red paint. I cannot say whether this is a prescription of the Koran, or the «nick of fashion»; but it is abominably ugly—worse than waterfalls.

„Donkeys are all the go—in fact, «quite the thing,» out here. They are small, but spirited, and very lively; you meet them at every corner, and the Arabs tease you, in broken English, to «get up, sir;» «goot tonkey, mister;» «go fast, sir.» If you do mount, you find yourself in a great red saddle, with very high pommel. You can hold on to this or the reins, as you choose. I preferred the former. When your feet are firm in the stirrup, the little guide, a fine little Arab brute, asks you : «Where you go, sir?» «Any where you like.» I replied, «so long as you bring me back to the hotel in twenty minutes.» Bang! bang! goes the stick on the little donkey's hind-quarters; gingle! gingle! go the bells round his neck. I shut my eyes and hold hard. Off we go at a furious gallop, the Arab urchin keeping pace all the time, and shouting like mad. Oh! if you had but seen your brother then, dear St. C., flying through the streets of Alexandria on an ass, pursued by a fierce-looking Arab! It was not so dangerous, however, as I imagined; and I was not a bit ridiculous—for, as I said, *it's all the go* here.

„But, oh! if you could see the camels! They are not over-handsome when you see them in pictures; but when they are in the streets, passing along in caravans, with loads of hay or stones tied up to their humps, they are absolutely frightful. Their great awkward necks are poked out as if they were looking for some one to cut it off and have done with it. Their skin is as shrivelled as a cross old maid's, only a shade browner; their knees are knock-knees, and their feet are *splaw-feet*, fine for killing cockroaches, but by no means neat. As to their gait, I can compare it to nothing but the *Grecian bend*. Did you ever see the Grecian bend? I witnessed it on the

Boulevards in Paris for the first time, and here for the second.

Dogs are very numerous, and belong to no one. I counted fourteen of them basking in the sun on one of the squares. This basking is not exclusively confined to dogs. You very often come across a full-grown nigger stretched at full length, and enjoying a comfortable nap under the scorching rays of the sun; and though the heat is strong enough to roast a leg of mutton, the sleeper appears to take it quite coolly. There is no use disputing taste, however; so I did not disturb any of them.

Nous (¹) avons acheté nos billets pour Jaffa, et à deux heures de relevée nous sommes partis de notre hôtel, avec notre guide, le bon Philippe. Il nous a conduits à bord d'un vaisseau des Messageries Impériales, et nous a quittés après nous avoir souhaité bon voyage. Nous avons attendu jusqu'à 3 heures le complet chargement du navire. Alors on entendit un coup de sifflet, l'ancre fut levée, et l'*Eridan* se mit en mouvement. Peu à peu nous nous dégageâmes des nombreux vaisseaux de toute espèce et de tout pavillon qui encombraient le port, nous passons devant la douane,—un établissement magnifique en pierre de taille,—puis la ville s'efface rapidement; bientôt nous ne voyons plus que le haut de la colonne de Pompée, voici enfin que nous n'avons plus d'un côté que la vaste mer et de l'autre un banc de terre basse et sablonneuse. Le temps est au beau fixe; le vent est bon, nous serons au Port Saïd demain

28 *Décembre.*—A notre réveil ce matin nous trouvâmes notre vaisseau à l'ancre dans le Port Saïd. Comme nous devons passer la journée ici, nous profitons du retard pour aller voir la ville. Des bateliers Arabes nous conduisent à terre pour la

(¹) Here, again, Mr. Doherty breaks out in French for a few pages.

modique somme de 2 francs. La ville est située sur une pointe de terre séparée du continent par un port très-considérable qu'on a creusé à l'entrée du canal de Suez. C'est un marais qu'on a rehaussé et desséché au moyen de terre apportée à dos de chameau. Juge un peu quel travail cela a dû coûter.

Nous trouvâmes le quai encombré d'Arabes flâneurs, et probablement voleurs par là même ; mais, sans nous occuper de leurs demandes pour des *backshiche*, nous nous rendîmes à la ville. Elle est tout entière de bois, et me fait la mine d'un immense champ de foire. Elle n'a pas l'air stable ; on voit qu'elle ne tire son importance que de l'activité passagère des premiers travaux, mais elle ne durera guères. Les maisons sont plus ou moins allignées. Chaque nation a son quartier. Il y a des consulats français, anglais, prussien, espagnol, italien, portuguais, chacun ombragé du pavillon national. Ici, comme à Alexandrie, nous voyons les Arabes couchés au grand soleil. Les femmes ont encore le bambou et le voile. Mais j'ai remarqué une particularité qui ne m'avait pas frappé là-bas. Chaque femme porte, attachées au bambou dont je parle, plusieurs pièces de monnaie d'or ou d'argent. C'est sa dot. Chacun est à même de compter sa fortune. De cette façon le *cavalier* sait à quoi s'en tenir avant de faire ses avances. Mais, mon Dieu ! la femme est ici comme ailleurs, on me dit que les pièces sont souvent fausses ou empruntées.

Nous sommes allés rendre visite aux Pères Capucins qui sont encore logés dans un couvent provisoire. Ils sont trois prêtres et quelques frères. Ils construisent actuellement un beau couvent et une église assez grande. Le tout vient d'un généreux bienfaiteur autrichien qui leur a défendu de dévoiler son nom. Mais Dieu le sait. Il y a environ 4000 catholiques dans la ville. A l'extrémité de la pointe et en avant de la ville, est un phare de 182 pieds de

haut. En arrière de la ville et de l'autre côté du
port, on voit le canal, dont l'entrée est marquée par
deux grosses tours peintes en rouge et affectant la
forme. d'obélisques. Tout autour s'étend le désert
silencieux et solitaire, sans le moindre signe de
végétation.

À 5 heures P.M. nous quittons le Port Saïd. Le
temps est superbe. Demain, enfin, nous verrons la
Terre Sainte.

29 *décembre.*—Nous voici donc en face de l'objet
de nos désirs! La Terre Sainte est devant nous;
nous contemplons, les larmes aux yeux, et le cœur
rempli d'émotions les plus douces, ce sol béni, té-
moin de tant de miracles, la patrie de Jésus, Marie,
Joseph. Notre vaisseau est à l'ancre devant Jaffa,
l'ancien Joppé, à un demi-mille du rivage. Encore
quelques minutes, et nous aurons touché au terme
de notre voyage. Nous avons fait le grand trajet.
Dieu nous conduit comme par la main. *Sit bene-
dictus per sæcula.*

Jaffa rises in amphitheatre, by the border of the
sea, to the height of about a hundred feet. Oh!
what a host of souvenirs hover round its rock-bound
summit! Here Noah, at God's command, built the
ark, one of the beautiful figures of the Church of
God. Here Jonas was sent on his prophetic mission
to Nineveh. Here Peter had the vision of clean and
unclean animals ; here he preached and performed
miracles. Here, too, came the warlike hosts of the
Crusaders to do battle in the cause of God ; and
here, still, I can see the cross which stands over the
Franciscan convent, shining out brilliantly as it
catches the rays of the morning sun, like a beacon-
light to guide poor wearied travellers in the path
that leadeth to rest !

In front of the port lies a ridge of breakers,
through which a narrow passage leads to the wharf.
It appears that, in stormy weather, the landing is

very dangerous. A few weeks ago the Emperor of Austria was on the point of being lost as he came through. We have, therefore, every reason to thank God for the splendid weather and the calm unruffled sea. After a good deal of fighting with the rascally Arab boatmen, we hired a small craft, and in ten minutes we landed at the pier. The customhouse officers made no secret about telling us that by paying a small *backshiche* they would forego the examination of our baggage. Of course we made ourselves agreeable. We jostled through a motley crowd of hangers-on, sternly refusing to accept their services, and made our way to the convent. We were warmly received by Father Daniel, whose office it is to see after the pilgrims ; and on our expressing a desire to say mass, we were conducted to the sacristy. I need not tell you with what emotion I offered up the Holy Mysteries for the first time in the Holy Land. The church-floor is covered with mats, on which are a lot of little Arab children in the Turkish dress, and, behind them, about 100 women, all dressed in white. The effect is handsome. They are half-kneeling, half-sitting. There are some men also, with their turbans in their hands, and who have taken off their shoes at the door. All are seemingly devout and prayerful. On the grand altar is a picture of the miraculous vision of St. Peter. I said mass here in thanksgiving for our safe journey. The church is all hung round with *ex-votos.*

After the morning's devotion we were conducted to the pilgrims' refectory, and got some very good coffee without milk, and very good bread without butter. We must not expect to see much more butter till we reach home again ; but the coffee is delicious. You can have no idea of how the coffee tastes out here. Whether the plant is different, or whether they have some secret in making it, I do not know ; but it is not the same beverage at all as we drink in Canada.

It was now 10 o'clock, and we had hardly reached the parlour of the monastery, where we were surrounded by the Arabs again, who wished to hire horses to take us to Jerusalem. Father Daniel, an old Austrian soldier, drove them out, not at the point of the bayonet, but with a robust broom-handle, and, selecting one from amongst them, told us that he was the only honest man in the crowd. We gave him 50 francs to furnish us with 4 horses, a mule for our baggage, and an Arab guide with an ass. Twenty-five francs were deposited in the Father's hands; the rest was to be paid when we should reach Jerusalem. We were to start at one o'clock, after dinner; and to remain all night at the convent of Ramleh. Padre Daniele gave us, in broken French and Italian, a few useful hints as to the manner of treating with the Arabs, and they agree with what had been told us before. A little blustering must be done ; otherwise they would play tricks upon travellers. They are the most unprincipled set of fellows I ever came across. They make a bargain with you, and when they get you on the road they insist on getting more money, together with the eternal *backshiche*. This *backshiche* is an Arab word corresponding to the French *pourboire* and the Italian *qualche. cosa per l'amor di Dio*. Every Arab, man, woman, and child, asks you for it. They appear to think that Europeans have no right to pass them without opening their purses.

We dined at twelve o'clock with a French doctor who had just returned from Jerusalem and a Turkish gentleman who belongs to the household of the Pacha. Padre Daniele tied up a few bottles of wine and some oranges and cakes, and prevailed on us to take them with us for the journey. At one o'clock exactly we mounted our sorry beasts, and, preceded by the guide, we bade adieu to the good monks, and set out on our journey under a boiling sun.

Before we got clear of the town we had to pass through a lot of little steep, narrow streets, narrower even than those we had seen in Alexandria. They were filled with all sorts of persons—working, talking, sitting, or drinking coffee, and smoking. There were shoemakers, carpenters, tinkers, and weavers; there were old women selling oranges, and old men selling wine; some scolding, some laughing, but all bawling lustily at the top of their voices. I threw the reins over my horse's neck, and delivered myself up to his instinct to extricate me from this Babel. I shut my eyes twice, as I saw him (as I thought) about to crush a few naked children that were lying in the road, and twice more, as he slapped an old woman's face by whisking his tail. He managed, however, to escape any very untoward accident; and after about a quarter of an hour thus picking our steps, we found ourselves at the outskirts of the town, on the plains of *Sharon*.

As you leave the precincts of the town you find yourself on a very beautiful road, bordered on each side with groves of orange-trees and cactus. The effect of the golden fruit, half-hidden amid the luxuriant foliage, is strikingly handsome. It continues thus for about a quarter of a mile ; and then, just as you arrive at the tomb of a Dervish—a small Turkish temple with nine cupolas—you are issued into a vast plain stretching away as far as the eye can reach, in gentle undulations, and covered with a mantle of rich green. This is the plain of *Sharon*. It is the former country of the Philistines. Here Samson burned their crops ; here he took to himself for wife that *upsetting* young female called Delilah, who was the cause of all his troubles ; here, too, David fed numerous flocks of sheep. At the entrance of the plain we fell in with a caravan, composed of the Protestant bishop of Jerusalem, his wife, his son and *his* wife, a Scotchman from Glasgow, an Austrian officer, a Prussian count, and two old Russian ladies. They were all on horseback, except the bishop's wife, who travelled in a palanquin. We joined the party, and formed altogether a very numerous cavalcade.

The road is level and very good. The journey would have been very pleasant had the sun been less hot and our saddles something softer. My horse ran away with me when we were about half a league from Ramleh, and stopped, of his own accord, at the convent-gate at 4½ P.M.

I introduced myself to the good monk who is always in attendance on pilgrims, and explained to him the reason of my appearance in advance of the party. He laughed at my adventure. In about three-quarters of an hour the rest of the party arrived, and we were all shewn to our rooms. The bishop, however, did not come; he, with his family, remained at a house in the town.

Ramleh was formerly called Arimathea, and in the convent is still the room where St. Joseph of Arimathea was buried. The town is built of white stone ; the houses are of one story, with flat roofs, and surmounted by flattened domes. Here and there are tall-spreading palm-trees that rise gracefully and throw a grateful shade over the houses. We were joined at supper by two German nuns, who came on horseback from Jerusalem, and are on their way back to Jaffa.

To-morrow we start at 5½ A.M. for Jerusalem. We start thus early for two reasons : first, to make as much of the journey as we can through the plains before the sun becomes too hot ; secondly, to arrive in Jerusalem before sundown. The gates of the city are closed by the Turks at sunset, and are opened at sunrise next morning.

JERUSALEM.

«Jerusalem, my happy home !
«How do I sigh for thee !
« When shall mine exile have an end ?
«Thy joys when shall I see ? »

Thus sang, in days long gone by, the children of
Israel as they sat and wept by the borders of the
river of Babylon. But the joys and glories of the
Holy City have long since departed ; and on seeing
the desolation that surrounds her, the words of
Jeremiah recur to the mind as being fitter of application to the present time : «How doth the city
sit solitary that was full of people ! How is she
become as a widow ! She that was great among
the nations, and a princess among the provinces,
how is she become tributary !» Aye, mournful
and sad she sits amid the ruins of her former
greatness. The howling wilderness stretches its
dreary barrenness on all sides; the Crescent of
the infidel Mahometan stands on the mount of
Moria, where once arose, in wondrous splendor, the
temple of Solomon ; her narrow, ill-paved streets are
filled with an unsightly rabble—a population of
beggars, filthy and dishonest ; ruins and decay meet
the gaze at every step ; and were it not for the
softening influences of the memory of Christ that
abound everywhere, the soul would be filled with
sorrow and disgust.

30th December.—I write to you now, my dear
St. C., from the Holy City of Jerusalem. We arrived
at $4\frac{1}{2}$ P.M., and I am now sitting in my little room
in the Franciscan convent of Casa Nova.

We set out from the little town of Ramleh this
morning at six o'clock. The sun had not yet risen,
and the morning-air was somewhat sharp. As we
left the convent-gate and issued through a grove of
cactuses into the plain of Sharon, our refreshed

senses were more fully enabled to enjoy the beauties
of the scenery. Around about us, on every side,
lay the wide, level plain, bounded to the north by
the mountains of Israel, whose rugged tops stood out
boldly against the clear, cold sky. In front, directly
eastward, were the mountains of Judea, their sum-
mits all aglow as the horizon reddened at the
approach of the sun. Blue smoke was curling up
from the midst of the little Turkish hamlets. A
solitary turbaned fellah might be seen wending his
way, at intervals, leading his camels towards
Jaffa—on their way to market, I presume. Immense
flocks of sheep, calves, and asses, were grazing
quietly in the fields; a little bird now and then
flitted across our path. We could follow the windings of the road for miles and miles by the Turkish
guard-houses that border it all along from Jaffa to
Jerusalem, at intervals of three-quarters of a mile.
One might, with a very slight effort of imagination,
fancy himself away back through the course of
ages, to the very days of Samson or David, so
Eastern (if I may say so) is the whole prospect,
were it not for the telegraph-poles and wires that
break in on your dream, like some unpleasant
truth, and disturb your imaginings. However useful
modern inventions are, they certainly destroy the
poetry of the landscape here.

I had remained behind the rest of the cavalcade
with our guide, a very chatty little Sicilian,
whose acquaintance I cultivated for the want of
better, and also to practice and augment my slender
stock of Italian. He was seated on a sober mule,
which also carried our baggage, and I bestrode my
«milk-white steed.» As I felt my saddle rather
hard, and, consequently, trying on my nerves, I
requested him to change seats with me for a time.
He got down, and I was *hoisted* into his airy seat;
but while he was attending me, the horse I had

just left profited of a moment's liberty, and took to
his heels over the plain. My companions were
somewhat frightened when they saw the beast come
thundering after them without its rider, and thought
that I had been unhorsed. I soon, however, came up
with them, and the whole caravan came to a halt
and set about coaxing back the fugitive. He was
caught, like many a one else before him, by false
promises; the Sicilian got up, and we continued our
journey.

At half-past nine we reached the foot of the
ravine at the entrance of the mountains of Judea,
close to the spot where, according to tradition, the
«good thief» used to live and ply his trade. The
heat, by this time, had become intense. The mountains at first are picturesque and pretty well cultivated : there are some good olive-plantations and
pasture-grounds, filled with black and yellow goats;
but after an hour's ride the soil becomes barren
and rocky, till, at last, every sign of vegetation
disappears. The little villages are all passed, and for
three hours you see nothing but one immense sea
of stony hills, without the slightest sign of any kind
of life or movement. I never saw anything more
dreary or monotonous. Sometimes the mountains are isolated and conical-shaped, and give an
idea of the «high places» so often mentioned in the
Bible. At twelve, or a little after, we reached a
little café, a miserable hut, or open tent, where two
half-nude Arabs were making coffee. We rested
here for a while, took some refreshments, and
started again under the broiling sun. Oh! such
heat! Nothing except Nebuchadnezzar's furnace,
seven times heated, could give you any idea of it.
At times I really thought I was melting down and
running off on the ground. However, I went
through it for three long hours, crossing, at about
two o'clock, the brook where David got the stones,

and the valley where he slew Goliath. After going up the face of the mountain that bounds this valley to the east, we reached a high level plateau, covered with the ruins of palaces and temples ; then we came to a gentle ascent, crowned by a Turkish guard-house. When we reached the summit, Jerusalem suddenly burst upon our view.

We immediately alighted from our horses, and, kneeling by the roadside, recited the psalm : « *Læta-tus sum in his quæ dicta sunt mihi: in domum Domini ibimus.*» I had read, in the history of. the Crusades, of the emotions experienced by the Chris-tian warriors when they first caught sight of the Holy City. I could now almost fully realize them. The fatigue of the journey had completely dis-appeared. My soul was filled at once with joy and sorrow; but the prevailing sentiment was one of profound reverence and devotion. I kissed the ground, and, with as much humility as I could, asked pardon of God for all my sins. The scene, from the eminence on which we were placed, was one which shall be ever present to my mind. On either side of the road, and at a distance of about half a mile inwards, stood two very handsome and im-posing buildings, of yellow stone. The one on the left is a convent, and the other a consulate, hospital, pilgrim-house, and chapel, all connected. Both belong to the schismatics. The road itself, which lay down a gentle slope to the gate of Jerusalem, was bordered by dwelling-houses thinly scattered, some tenanted, and others in course of construction. Olive-plantations variegated the rocky soil, and here and there a stately palm-tree towered high above all. Behind us, nestling among the arid mountains, was Bethlehem (the house of Bread), and directly in front, but far beyond the city, and blue in the dis-tance, stood the mountains of Moab. The declining sun lit up the white turretted walls of the city, and burnished with equal refulgency the cross over the dome of the church of the Holy Sepulchre, and the crescent over the Mosque of Omar.

We again mounted our horses, and rode down at a trot towards the gate called, by some, «The Pilgrims' Gate,» and by others, «The Gate of Jaffa.» Immediately outside the gate, which, I may as well remark at once, stands almost beneath the Tower of David, is the Custom-House. We were, of course, surrounded at once by a crowd of idlers and officials, all in some way eager to fleece poor strangers. There were women enveloped in white from head to foot; Turks with green turbans and wide pants; Arabs with their heads tied up as if they suffered from a chronic headache, and others, who, as I learned afterwards, were Russians, with top-coats and large fur-caps,—all babbling, talking, screaming, and endeavouring to make us understand that we stood in absolute need of their assistance. Amongst them we descried the Turkish soldier charged with the direction of the post, and driving the rabble before us in a very unceremonious manner. We accosted him in French:—«Qu'est-ce qu'il faut faire avec ces gens-là, soldat?» He shrugged his shoulders. We then tried him with Italian, and fortunately he spoke it, as he said, *un poco*. He was very civil, took our passports, telling us. that we would find them at the consul's office next morning, accepted our proffered *backshiche* on condition that he would not examine our baggage, cleared us of the howling crowd, and let us «pass on.» Two minutes after, we passed under the arched gateway; and at last I stood within the walls of Jerusalem!! Oh! how far away from home!

Our Arab guide led us across an irregular, ill-paved piazza, up through a narrow winding street, and we dismounted, tired and jaded, at the convent-door. The good *frère Pierre* received us with open arms;

we then shewed him our credentials as priests, upon
which he insisted on kissing our hands. We paid
our Arab for the horses, and dismissed him with a
backshiche. We drank some very good and refreshing cordial. We then were shewn to our rooms,
and, while waiting for the supper, performed
ablutions, which had become extremely necessary
from the dust which had accumulated on our faces,
hands, and necks, during the day's journey.

At 7 o'clock the bell summoned us to the supper-
hall, where we had the pleasure of meeting a number of pilgrims,—four Frenchmen, three Italians,
two Spaniards, and a Polish gentleman. As no
ceremony is used, we were soon all joined in general
and pleasant conversation. We, being the *new-
comers*, and from the farthest part of the world,
were naturally greater objects of curiosity than the
rest; so we had to give them all sorts of details
about America and Canada. After supper we
adjourned to the terrace formed by the flat roof of
the convent, and enjoyed a moonlight view of the
city. The calm silver light covered the silent house-
tops, minarets, and cupolas with a mantle of beauty.
Mount Olivet was especially resplendent as it stood
out in bold relief against the clear sky, and contrasted
trenchantly with the sombre darkness of the Valley
of Josaphat, which lies at its base. We enjoyed a
pleasant evening until 9 o'clock, when we retired to
our rooms.

31st December. — The description of yesterday's
adventures was, I fear, long and tedious; but the
journey was so long, and the impressions so numerous, that I could not in any way manage to
condense my narrative. To-day I will be more
concise.

I rose at half-past five, and, after my morning
devotions, set out to say mass in the church of the
« Holy Saviour. » This is the parish-church, or,

rather, the cathedral of Jerusalem, and will continue
to be such until the Patriarch's church will have
been completed. It is quite close to the convent
where we are now remaining, and is attended by
the Capuchins. The good brother Pierre conducted
us through a narrow winding street ; then through
an archway; then up a flight of stairs, through
the corridors of the monastery ; and, finally, we
arrived at the sacristy, where we found two monks
and a lot of little orphans (Arabs) waiting to serve
mass.

I immediately robed, and was conducted to the
chapel standing at the left of the grand-altar. You
may easily guess my joy when the monk told me
that the altar at which I was going to say mass
bears the indulgences of the « upper room,» in
which the Blessed Eucharist was instituted. The
indulgences have been thus transferred because the
room itself is in the possession of the Turks. I said
mass in thanksgiving. for our safe arrival. It is
needless to add how solemn the words of Consecra-
tion became in this place. After my mass I assisted
at grand-mass, which is celebrated every morning
at half-past seven. The congregation, exclusively
composed of Arab Catholics, was large and very
edifying. The men wore their turbans in church,
and the women were, as usual, closely veiled and
enveloped in the large white cloak, or shroud. An
old hump-backed monk played the organ with as
much vigour as if he were thirty, though he counts
every day of 82 ! Two kettle-drums helped to give
effect, and the harmonious. voices of a choir composed of little Arab orphans was extremely pleasing.

The church is in nowise remarkable, but·its
treasury is very rich. I was so very fatigued after
my journey of yesterday that l made only one visit
to the Holy Sepulchre. I will give you a full description of the church in a few days. We have

arranged to make the «True Way of the Cross» to-morrow, with one of the monks as our guide. What happiness on this new-year's morning!—to begin the year by following the footsteps of our suffering Lord! God grant I may never stray far from them. We went to see the *Révérendissime* Father Seraphino, the Superior and Provincial of the Franciscan Order for the Eastern countries. He was most affable, and told us that we could say mass at any of the sanctuaries we. chose. He served us with coffee, and then a delicious *liqueur*. From the window of his room we had a full view of Mount Olivet.

NEW-YEAR'S DAY, 1870.—Would you have thought, dear St. C., last new year's day, that I would address you on that-day-twelve-months from Jerusalem? I myself had not the least notion of it. However, you see, such is the case; and I give thanks to God for such a favour. I wrote you all my good wishes in a letter, so I need not repeat them here. I will, therefore, give you a short account of what happened me since yesterday.

At 6 o'clock this morning Père Clément came to our rooms to guide us through the «Way of the Cross.» He is an Italian, and is employed as a teacher in the school held by the good Fathers. As we wended our way through the rough, uneven streets, he told us about his school. His pupils are chiefly Arabs, but there are some Turkish children and a few Europeans. They are taught the ordinary branches of primary education in Arab and Italian. When they attain the age of 14 they are generally apprenticed to some trade, and continue still under the immediate surveillance of the monks. The Franciscans have workshops here for every trade, and one of the lay brothers superintends each. The poor little children are generally very disgusting (excuse the word) and slovenly, having no domestic education, and being, consequently, in blissful ignorance of anything approaching to cleanliness or good manners. Besides their schooling, the Fathers are often obliged to give them clothes. The first thing done in class every morning, even before prayer, is to wash their faces, hands, &c., &c., besides making a raid on the *creeping things* that abound on their persons. Then they are furnished with a good breakfast, a little recreation, and class begins. All this is very onerous; but the monks are glad that the parents allow them to come to school at all, for in the education of the children and their early training lie all the hopes of converting the population. «Nous n'avons guère de consolations,» *said* Père Clément; «mais nous faisons toujours ce que nous pouvons, et laissons à Dieu le reste.»

I found this sentiment very beautiful : it pourtrays the patient resignation of the missionary, and gives the spirit requisite in all those who labour in God's cause. Indeed, nowhere could that sentiment be more opportune than here, in this very city, where Christ—the first missionary—toiled and preached with such little apparent success. He worked and prayed for three years, desiring that all sinners might « be converted and live » ; yet, after all He did, at the hour of death He only had Mary and John at the foot of the cross ! His mission appeared to have been a complete failure ; still, in God's own time, the seed which he had sown sprang into maturity, and the world was converted. In such a spirit does the holy Franciscan friar work in his own obscure but powerful way, amid the trials and poverty of the Eastern missions. He labours and waits in the spirit of hopeful prayer, and he must eventually succeed.

At half-past six, amid the loneliness of the deserted streets, and in the gray dawn of morning, we knelt at the first station. The whole length of the road, from the first station to Mount Calvary, might

be computed, I think, to about the three-fourths of
a mile. The first three stations are made in one street,
which runs downwards with a slight inclination.
You then go along a level street, and come to the
fourth station, where a narrow lane intersects the
main road. It was at this place, on a stone step, that
the Blessed Virgin caught sight of her Divine Son.
You continue to follow the same line till you arrive
at the fifth station. Here you meet the first houses,
for the road we have first travelled is bordered on
either side by high stone-walls. Here, too, the ascent
begins ; and it must have been very painful for our
dear Lord to drag the heavy cross up its rugged
pavements. It is about as steep as Mountain-hill in
some parts. From the sixth station to the seventh you
pass under a long archway formed by houses which
are built right across the road ; and here you come
to a high stone-wall, where a high column stands.
This was formerly at the gate of the city ; and as
criminals always passed through it, on their way to
execution, it was called the « Judiciary Gate. » Here
Jesus fell fainting for the second time. The sentence
of death was read over Him for the last time, and He
was hurried on to Golgotha.

He continued His upward, toilsome way ; and after
going about twelve feet, He met the pious women,
and, forgetting his own sufferings, He turned to
them and sweetly consoled them, saying : «Weep not,
daughters,» &c. The 9th station is close to the church.
Finally you enter, and the 10th, 11th, 12th and
13th are all on Mount Calvary. The 14th station is,
of course, at the Holy Sepulchre, in the middle of
the church, under a large dome or cupola, at about
fifty paces from the summit of the mount.

After performing the station I went to the sacristy, and prepared for mass. When I was vested,
I was conducted by the servant to Mount Calvary
again ; and there, at the altar erected on the very

spot where Jesus was nailed to the cross, and at about ten feet from the place where He hung for three hours, I began the mass called *Missa de Passione.* ([1])

Oh! my dear St. C., shall I ever forget this moment—so solemn; so sweet and consoling, and yet so dreadful! I am not ashamed to confess that I had wept bitter, scalding tears, at the different stations; but here I was seized with a sort of tremor, which rendered it impossible for me to begin the Holy Mystery for some time.

Methought that the rich ornaments, the golden chandeliers, the thousand bright lamps, the wondrous flowers, the marble-vaulted roof—in a word, that all the riches with which piety has bedecked this thrice Holy Place had disappeared. The numerous pilgrims who were kneeling around about the altar had also vanished, and the hill was once more naked, rugged, and reddened with blood. The ruthless bronzed Roman legionaries, the triumphant High-priest, the jeering Pharisees, the excited rabble, started once more into life. They were all there, exulting, with hideous, fiendish joy, at their brutal victory. I heard their cries and vociferations and blasphemies ringing out on the clear air and mounting to the skies. I listened to the cruel echo, as it came reverberating back over the city from Mount Olivet, and then went on defiantly till it died away in the mountain-gorges near Bethlehem. I raised my eyes to the cross. The large, life-sized image of the crucified Redeemer that stands on the hallowed spot became suddenly animated; the rich, generous blood of the Lamb flowed in torrents; the huge nails clang to the festering wounds; the dying eyes were mournfully and tenderly turned towards me; the lips moved, and I heard a voice

([1]) Passion-Mass,

whispering affectionately : " My child, see how much I love thee." At that moment I would have willingly laid down my life ; and since this was neither possible nor required, I promised, from the very depths of my soul, never, never more to mortally offend Him who had thus suffered for me. And, oh ! do believe me, dear St. C., you were present to my memory then, and I prayed that you might ever be a worthy spouse of the Divine Master, ever near Him, ever close to Him, till He would take you to Himself, and crown your life of sacrifice amid Heavenly joys.

I made my thanksgiving-act in the Holy Sepulchre, leaning on the marble slab that covers the tomb of Christ. How happy if I could have felt some of those delicious throes of Divine love, such as the seraphic Francis felt in the contemplation of Heaven's gifts! But, alas ! the field of my heart had not been sufficiently cultivated to produce those pure flowers of devotion. I had, therefore, to content myself with some acts of Desire, and especially of Resolution.

It was late when we got back to the convent, somewhat tired, but well satisfied with what we had seen and felt. I have obtained permission to sleep in the church to-night, and say mass in the Sepulchre to-morrow morning.

2nd January.—Any one wishing to say mass in the Holy Sepulchre must pass the night in the adjoining convent, where there are a few rooms set apart for pilgrims. The reason of this is, that the Turks, possessing the keys of the church, lock it up after sunset, and do not open it until pretty late in the day ; on some days they even keep it closed the whole time. Such is the established rule ; and this is why the different rites, or, at least, the priests that profess them, are obliged to reside permanently in cells that open on the church.

It is curious to see with what jealousy the allotted portion is guarded by each. But of all this I will speak more at length th on a future day. Let me only remark that the Catholics have the right of saying three masses every day (two low masses and one high mass), at the appointed hour, in the Holy Sepulchre itself. The two low masses are at 4 o'clock and half-past four A.M., and the high mass at 5.

For these motives, then, I was obliged to take lodging, as I have said, for the night, in a little room that opened out on the Latin part of the gallery that surrounds the cupola. I, however, considered this more in the light of a great favour than anything else, for it gave me the opportunity of passing the solemn night-hours alone in the Tomb and on Calvary.

Accordingly, at 4 o'clock yesterday evening, we all went together to take part in the grand procession that takes place at that hour every day to the different stations which are in the church. They are as follows : 1o. The chapel where our Lord appeared to His Blesse dMother after His resurrection; 2o. The prison, or place where He was kept whilst they were making the last preparations for His crucifixion ; 3o. The chapel of St. Helena, the place where the cross was found ; 4o. An oratory where St. Helena prayed whilst the search for the cross was being made; 5o. The *Improperium*, or chapel containing the stool on which Jesus sat blindfolded whilst they crowned him with thorns ; 6o. The place where He was nailed to the cross ; 7o. The place where the cross was planted ; 8o. The stone or rock on which His body was anointed after death ; 9o. The Holy Sepulchre ; 10o. The place where He appeared to Mary Magdalen on Easter-morning ; 11o. Finally, the procession returns to the starting-point, the chapel of Our Lady, where the ceremony terminates by a solemn benediction of the Blessed Sacrament.

All this is very solemn and impressive, I assure you ; and I took part in it as often as I could while I remained in Jerusalem. The cross-bearer, accompanied by two acolytes, go first ; then come the surpliced monks, followed by the pilgrims. All bear in' their hands lighted wax-tapers. Between each station a psalm is sung, and when arrived at the station itself a prayer recalling the mystery is chaunted, incense is offered up, and then all proceed to the next one. The ceremony lasted about an hour and a-half. You may fancy the thrill that runs through you as you hear the words : «*Here* Christ appeared to Mary ! »—«*Here* Christ was nailed to the cross ! »—« *Here* Christ expired ! »—« *Here* Christ was laid in the tomb,» etc., according to the different stations.

At seven o'clock the doors of the church were closed, so that I was left alone in the vast edifice with a few more Russian pilgrims. After a while the monk came to conduct us to the refectory, where we were served with a good supper, consisting of beans, meat, salad, and wine. We were then shewn to our rooms, and, after a little recreation, we went down again to pray at the Tomb and on Calvary. I will not attempt to describe my feelings during the solitary hours of watching I passed at both those places. They will be ever amongst the treasured remembrances of my life.

ALONE ON CALVARY ! ALONE IN THE TOMB OF JESUS ! And, oh ! if those moments be so delicious, dear St. C., what must it be in Heaven !

We retired after midnight, and about one o'clock I was awakened by the voice of Psalmody: the Armenians were just beginning their hour of devotion at the Sepulchre. They would be succeeded by the Coptes, these by others, and so on, for each rite has its turn. At 4 o'clock I was at the Sepulchre. I heard my companion's mass, and then said my own, by the light of the numerous lamps that burn all around the interior, and amid the fragrance of sweet perfumes. It was a mass that I never shall forget.

I made my thanksgiving-act on Calvary, and, after making an offering to the good Father *Sacristain*, who invited us to return again, we came back to the convent of Casa Nova, and enjoyed a good hearty breakfast of coffee and bunns.

Some time after breakfast we started on an excursion down to the valley of Josaphat. We saw many things to interest us, as you may imagine; but all these I will describe in regular order when we visit them after our return from the Dead Sea. We completed our arrangements with the *Moukhre*, or Arab guide, named *Jean Aouad*. We are to leave to-morrow morning by 9 o'clock for Jericho, the Dead Sea, St. Saba, and Bethlehem. We shall be three days on horseback, and intend reaching Bethlehem for the feast of the Epiphany. The bargain is as follows: We each give *Jean* 80 francs for the three days; in return, he furnishes everything—tents, beds, mules, horses, provisions, and an escort of Bedouins. It is pretty dear; but we shall thus travel in perfect security, and with every comfort.

After thus providing for material wants, we determined to secure the spiritual advantages also; and with this view, it was arranged that, after dinner, we would all go to confession to Mr. Ratisbonne, who lives in the convent on the «Sorrowful Way,» formerly the site of Pilate's palace.

When we went any place all together I was always named leader, so that when we left the convent I took my station in the first rank. I mention the *first rank*, for the streets are so narrow, and withal so encumbered, that it is impossible to walk two abreast as a general thing. To explain my

being chosen *leader*, I may as well say that it was
found that my *forte* (like that of four-footed animals)
lay in my skill in finding out any place to which
I had once been. But, alas! this once my instinct
was at fault. I missed one turn, and, coming to
the *Tower of David*, we found ourselves at the
entrance of the «Grand bazaar,» or chief commercial
street of the city. We were bewildered, not knowing
which way to turn. Poor old Mr. A., who is exces-
sively timid, urged us strongly to retrace our steps;
but this would have been disgraceful and cowardly.
I, therefore, bid them be of good cheer and follow
me, pledging my reputation to bring them safe to
our destination. Away we plunged headlong into
the filthy crowded *bazaar*. The street was narrow,
for the most part arched in, bordered by shops of
all descriptions, and workshops, varying from the
baker to the tin-smith. And, oh! such a Babel of
confused noise—bellowing, shouting, and cursing!
camels, asses and horses! men, women and children!
—it was worse than anything I had seen heretofore
in Alexandria or Jaffa. Mr. A. was now all in a
tremor. He begged of us, for God's sake, to turn
back; but still we pushed on through the dense
crowd, hoping that some lucky turn would afford
an escape. None, however, offered, until, after travelling a mile or more, we found ourselves obliged
to come to a full stop before a high stone-wall,
having a ponderous gate, which apparently led into
an extensive field. Here we were completely non-
plussed. I enquired from several the way to Mr.
Ratisbonne's. I made use of English, French, and
Italian; I think I even made a desperate effort at
German; but I might as well have been talking
Connemara Irish. They shrugged their shoulders,
and some did not even give me the honor of a reply.
After some consultation, I suggested that we should
enter the gate, and, once in the open field, we would

be in a better position to sea the environs and take
our bearings. This advice was acted upon reluctantly, however; for Mr. A. now loudly called for a
« turn-back, » *coûte que coûte*. It would have been
better for us if we had done so ; for we had hardly
passed the gate when we heard shouts from all
sides, and, turning round, we found that we had
suddenly become objects of *popular odium*. What
crime had we perpetrated? Nothing less than a
sacrilege, for which, twenty years ago, we would
have been stoned to death on the spot! With
unhallowed feet we had, however unwittingly,
sullied the sacred precincts of the Mosque of Omar!!
A fierce, ugly-looking little Turk immediately
rushed at us, and, happening to meet first with Mr.
A., caught him by the arm, and waved a stick over
him in a most threatening manner. I could not
understand what he said, but it was clearly a «notice
to quit» at the shortest possible delay. You may
depend we lost no time in questioning his authority,
but beat a hasty retreat, and were glad to slink
away through the angry, murmuring crowd of by-
standers. Mr. A. was as pale as the sheet I write on ;
but when we got out of danger, he relieved himself
by a round volley of abuse, discharged full at our
devoted heads, bewailing his hard lot at thus having
been on the point of losing his life for the sake of
three asses! Once before, he said, in Greece, he
had been led astray by following us ; but this, he
vowed, was the last time, even if he had to perform
the rest of the journey alone.

We had to go again through the filthy bazaar, and
arrived at last at the convent. It was only by great
coaxing and professions of sincere sorrow that we
could prevail on the irate old gentleman to «come
and try again.» He did so, protesting that it was
only a desire to go to confession that could induce
him to risk his life in our hands. This time we

were more fortunate, and reached Mr. Ratisbonne's church without any outward adventure. Here, after composing our minds and duly preparing ourselves, we had the consolation of receiving absolution under the very arch from the summit of which Jesus was condemned to death. « My son, » said the holy convert of Mary, «you are now going to receive the sentence of life on the very spot where your Master received His condemnation. »......... We start for Jericho to-morrow.

JERICHO, 3rd January.

My dear St. C.,

I date this, as you see by the superscription, from the plains of Jericho. We have just retired to our tents for the night; but, before going to sleep, I must, as usual, take my notes for your special benefit.

It was ordered last night that we should leave Jerusalem at 9 o'clock this morning. I said .mass in the church of the Holy Saviour at an altar dedicated to St. Thomas. After our masses we took a hasty breakfast, made our last arrangements, tied up our heads in white towels to preserve them from the sun, and mounted our « Arab steeds » that stood waiting for us at the convent-door. The weather was beautiful, but the sun was very hot. We left the city by the « Pilgrims' gate, » passed round the walls, and came to the place where Godefroy de Bouillon took the town by assault in 1099. Continuing, then, our easterly direction, we descended into the valley of Josaphat, crossed the torrent of Cedron, passed by the garden of Gethsemani, and ascended Mount Olivet in an oblique manner, till we came to a turn about half-way from the top. Here we enjoyed a splendid view of Jerusalem, which lay a little below us, on the opposite side of the valley, but soon lost sight of it by going round

the mountain, thus placing it between us and the
city. We were now within the precincts of Betha-
nia, a little village so often sanctified by the presence of our Lord, and where many interesting
souvenirs still arrest the attention of the traveller.
Here is the place where formerly grew the fig-tree
cursed by Jesus, and—singularly enough—a with-
ered specimen of the same tree still stands on the
same spot. Here is the site of the house of Mary and
Martha. Further on, our guide pointed out the
stone on which Jesus was seated when the two
sisters came to tell Him of the death of Lazarus,
their brother. Finally, after descending somewhat,
we arrived at a little Arab village containing the
tomb of Lazarus. We dismounted, and, being furnished by the guide with wax-tapers, descended
27 steps into the long narrow tomb, in which mass
is sometimes said by the monks. We were, of course,
on our return to the *upper* air, surrounded by the
villagers, men, women and children, all clamouring
for *backshiche*. We threw them some pieces; but
this did not satisfy them : they followed us with
persistency for about half a mile, and we only got
rid of them when the guide turned his horse and
made a charge into the midst of them.

We then continued our way, and, after going
down a break-neck hill, found ourselves in a
deep valley, in the midst of which flows the *Fountain of the Apostles*, so called because Jesus and His
chosen ones often rested here to refresh themselves
on their way to or from Jericho. It being now
twelve o'clock, we halted in a little cavern ; the
guide prepared an excellent dinner, and we reposed
until one o'clock.

When all the dinner's things were washed up
and packed safely on the mule's back, our Bedouins
started on before us, and we quickly mounted and
followed them. The heat now surpassed anything

6

that I had hitherto experienced ; the rays shot down
vertically on us, and I thought I could actually
hear the blisters crack and boil over, both on myself
and on my companions. I was also kept in a fever
of excitement by my brute of a horse, who had, in
my inexperienced hands, become perfectly unman-
ageable. He was a great white beast, of pure blood,
that the guide had reserved for me under the mistaken notion that I was «a capital rider.» Shortly after
we left Jerusalem he rode over to me, and, wishing
me to know how much I was under a compliment
to him, said, in a confidential tone :

«Sir, you have good horse—the best.»

«Rather hard to manage, I think,» said I, trying
to keep my seat, as he curvetted and pranced down
the hill.

«Oh!» said Jean, admiringly, «oh! no, sir; very
fine horse; you'll see just now when he *gets heated.*»

I got alarmed. «Look here, Jean,» said I; «what do
you mean? What will he do when he *gets heated,*
as you say?»

«Very fiery,» Jean replied; «and then,» he added, in
an under-tone, «I gave him to you because you ride
better than the other gentlemen, and have more
pleasure.»

If I had had my whip hand at liberty I would
have given the fellow a blow over the head; but I
was not able to do so, as my left hand held the reins
tight, and my right clutched the saddle convulsively.
I had, therefore,—however humiliating it was—to
assure Jean that I was no rider at all, and I begged
of him to exchange horses with me.

But Jean was an Arab, and could not understand
how it could happen that any one would not prefer
a fiery horse to a tame one ; as to good riding, the ras-
cal imagined that it comes as natural as eating. He,
therefore, only smiled incredulously at what he

thought a poor joke, and rode off to attend to another part of the caravan.

So, dear St. C., here was your unfortunate brother, in one of the worst *pickles* ever he remembered in life, given over to the tender mercies of a great, high-boned, round-necked, full-eyed devil of an uncivilized horse, cursing my ill-luck at having found favour with Jean, and doing my best to keep the reins tight and my animal quiet, lest he might *get heated.*

All went well enough until dinner-time; he, not being, I suppose, up to the proper heat as yet, behaved in a semi-decorous manner, and landed me safe at the *Fountain of the Apostles.* I should have exchanged him then; but I fear my vanity prevented me from making the proposal, and, besides, I half-fancied that I would be able to manage him, after all.

I was not, however, a league from our resting-place when I had good reason to repent for my temerity and foolish pride. While the other horses kept a sober and steady gait, mine went on prancing, pawing the air, and betimes stopping of his own accord to paw the ground, till, at last, having, in all probability, acquired the necessary quantum of *heat*, he suddenly shot past the rest, and carried me, body and bones, at the rate of a mile a minute, up the stony side of a mountain. I clung closely, like John Gilpin of old, with might and main, to my unsteady seat ; but I would have soon been on the ground and he out of sight if I had not, by a desperate effort, driven him right up against a high wall formed by the ruined turret of the *Hospital of the Good Samaritan.* He eyed the obstacle fiercely, as if he were going to leap over it ; but before he could do anything more perilous than he had already accomplished, I had leaped off, and was holding by the mouth-piece like grim death.

Jean soon came up with us, and I insisted, this time in good earnest, on an exchange. Jean, though he demurred somewhat, was evidently very glad at the offer, and I was soon on a red mare,—not very handsome, but quiet and gentle,—thankful for my escape, and fully resolved never again to mount a horse liable to *get heated*.

Tradition places on this spot, at the head of a mountain-gorge, and at about three leagues from Jerusalem, the scene so beautifully narrated in the Scriptures of the Samaritan's charitable act. There were formerly a church and an hospital here, but the ruins are now fast disappearing ; yet, though nothing marks the spot, I think I shall be able to find it out again if ever I travel over the same road.

We were now in the very middle of the mountains, and, indeed, a more frightful solitude could hardly be conceived. No living thing appeared for hours,—not even a stunted tree nor a blade of grass. The great, bald, ashy piles of succeeding mountains reminded one of the mountains of Gelboe, cursed by the prophet; and many a time, as I wiped the streaming perspiration from my face, did I almost wish myself safely back in Quebec, or at least in Rome. At length we came to a high mountain-ridge, and got a full view of the plains of Jericho, that lay far down beneath us. To the right glistened the Dead Sea, and on the farther side of the plain we could trace the wanderings of the Jordan by the reeds that grow on its banks. The plain itself appeared covered over by white patches, saline deposits that had formed on the soil. We again plunge into a ravine, and after innumerable windings between barren hills, sometimes following the beds of dried-up torrents, we were issued into an upland, forming, as it were, the foreground of the valley. Jericho was now at a

short distance below us; but we turned to the
left, and galloped along the base of the mountains
for about twenty minutes, when we came to Elisha's
Fountain, opposite the mount of the Forty Days'
Fast of our dear Lord. We drank of the waters of
the little fountain,— no longer bitter since the
prophet made them sweet, thousands of years ago.
We admired the bold perpendicular front of the
holy mount, all honey-combed with grottoes, where
the Fathers of the Desert lived and died, in the
first ages of Christianity; then, mounting again,
we turned back and reached the middle of the plain
where formerly stood Jericho in all its pride, but
which is now a miserable village, inhabited by
200 poor infidel Arabs. We found our camp already
formed and comfortable quarters awaiting us, for
the heavy.baggage and mules had gone on before us.

In one tent were four beds ranged around the
centre pole, the sheets and blankets being clean
and well aired. In another tent, alongside, was a
long table loaded with a first-rate supper. Further
on was a third tent for our Arabs and Bedouin
soldiers. All around the camp were picketed the
mules and horses, which, with our own, amounted
to fifteen. Fires were built at intervals, as well to
keep away the chacals as to cook the victuals. The
sun was just descending; the air had become cooler;
and, while awaiting the final preparations for supper,
we passed a pleasant time, resting and recalling the
souvenirs of the place. This, as you know, is the
famous plain of Sodom and Gomorrah, whose towers
and minarets lie beneath the waters of the sea
yonder. Here, on the very site of our encampment,
once rose the walls of Jericho. On the summit of
that bold mount, behind which the sun has just
gone down, the tempter dared to try the virtue of
Man-God. It was here that he shewed Him all the
empires of the earth. « All those will I give thee if,

falling down, thou adorest me. » « Begone, Satan, » etc. On the other side of the valley, at the distance, I believe, of two leagues, is the spot, the very place, where St. John the Baptist baptized our Lord. We shall go there to-morrow morning.

These and many others we were going over, until supper was announced. You may be sure that we had good appetites; and I must do our cooks the justice of saying that their culinary efforts were both successful and satisfactory.

After a hearty meal we came forth from the tent to smoke our *narguillé* and drink coffee in the cold air. The inhabitants of the village came to dance for us. This being the only way they could be of service to us, they did their best to merit the *backshiche.* We let them go through their monotonous performance, gave them the usual fee, and requested them to retire, finding greater enjoyment in a pleasant chat than in the spectacle of their somewhat hideous contortions.

And now, ten o'clock has come; our solitary campfire is burning; around it the Arabs are sitting telling stories; I can hear the chacals barking close enough to the camp; two sentinels are pacing up and down. I am getting sleepy, and so must bid you « good-night. »

4th JANUARY.—I write to you this evening, dear St. C., from the borders of the torrent of Cedron, beneath the walls of the Greek convent of Saint Sabas, in the very heart of the mountains of Judea. I am tired and jaded out; nevertheless, I will endeavour to record the day's adventures faithfully, but as succinctly as possible.

We arose this morning at half-past five. I had already time to shake the fatigue of yesterday off, and would fain have taken an extra nap; but my companions were inexorable, and our guides were calling for permission to strike the tents and set out for St. Sabas. I, therefore, had to rise, though sore against my will. I performed the morning ablutions and made my toilet in the tent; then we all went forth, and made our morning-prayers kneeling in the open air, in view of the «Mont de la Quarantaine.» From where I knelt I could see the cave in which Jesus passed the forty days; and though He was not visible to the eyes of my body, I knew that He still looked on me and heard my petitions.

While we were thus engaged breakfast was preparing. We relished the *stew* very much; we then had some good Arab coffee and bunns, and took, by way of final preparation for the journey, a stirrup—cup of Cyprus-wine. All was now ready; the tents, bedding and baggage were packed on the mules; we mounted our horses, and off we started towards the Jordan, kissing our hands to the villagers who stood at their cottage-doors.

We struck right straight across the plain in an easterly direction, and, after two hours' ride, came to the spot where Jesus was baptized by St. John. The Jordan is at this place about 400 feet wide. The stream was swollen and very rapid; the waters were of a dark-yellow tint; the borders are covered by tall reeds and underbush. The church and marble pavements that were formerly here have long since disappeared. We here renewed our baptismal vows, washed our hands, feet, and heads, took some of the water, and, after a delay of about three-quarters of an hour, started for the Dead Sea, which lies at about a league and a-half to the south. Following more or less the wanderings of the Jordan as it rushes towards the great salt lake, we galloped over a sandy plain, and, exactly at ten o'clock, dismounted on the shores of this far-famed body of water, amid a scene of desolation that bears evident marks of the wrath of God.

The Dead Sea is twenty leagues long by four

leagues wide. It is embedded between the mountains
of Moab, that rise perpendicularly to the height of
400, or 500 feet along its eastern shore, and the
mountains of Judea, which border it to the west. Its
northern waves expire on the sands of the plain of
Jericho, on which we were then standing. No better
place could be chosen to meditate on the innate
malice of sin and the hatred God bears to it. A death-
like silence reigns all around ; no living thing is seen
within its precincts ; the very stones that lay on the
sand are scorched and blasted. The waters are very
dense, of a dark-blue colour, and so impregnated
with salt that if you immerse your hand in them,
and then let it dry in the sun, it is totally covered
with thick scales.

We remained here about half an hour, not wishing to prolong our stay, on account of the great heat.
The Bedouin cheik that accompanied us gave us,
while here, a specimen of Arab horsemanship.
While the horse was in full career, he threw
himself to the right, then to the left, clinging to the
saddle by one knee, and pointing his long musket
as if about to fire. Sometimes he made the horse
turn suddenly to the right, then wheel to the left,
while he himself swayed from one side to the other
in the opposite direction to the supposed enemy. I
assure you that I envied him his skill. The timid
Mr. A. became quite alarmed when the young cheik
rushed up to him, and swept by with the rapidity
of lightning, holding his gun so close that it brushed
Mr. A.'s umbrella. « Voyons, voyons, c'est assez,»
said he ; « avançons.»

We accordingly advanced, leaving the plain, and
again beginning to ascend the mountains of Judea
on our way to Saint Sabas. The same tortuous,
climbing, dizzy road as formerly had again to be
affronted. At one o'clock we halted in a sheltered
place, and, tying our horses to projecting rocks,
- waited till Jean prepared dinner.

At two o'clock we were once more *en route*, replenished and refreshed. Up steep mountains, down perilous ravines, now suspended between heaven and earth as the steed balanced himself on a *dos d'âne*, where a single *faux-pas* would have hurled horse and rider a thousand feet into the yawning abyss,—and, all this time, not the shelter of a tree nor the ruffle of a breeze to temper the fierce meridian heat. At length we came to the torrent of Cedron, which had made its way through the ravines all along from the valley of Josaphat. But one would say that it has caught the spirit of the scene as it wended its way through the desert. From being a gentle little stream, rolling between mossy banks yonder, it has become a fierce mountain-torrent, encased in rocky shores of two hundred feet in height. We crossed its dried-up channel, and ascended the opposite side by a very good road which the monks have cut in the hard rock for the benefit of pilgrims. It wound around the mountain in a zig-zag fashion for twenty minutes ; and when we turned the last angle we came in sight of the convent, actually built on the steep sides of the cliff, and surrounded by massive stone walls. A little beyond we descried our tents, and by the smoke of the camp-fires we knew that supper was ready, or nearly so. It was just half-past five as we alighted from our horses.

The convent, which is inhabited by schismatic monks, is built, as I said, on the sloping sides of the mountain. A palm-tree, which is as near as possible to the walls of the building, was planted by St. Sabas himself, in the early ages of Christianity, and is, of course, much venerated by the monks as an interesting relic of their founder. He, however, was a good Catholic, whilst they have embraced the errors of Photius ; and it is sad to think that their penitential life is not consoled and

vivified by union with the true fount from whence
flow grace and merit. Having been furnished with
a « pass » from the Greek Patriarch before we left
Jerusalem, we were enabled to visit the interior of
the convent. There are several chapels and oratories,
highly ornamented ; pictures of the Blessed Virgin
and Child recur very often. The tomb and cell of
St. Sabas are in the lower tier of buildings, though
the saint's body is, I believe, in St. Mark's church at
Venice. On the opposite side of the cliff are the cells
formerly inhabited by Catholic monks, but who
were all massacred in the 6th century by Chosroes,
king of Persia.

After a short visit we returned to our tents,
where we supped, chatted, and went to bed.

BETHLEHEM, 5th January.

This morning we were again in the saddle at half-
past seven. The road was a repetition of what I have
already described till about ten o'clock, when we came
in sight of Bethlehem. The ground here becomes
less broken and more level ; a gentle declivity leads
into a fertile valley running from east to west, and
planted with corn and olive-trees. At the end of
this, and rising on an eminence, stand the whitewashed, flat-roofed houses of Ephrata (the House of
Bread), or Bethlehem, the birth-place of Jesus.

The shepherds were on the hill-sides tending their
flocks, or stretched in grottoes, just as they must
have been on the night when the Angels brought
them the « good tidings of great joy.» You would
have almost said that nothing had been changed
since then. The costumes were antique and strictly
eastern ; I saw several little children with crooks,
and dressed in the same manner as the personifica-
tions of St. John the Baptist on the Canadian
national feast in Quebec ; the women were dressed

in red tunics and blue cloaks, such as you see in pictures of the Blessed Virgin ; in a word, everything appeared to have remained stationary, as if to impress with greater vivacity on the pilgrim's mind the great souvenirs from which he had come to seek piety and consolation.

At eleven o'clock we arrived at the Franciscan convent, and were received by the good monks with their usual open-hearted hospitality.

As you may easily imagine, we hurried immediately to visit the grotto of the Nativity and humbly kiss the sacred spot where « The Word was made flesh. » We knelt in lowly adoration, and wept tears of joy in this holy sanctuary. There I thanked God and the Blessed Virgin for the immense favour of being enabled to make this consoling pilgrimage, and promised that my life would henceforth be an act of gratitude for *such* a privilege.

At twelve o'clock we were called to dinner, and found a numerous company already seated around the table from various parts of the world. The Austrian consul — Count *Something* — sat at the head ; a Prussian baron *Somebody* sat at one side of him, and a French countess at the other. There were a Pole and an Austrian, with whom we had previously become acquainted, two Greek ladies in full Bloomer costume, and some others. All passed off very pleasantly.

It was arranged that we should say our masses at seven, eight, nine, and ten o'clock. I chose 9 o'clock, so that at that hour—corresponding, I think, to five or six o'clock A. M. in Canada—I shall have the glorious privilege of offering up the Holy Sacrifice in the stable of Bethlehem, and that on the Feast of the Epiphany.

I was so tired, after my long ride, that I remained in my room all day, looking through my window at the busy crowd on the square opposite. There are a great number of Greek pilgrims from all parts. I witnessed the processional entry of the Greek Patriarch into town this evening. He bore a crozier in one hand, and in the other a little silver cross, with which he distributed blessings right and left. There were a great many priests dressed in flame-coloured cassocks, singers in yellow copes and banner-bearers in long surplices. Clouds of incense rose up around him, and flowers were strewed along the way.

Though it is only half-past eight P. M., my companions are all in bed, and Mr. A. is snoring as if he never more intended to awake.

MEDITERRANEAN SEA, 21st *January*. ([1])

My dear St. C.,

......We remained three days in Bethlehem, and visited thoroughly all its interesting places, the shepherds' grotto, the house of Joseph, the grotto of milk, &c.

We then went to St. John's in the desert. I said holy mass on the spot where St. John the Baptist was born. The next day I said mass in the chapel of the *Magnificat*—that is to say, where the *Magnificat* was first sung by the Blessed Virgin. I saw the rock from which St. John the Baptist preached, the grotto in which he did penance, the tomb of St. Elizabeth, and the fountain whence the Blessed Virgin used to draw water for the household uses of her cousin.

([1]) We have found nothing in Mr. Doherty's papers from the 5th to the 31st January. He contents himself, in this letter dated from the sea, with rapidly noting down the principal events of his sojourn in the Holy Land. We have then to follow him back again to Rome, from which place he wrote many most interesting pages.

We remained here two days, and then returned to Jerusalem on foot, in order to follow, if possible, the footsteps of Mary in her journey through those self-same mountains.

We passed the next fortnight visiting the sights in and around the Holy City, drinking in the inspirations they lend the Christian soul, and trying to strengthen our love for Jesus on those hallowed spots where He deigned to suffer so much for us. I need not tell you that the traditions which fix and determine those spots are most authentic. They have been handed down through ages, and are venerated by every sect and every rite; even the Mussulmans look on them with respect. Therefore, not the slightest doubt can be raised as to their correct location; so that the cavilings of some infidel writers are quite silly and without the slightest foundation.

This said, I will just mention some of the places I saw, leaving to your imagination the task of picturing to itself what feelings of awe, veneration, and profound contrition fill the heart when we approach them.

I slept two nights in the church of the Holy Sepulchre, and said mass the first morning in the Holy Sepulchre itself, and the next on Mount Calvary.

I made the way of the cross several times in the early morning, following in the footsteps of Jesus, passing through the same streets. To my mind, the most affecting place of all is the corner of the two streets where Mary met her Divine Son. It is called the *Fourth Station*, and is in sight of the house of *Dive*, the *rich man* mentioned in the Gospel.

I saw and kissed the footprint that Jesus left on Mount Olivet at the moment of His ascension into Heaven; and the next morning I said mass on the spot where He taught the Lord's prayer. This little chapel was raised by the Princess de la Tour d'Auvergne, who resides on the mountain. A little farther on is the *well* where the Apostles composed the Creed, previous to their separation. Then comes the spot where Christ wept over Jerusalem. All these beautiful souvenirs are on Mount Olivet, from the summit of which there is a splendid view of Jerusalem and of the valley of Josaphat. Below the mountain, directly at its foot, is the garden of Gethsemani, in which still grow some of the olive-trees beneath which He prayed. Here, too, is the place where Judas gave Him the kiss of treason; here is the rock where the disciples slept while He went further on to pray. Here is the grotto of the *bloody sweat;* and in it I said mass with greater emotion, I think, than any where else.

But I find I must stop, dear C.; the weather has got very stormy, and the vessel is rolling from side to side. My only consolation, therefore, is that I have taken notes [1] of all the places I saw, and will be able to tell you all about them.

ROME, *Tuesday, 8th February,* 1870.

We arrived from Naples on Tuesday evening. I found quite a number of letters from home. Read every one of them, from end to end, before I blew out my candle at 2 o'clock in the morning. What a beautiful thing *home* is! How pleasing to know that thousands of miles away there are hearts that beat in unison with your own!

> "To think that some dear one is sighing,
> And saying: 'I wish he were here!'"

God help those that have neither friend nor home! they are deprived of one of the holiest, purest, and deepest sources of joy that sends its thrill through

[1] What has become of these notes, and how considerable they were, we do not know.

the soul. And may the Almighty bless you, dearest sisters and kind friends, whose warm love and affectionate words have caused me such happiness this night.

Wednesday.—We sat for our portraits this morning in full travelling-«rig.» I went to see His Grace the Archbishop, before allowing the ruthless hand of the barber to raze my tufted chin. I fancied I would create an impression; but he merely laughed at me, and said that it was a very poor two-months' growth. This from any one else I would attribute to jealousy; but from the Archbishop!—really, I cannot explain it. Wrote letters from twelve to four. Went for a walk. Wandered across the Tiber, and got as far as the summit of the Janiculum. A church stands on the brow of the hill, on the spot where St. Peter was crucified. The view of Rome is splendid from this point. To the west are the snow-clad Apennines; to the north stretches far away the rich Campagna of Rome, intersected by aqueducts older than Christianity. Here and there are princely villas and stately churches. The glistening Tiber rolls its rapid stream through the city and loses itself among the green hills yonder. I can see the place where A. Martius built the famous wooden bridge, 600 years before Christ.

And Rome itself is at my feet—Rome! once the despotic mistress of nations, now the centre of civilization, and still potent in the authority she holds from Christ. I can count 13 cupolas; and above them all, like some protecting genius, soars the mighty dome of St. Peter's. What great changes have taken place since the inverted cross of the Prince of the Apostles was first planted on this spot!.

Peter's cross was sunk in derision and ignominy; it now stands upright and glorious on the highest pinnacle of the most superb edifice raised by the hands of men. Peter stood here, alone of his faith.

His only attendants were the fierce executioners and
the satellites of the pagan emperor who had issued
his death-warrant. To-day, while the forum is in
ruins, and Nero's palace is deserted, the successor
of Peter reigns triumphant. He is surrounded, not
by enemies, but by his fellow-labourers in the
Lord's vineyard. At his call they have come from
the earth's extremities, in obedience to his voice, to
prove that Peter's faith is in their hearts,—to shew
that Peter's authority is recognized throughout the
universe,—to make it manifest that the cross of
Peter *has triumphed.*

The monument commemorative of the Council
has been very appropriately placed on this spot. It .
is now in course of construction. And, oh ! it is
consoling to know and feel that the great assembly
will outlive in effect this monument, though strong
and solid. Its enactments will be in vigour, its canons
respected, even when the marble column will have
crumbled into dust,—aye ! even to the end of time.

The sun was just sinking to rest, and the air was
soft and balmy. I was loth to leave this beautiful
place ; but, alas ! the supper-hour had come, and at
its imperative call I turned my steps homewards,
mingling with the thoughts of Rome and its
wonders the thought of friends to whom I might
one day be able to give an imperfect account of all
I saw and heard.

Thursday, Friday, and Saturday, we chiefly spent
in letter-writing, receiving and paying visits, and
the thousand little *et-cæteras* that sometimes steal
away your whole day without your knowing at the
end of it what you have done or where you have
been.

On Sunday I went to hear Mgr. Mermillod preach
to the Zouaves in the church of St. John the Baptist.
The church was crowded with gray coats and
white leggings. I love to see those noble fellows

kneeling piously at the foot of the altar, and hear
their manly voices unite in the chaunt of the *Tantum Ergo*, or some simple hymn to the Blessed
Virgin which we used to sing together at the com-
munity-mass in college. The clanking of their
sabres on the marble pavement reminds one that
while they fortify their souls with the nourishment
of prayer, their right arms are ready to defend the
good cause. Indeed, it is most edifying to see those
dear Zouaves in the Holy City. You cannot enter
any church, whether morning or evening, without
meeting some of them in the performance of their
religious duties ; and, believe me, if the trumpet of
battle sounded, they would prove again, as at Mentana, that piety and true courage go hand-in-hand.

On Monday several of us went on an excursion
to Monte Rotondo and Mentana, the scene of the
late combat between the Pontifical army and the
hordes of Garibaldi. We came by rail to Monte Rotondo, and returned to Rome in a carriage through
the little town of Mentana. This was going over the
battle-field backwards ; so, my dear Christine, to
give you a better idea of the brilliant affair, I will
begin by the end of the journey, which will allow
you all the better to follow the movements of the day.

On the night of the 2nd November news came to
Rome that Garibaldi had crossed the frontier and
occupied Monte Rotondo. He was, therefore, within
four hours' march of the capital, and it became
urgent to meet him at once. The drums beat to
arms in the dead of night ; the troops were collected,
and at two o'clock in the morning they left Rome
by the gate called *Porta Pia*. After leaving the city
the road winds for some time through the splendid
villas of the Roman patricians. A range of heights
are then gained, and, after crossing the Tiber on a
huge stone bridge, you enjoy a wide prospect of the
environing country. Away to the right rises Monte

Mario, where Constantine defeated the tyrant Maxentius; directly in front are the hills that hide the foe; behind is Rome, faintly seen through the grey light of the breaking day. Many were the eyes, I am sure, that turned backwards to gaze on the cupola of St. Peter's; and many, alas! saw it there for the last time.

After three hours' march the advance-guard engaged the enemy, who lay in ambush behind a long range of brushwood. The Zouaves were immediately deployed as skirmishers, and they were not long clearing the road for the rest of the troops, who came on in close order. A convent and church were next taken by storm: it was here that the two Canadian Zouaves fell wounded, and the Garibaldians retreated to the town, where they intrenched themselves behind the stone walls of the houses. But the blood of the Zouaves was up; they were enraged at the cowardly manœuvres of an enemy who declined to meet them on a fair field; the town was surrounded on all sides; the order to charge with the bayonet was given, and a most murderous conflict ensued. The Pope's soldiers dashed at the barriers, up the steep hill, through the streets, and into the houses, where they massacred all those that resisted them. In an hour's time after the assault all the Garibaldians had fled or lay weltering in their blood. The order was given to push on to Monte Rotondo, whither Garibaldi had retreated; the place was taken after a short struggle; and the general, who had loudly proclaimed that he *should have* "Rome or death," was in the advance-guard of the fugitives over the border.

The churches had been fearfully desecrated during the short stay of the revolutionists: the tableaux were turn down, the statues of the saints mutilated, the altars overturned, and, in some cases, the sacred host trampled under foot. I saw one of those churches in Mentana, which is still in the state they left it, and it almost made my heart turn sick. In Monte Rotondo I said mass in the church into which Garibaldi had entered on horseback. I offered up the Divine Victim in reparation for the blasphemies and outrages that had been committed in the sacred edifice. I spent a very pleasant evening with Bishop Horan and Mr. McCarthy at their rooms in Santa Chiara.

Tuesday.—Nothing worthy of note.

Wednesday.—A few Canadians left for Canada. We accompanied them to the railway-station, and « saw them off. » On our way home we had the happiness of seeing Pius the Ninth on his way to open the « Grande Exposition des objets d'art Chrétien. » The whole Roman court was present, with the greatest part of the Fathers of the Council. It was a very grand sight. I got a full-faced view of the Holy Father, as he was turned to our side of the carriage at the time it passed us. Of course we joined in the lusty cheering.

On Thursday I went to pay a visit to the Archbishop of Tuam. I read to him the part of Mr. W.'s letter relating to him. He was quite pleased. His conversation is quite *sans cérémonie*, pleasant and fatherly. He invited me to call on him often, and promised me his portrait.

On Friday, after saying mass in St. Andrea delle Fratti, the church in which the Blessed Virgin appeared to M. Ratisbonne, I went to the Propaganda to ask Mgr. Simeoni if he would obtain an audience for us from the Holy Father. He very kindly consented, and told us to be ready for Sunday evening.

Saturday.—Nothing very important. The carnival began to-day.

Sunday.—I have just come from the private audience with the Holy Father. You may be sure that we are all overjoyed. I will give you all the details in Wednesday's letter. It is one of the happiest days of my life. No wonder that all those that see Pius the Ninth love and venerate him. He has the heart of a father, and evidently loves all his children.

The carnival commenced on Saturday, and was continued to-day, Monday, throughout the whole length of the *Corso*. The shops are closed, and the people are all in holiday attire. In the aforementioned place the balconies are crowded with English, French and Americans, who shower down small round lumps of flour, called *confetti*, on the passers-by. These latter, a good many of whom wear fantastical dresses, attack their assailants, and a regular combat takes place. The two parties are soon completely *whitewashed*. The ceremony opened on Saturday by the booming of cannons and a very gorgeous procession of the senate and military from the Piazza del Popolo, at the entrance of Rome, to the Capitol, and each day's amusement ends with a race of riderless horses. It will close on the Tuesday of next week. The amusement begins at three o'clock and ends at six. It is exclusively confined to the Corso.

I visited to-day the churches of St. Mary Major and St. John of Lateran. They are noble edifices. In the former is the Manger of Bethlehem, and in the latter the Holy Staircase brought from Jerusalem. I came home by the Coliseum and the Capitol.

Tuesday.—This morning I went with two friends on an excursion. We reached the Capitol by the Piazza di Venezia, and, mounting by a staircase of 128 stone steps, we found ourselves at the door of the church of *Ara Cœli*, belonging to the Franciscan monks. It is said that the pagan Emperor Augustus had a vision of the Blessed Virgin and child Jesus, in consequence of which he raised an edifice or

temple in honour of the « Unknown God. » St.
Helena built a temple in the same place, and lies
buried in a beautiful tomb surmounted by a noble
altar and baldaquin near the Grand Altar. There
are 24 altars in the church. A double row of
columns reigns on each side of the middle nave.
They are all ancient, and of different orders of
architecture. Some of them belonged formerly to
the temple of «Jupiter the Thunderer.» In the
sacristy is the *Bambino*, a wooden statue of the
Infant Jesus, which was made by a monk in Jerusalem, and miraculously transported to Rome. It is
very richly dressed, and all covered over with precious stones. It has its cradle and coverlets, which,
together with itself, are all under lock and key in
the Treasury. There have been several very sur-
prising miracles performed in favour of those who
honour it. When a sick person sends for it, it is
conveyed to the house in a handsome carriage ; a
stole is thrown half-way out of the window, so as
to let the Romans know of its passage. They invariably uncover themselves, as a mark of respect, as it
passes by. We next went to the church of St.
Martina, a Roman lady of noble family, who suffered
martyrdom during the reign of Diocletianus. The
church is very beautiful ; a remarkable statue of
the saint, in marble, is placed directly over the front
altar. To the right is the *Forum Romanum*, one of
the most interesting ruins in Rome. It was here
that the people used to assemble to deliberate, to
hear the orators who addressed them, and to vote
on the destinies of nations. Here stand the remains
of the *rostrum* from which Cicero pleaded so elo-
quently. Here is the *Sacred Way*, which the triumphant *generals* crossed so often on their way to the
Capitol. All around stand decaying columns of
temples, grand and sumptuous, now awaiting the
last stroke of time to crumble into dust.

From St. Martina's church we went to that of St. Frances the Roman, passing by the temple,—the actual temple of Romulus and Remus, erected 2600 years ago, now dedicated to SS. Cosmus and Damian. St. Frances's is built on the spot where Simon the magician wished to imitate the Saviour and outdo the Apostles by publicly ascending into heaven. St. Peter was present among the crowd that came to witness the spectacle. He prayed that God might reveal the imposture, and his prayer was heard; for when *Simon* had reached a certain height, he fell to the ground and was instantly killed. The rock on which St. Peter prayed is still preserved in the church; it bears the impress of his two knees. The church is now undergoing repairs. As you already know, St. Frances used to see her Angel Guardian: this fact is represented in a beautiful marble-group under the altar.

From this we went to the Coliseum, passing under the triumphal arch raised by Titus as a remembrance of the taking of Jerusalem. To this day the Jews will not pass under it. When business or pleasure takes them this way, they take a circuitous route on one side of the trophy. The Coliseum is an immense amphitheatre. It used to contain at least 100,000 persons, and many a holy martyr here found death and victory. The stations of the Cross are placed around it; and every Friday they are publicly performed in the presence and with the accompaniment of vast numbers. So much has been said of the Coliseum and the reflections it inspires, that I will refrain from repeating what, I am sure, you have already read.

From the Coliseum we turned to the right, and after twenty minutes' walk had arrived at the church of St. John of Lateran. It was here that Constantine was baptized; here several councils were held; here, too, the Popes lived for some time, if I mistake not. Here, in an adjoining church also, is the Holy Staircase—that is, the staircase belonging to Pilate's Palace. Jesus mounted it four times during His passion, and it has still marks of His Precious Blood. We mounted it, with many other pilgrims, on our knees, praying at each step. I then went to the church of the «Holy Cross,» beyond St. John's gate. You perceive on your way the ruins of the Roman aqueducts, ivy-crowned and time-worn, but still strong. The church is very fine. The relics, especially, are numerous and precious. I venerated a large piece of the *True Cross* and the traverse-beam of the cross belonging to the *Good Thief;* one of the nails that pierced our Saviour's hand ; a finger of St. Thomas ; and many others. I also saw the inscription that was placed on the Cross of Our Saviour—I. N. R. I.

There is also a chapel, called the Chapel of St. Helena ; the earth underneath the marble floor is *holy earth*, having been brought from Mount Calvary by the orders of St. Helena. I do not know why women are excluded from this place, but it is a fact. A written placard forbids them to cross the threshold, under *pain of excommunication*, except once a year.

Returning home, I again visited «St. Mary Major.» This is a miraculous church, and is richer than any other in Rome, I think, except St. Peter's. The *Manger* of Bethlehem is kept in the *Confession;* I had the happiness of venerating it.

My road then lay by the Quirinal, a former palace of the Popes : I had already visited it before. It was here that Pius the Ninth lived before the revolution of 1848. I saw the room from which he fled in the dress of a *Priest*. I saw the gate through which he passed. Both are now historic.

We had a very grand Italian dinner on the occasion of our hostess's feast-day, *la Signora Margarita.*

Two bishops were present, and a number of priests
and laymen. There were toasts to no end, and, at
least, six different sorts of wine.

Wednesday.—This is letter-day. I consecrated it
to remembrances of home and absent friends. I, however, had time to pay a visit to the *Gesu*. The altar
of St. Ignatius exceeds all description. Gold, silver,
and precious marbles are here in profusion. It is
said that the chapel of the saint alone is worth
more than $1,000,000 !

Thursday.—I said mass this morning in the church
of St. Agnes, the sweet little saint whom Cardinal
Wiseman popularized throughout Europe in his
Fabiola. The church is built on the scene of her
martyrdom ; it is a rotunda. Beneath the high altar
is the crypt—that is, the room where she suffered.
I shall say mass there to-morrow. The Prince
Doria is the patron of the church. A gratuitous
school is attached to it.

This is a dreary, cold, rainy day ; so that, with the
exception of a visit to the Archbishop, I have been
house-ridden all day long,—*or, que faire en un gîte, à
moins que l'on ne songe ;* and where could a better
place for thought be found than in Rome ? Some one
called Rome « the city of the soul,» and there is no
metaphor in the expression. It is, indeed, a place of
benediction ; it is a city where man does not appear
entirely to forget his God and the one thing necessary,—where religion is held in honor, and where
all ideas of devotion are not, as in other places,
jostled out of every-day life. I have seen many
great centres of population ; I have visited many
cities both in the new and the old world ; and in each
and every one of them, as a priest, I have been painfully struck by the exclusion of spiritualities manifest in them. I saw magnificent rows of buildings,
manufactories, warehouses, stores and palaces ;
splendid squares adorned with fountains, trees, and

the statues of great men. Everywhere people appeared absorbed in affairs; every one was busy; every brain was teeming with thought; every energy was put forth. I listened to their conversation : they spoke of commercial interests, of agricultural interests, of bank-stocks and rates, of politics, of ministerial or dynastic changes; but I never heard the name of God pronounced, except in blasphemy. I went to the churches, and they were almost empty : some women, a few old men, and little children, were, in most cases, their only occupants. The thousands, nay, the millions outside lived, moved, and breathed in an element far removed from religious influences. One might have said that the Deity of those vast reunions was « an unknown God.»

Nor was the spirit of indifference the only nor the worst side of the picture. Around about me and on all sides were allurements to vice : the statues were often lewd; the images in the windows, exposed for sale, were often infamous ; the walls were placarded with invitations to theatres, where vice was promenaded and held up amid the most gorgeous decorations every night, &c.

In Rome it is not so. There may be, there is, wickedness in Rome ; and there ever was and ever will be wickedness wherever men are congregated. But it is held in check ; it is less flaunting; it has no official, or, at least, no universal sanction here as elsewhere. On the other hand, the numerous churches, confraternities, religious orders, and philanthropic associations, while they give a religious colour to society, are so many incentives to virtue, so many means easy and open to all to serve God. And these act on society; they possess their influences ; people are not ashamed here to be seen in the church; they can afford a half an hour to hear mass; they come to the sermons that are given; they attend the devotional exercises ;—in a word,

7

. they are more religious, more devout, more God-
fearing, and hence better, wiser, and happier here
than I have seen them in other cities. They may.
have less riches; they are certainly not so well clad
as in Paris or London; the voice of trade, of commerce, &c., is not so loud as in those great marts;
but what does that prove in favour of real happiness?
Nothing.

You will understand that I do not mean to say
that there is no *good*, no examples of piety, in the
great cities to which I have alluded. This would be
not only an exaggeration, but a falsity. In Paris
itself, where there are so many wicked things said
and done, I saw the churches filled with pious,
prayerful people; the crowds that assisted morning
and evening at the devotional exercises held in the
sweet little church of « Notre-Dame-des-Victoires »
were edifying in the extreme. In Alexandria, where
vice, in its most degrading forms, reigns supreme, I
was happy to find the Jubilee well attended. Even
in Chicago, the number and beauty of the churches,
as I saw them some years ago, struck me with admiration; while in New-York I had seen the Irish con-
gregations, there as elsewhere, faithful to their God
and attentive to their religious duties.

No! there is a mixture of good and bad everywhere. But what I do affirm, from the observations
I have been able to make, is, that in Rome the love
of God is publicly, and, I might say, officially incul-
cated: religion is a state affair, and, receiving the
high sanction of authority, its action on the masses
is more powerful; while in other places its progress
is entirely left depending on individual action. The
shadow of indifferentism is thrown over it; and, not
unfrequently, sarcasm and ridicule are the public
rewards of those who take the side of God.

Friday.—I said mass this morning in the church
of St. Agnes, but this time in the subterranean

chapel—that is, in the very room where the dear
little saint suffered martyrdom. I prayed to God,
dear St. C., through her intercession, that as she
was miraculously preserved from material fire, so
you and I might be ever preserved from the fire of
worldly passions, and be worthy of our religious
vocation.

The devotions of the forty hours began to-day in
the church of St. Lawrence in Damaso. The Pope was
expected to come, so that there was a crowd near
the entrance of the church ; but he did not arrive ;
so, all we got was a good drenching in the rain. We
went to spend the evening with Messeigneurs
Langevin and Laflèche, and remained until after
nine o'clock.

Saturday, 27th *February*.—This morning I went to
« St. Lawrence in Damaso.» The Blessed Sacrament.
was exposed. The sweet Saviour had remained on
the altar all night ; and how many blessings had He
not imparted on the city and its inhabitants while
they slept !—blessings of comfort on the poor and the
disconsolate ; blessings of peace shed in the midst
of families ; blessings of mercy on the sinner who
had, perhaps, passed the hours of night in offending
Him ! And here He still remained, silent and bounteous, listening to the petitions that the kneeling
crowds were offering up to Him, forestalling all
their wishes, and giving them graces even a hundredfold more than they even dared to ask for.

Oh ! if we but reflected on the goodness of Jesus
under the veils of the Eucharist, how our hearts
would burn with divine love !

In the evening I went to visit St. Peter's. It was
not, of course, the first nor second visit, nor will it,
I hope, be the last ; for, besides devotional purposes,
the great cathedral offers artistic beauties which
it would take months and months to study. The

chief characteristic of St. Peter's, and the greatest triumph of the artist, lies, I think, in the exactness of its proportions. The details, whether of statuary, of painting, or of other ornamentation, are so nicely measured with the whole, that on your first entrance you are not struck by its immensity. It is only when you come to examine the height and breadth of each supporting-column, the hugeness of each statue, that the colossal dimensions of the building are revealed to you; and the more you examine, the more you are astonished and confounded. And this, if I may say so, almost gives a *divine* stamp to the work. Take the world, for instance,—the work of God's power. To a casual observer it presents nothing beyond a general fitness, a certain mark of beauty; but to him who examines the details, the variety, the perfection of each object, from the huge proportions of the largest animal to the admirable organization of the smallest insect, it will appear that none but a God of infinite power could have compassed it. So it is, on an infinitely smaller scale, if you will, with the Church of St. Peter. From the cupola, with its walls 22 feet thick, poised in mid-air at the height of more than 200 feet, to the little angels that hold the cup of holy-water at the door, all is perfect, without the slightest defect; and hence, all proves that he who conceived and executed this mighty work of art must have been the greatest artist that the world ever possessed. I saw the beautiful statue of St. Angela standing aloft, in the second row of niches, at the entrance of the side-chapel to the left; and I prayed that through her intercession all her daughters might be her imitators in this world and the participants of her glory in the next. As we left St. Peter's, the Pope's carriage was just passing through the Piazza; from all sides people ran to meet it, and dropped on their knees to receive the blessing of their King and

Father. If all the kings who rule nations were thus loved and venerated,—if all held the balance of justice equally poised,—if all administered to the wants of their subjects with as much mildness and paternal care, they would not want so many guards to surround their palaces nor uphold their authority. Alas that it is not so !

Sunday, 28*th.*—There was an exposition of the B. Sacrament in the church of the Gésu. This magnificent temple, one of the richest in Rome, belongs to the Jesuits. I told you before, I think, something of its richness. There were not less than 3000 lights burning on the altar and around it; the Sacred Host was placed high above the tabernacle, so that it appeared as if the stream of brilliancy all came from it. There were 26 cardinals at mass, and a number of bishops. The singing was very fine. I have seen Jesuit churches poor and almost empty; but here in Rome resides the royal splendour of their order ; and it is right that they should triumph here, for they have ever been, since their foundation, the firmest props, humanly speaking, of Rome and the Papal throne. Yet, this grandeur is confined to the church itself : the cells of the Fathers are as simple and as unadorned as your own.

Monday, 1*st March.*—I went yesterday to pay my first visit to the Ursulines, who have their convent in a small lane off the Corso, called *Vicolo* Vittoria, No. 13. Not being able to have an interview, as it was then vesper-hour, I returned to-day, and had quite a long conversation with Mother Margarita Teresa.

I passed the afternoon in a balcony on the Corso, viewing the pleasures of the carnival. As the end of the *Santissimo Carnevale* draws near, the merriment becomes faster and more furious. The whole line of the street is thronged with spectators and masqueraders. The balconies are elegantly dressed out in red, white, and gold ; they are crowded with male and female representatives of every nationality. The costumes are of every shade, from the hideous and grotesque to the handsome and refined : there are walking-fishes and horned animals ; troubadours and mailed knights ; Roman peasants, niggers, dominoes, and what not ?

The great business of the day is to throw little paste-balls at your neighbour. Fierce combats take place between the passers-by and the persons in the balconies. The gallants throw bouquets of flowers at the ladies, and the ladies throw bouquets at the gallants. The amusement begins at 3 o'clock, and continues until the *Ave-Maria.* A troop of dragoons then dash through the streets to clear the way, and in a quarter of an hour after, seven or eight horses without riders are let loose at the Piazza del Popolo, and come galloping up, amid the shouts of the people, as far as the Piazza di Venezia ; here they are stopped by immense blankets stretched across the street. The victorious horse immediately becomes a hero, and is promenaded through the city accompanied by drums and fifes playing lively airs. Such is the Carnival, an institution so dear to the Romans that to attempt to stop it would be to create a revolution in the whole kingdom. To-morrow is the last day.

Tuesday, 2nd March.—The Carnival closed this evening, or, rather, it will close at 12 o'clock to-night. The Corso was still more crowded to-day than ever, and the masqueraders in greater numbers. A little child was killed by one of the horses. At 6 o'clock the people came into the street with small tapers, and went about blowing out their neighbour's candle while they endeavoured to keep their own lighting. After dark the Corso was beautifully illuminated, the effect being very grand. As I write I can hear the singers prmoenading from place to place, serenad-

ing their friends; and, though the hour is far
advanced, they do not appear to have the least idea
of going to bed. I will set a good example to the
city, and retire. Good-night !

Wednesday, 3rd.—To-day all is silent, and people
appear as sedate as Quakers. There was a grand
ceremony in St. Peter's this morning. The Pope,
the cardinals, and the bishops held chapel in the
usual place. The Pope appears strong and young : his
fine full voice resounds through the church during
the solemn chant of the prayers.

Thursday, 4th of March.—I made full use of my
time to-day. We left the Corso this morning in the
bishop's carriage, and went first to the church of
St. Maria del Popolo, near the gate of that name,
and at the foot of the *Pincio*. It is built on the tomb
of Nero. It was formerly a place haunted by
apparitions. It was said that dismal sounds and
groanings were often heard during the night among
the ruins. To allay the fears of the people the
temple was raised and given in care to the Augus-
tinian monks.

It was here that Luther said his last mass!

Ascending the Pincio, we drove along the beautiful road that conducts to the Quirinal; and coming
to the Piazza di St. Isidoro, we stopped for some
time to visit the Irish convent of Franciscans. This
church and the convent attached to it are all full
of souvenirs of Ireland ; and in visiting it the mind
naturally goes back to the days when persecution
obliged the good Fathers to flee from the Isle of
Saints. Their love for fatherland did not decrease ;
wherever they went, they brought the memories of
Ireland with them, and worked strenuously to per-
petuate her glories. To them are due the Annals of the
Four Masters and the Irish Martyrology. There is a
beautiful painting of St. Patrick in the church. The
tomb of Curran's daughter is here, too ; if I do not

mistake, she was the celebrated poetess and beauty who was betrothed to Emmet, and whose reason fled when « her Emmet was no more.»

From this we went to the church of the Conception, which also belongs to the Franciscans. It is here that is preserved the body of St. Crispin. He died about a hundred years ago, and his body is as fresh as if he were still living. Beside the church is the cemetery where the bones of the dead brothers and fathers are symmetrically arranged in 6 chapels. There are arches, alcova columns, ornaments, and lamps, all made of the bones of the dead. Here and there are the skeletons of other fathers dressed in their religious garb—some sitting, others standing, and others in a reclining posture. On some of the skulls you still see portions of the skin and beard. All have little black crosses in their hands. The effect is not in the least hideous, though a sort of dread pervades you as you wander through those silent chapels, so full of the trophies of death.

In the evening there was a station at St. George's church at the foot of Mount Palatine. All the relics were exposed to the veneration of the faithful. In Rome they call a *Station* an exposition of all the considerable relics in a church; there is one in some church or other every day. I was glad to see a great many English Catholics in church during vespers. I venerated the relics of St. George; they also shew a portion of his banner and the end of his lance. He was a Christian warrior who suffered martyrdom in the fourth century, I think. Here, too, are the relics of 1100 virgin-martyrs, relics of sweet St. Philomena, and of St. Sebastian. The singing was very beautiful. The church is very old, many of the columns having belonged to pagan temples in times of old.

After coming from St. George's I went to see the ruins of a triumphal arch dedicated to Janus, and

belonging to the Augustan period ; then I visited
the *cloaca maxima*—that is, the great sewer of Rome.
It is still well preserved, though it dates as far back
as the days of Tarquin the Proud, some 500 years
before Christ. Quite near the filthy reservoir is a
source of pure limpid water, called the *silver* spring.
It is like virtue living in contact with vice pressing
its native purity, and shewing with greater effect
the hideousness of the latter. I then wandered
into the palace of the Cæsars, which covers Mount
Palatine, and forms one of the largest ruins of Rome.
It covers the whole mountain; the arches, which rise
to the height of 80 or 100 feet, are still wonderful in
their decay. What must it have been when it was
covered with the richest marble, adorned by statues,
softened by the verdure of hanging-gardens, and
cooled by the waters of a 1000 fountains ! Here
dwelt the masters of the world. From this place
emanated the edicts that were respected from the
shores of Britain to the Caspian sea. Here those
proud emperors received from the : sycophantic
senate of degraded Rome the title of *Divine.* But
the avenger since destroyed both the idols and their
idolaters, and the ruins of to-day tell in mute
eloquence of the emptiness of worldly pomp and
greatness.

It is the old story of the fall of pride.

After supper, Mr. G. came in the bishop's carriage
to take us to the « Baths of Caracalla.» They were
to be illuminated by *Bengal lights,* and a representation of an eruption of Mount Vesuvius was to terminate the performance.

I fear you will think me exaggerated or imaginative when you hear me so often apply the epithets
« immense,» « grand, » « magnificent,» to the names
of those palaces or buildings I am trying to describe.
But, really, it is not so, dear St. C. I do not amplify
in the least ; and, indeed, there is no want for high

colouring in the description of any of the ruins of
Rome. You will remember that all are the royal
remains of a kingly people ; that Rome was the
centre of that great empire which ruled the universe;
and that all those edifices were the conception and
work of men who allowed themselves to be called
Divine, and who built to themselves houses, baths,
palaces, and even tombs, in proportion to their newly-
acquired dignity.

This Caracalla, though one of the greatest mon-
sters that the earth ever bore, was, nevertheless,
voted a *god ;* and one of his endeavours to keep up
the illusion resulted in the immense baths, the
colossal ruins of which produce even a greater
impression than those of the Coliseum. Let me give
you an idea of their magnitude. Take the French
Cathedral of Quebec ; cut away the pillars and galleries ; make of it *one large room*, and you have just
one of the 17 or 18 departments of the Termini.

There were cold baths, and warm baths, and luke-
warm baths ; there were libraries and conversation-
rooms, dining-rooms and sleeping-apartments, etc.,
etc. The walls were adorned with the most precious
marbles ; every article that comfort and luxury
could invent here met the desires of the effete
monarch and his court. In a word, considering
himself a god, he naturally desired to possess a
material Paradise, and, as far as every earthly
pleasure can go, he succeeded.

But here, as in the case of Cæsar's Palace, the
revolving years have changed this scene of luxury
into one of desolation. The huge carcass lays strand-
ed on the shores of time, like the remains of some
monster whitening on the sea-beach where the
waves have left it. Its marble columns and coatings
have disappeared, discovering the vulgar brick
which had been disguised underneath the brilliant
exterior ; the wind moans through the vast halls ;

bats and nocturnal birds glance fitfully through its broken angles : the cold, clear starlight looks in through its roofless domes and arched windows ; its former occupants, so powerful in their day, have crumbled into dust ; and in their place we stand, 3000 spectators, assembled from every quarter of the globe. And it appeared to me as if we had come to exult over its fall and mark its disgrace, for the many-coloured fires that lit up each part in succession only served to render its ruins and desolation more perceptible to all.

The mimic eruption of Vesuvius, which closed the evening's entertainment, was something terrific. The ground actually trembled beneath the thunders of the explosions, and a feeling akin to awe hushed the voices of the thousands as the burning lava poured down the sides of the miniature volcano. What must the reality be !

During the intervals the military band discoursed sweet music. At about 6½ o'clock the eruption burned itself out ; the Bengal fires died away, and the spectators poured out in a vast living stream into the darkness of night to wend their way homewards, well pleased at all they had seen.

Friday, 5th March.—To-day I went to see the church of St. Gregory, where there was an exposition of relics. I saw the hard bed on which this holy Pope used to pass a few short hours of night in necessary repose, the marble chair in which he often sat, and some of his relics. There is here a miraculous image of the Blessed Virgin, which was carried through Rome at the time of the great pest that desolated the city during the pontificate of Gregory. On the occasion of the procession, or, rather, towards its end, an angel appeared on the summit of Adrian's mole, sheathing a fiery sword, and the calamity ceased. It was then that the *Regina Cœli lætare* was composed, and a commemorative statue of the

angel was placed on the place of the apparition. It
still stands on the highest pinnacle of the Castle of
St. Angelo.

It was St. Gregory who sent St. Augustin and his
monks to England to convert that island ; and I was
again happy to see a number of English Catholics
in the church, who were devoutly hearing Mass
in honour of their benefactor. I united my prayer to
theirs, and asked God, through the intercession of
the saint, to grant the English nation a speedy
return from the errors of heresy to the true fold of
Christ. On my way home, I visited, in the little
church of the B. Virgin near the forum, the image
of the Holy Mother painted by St. Luke. *It spoke* to
St. Mary of Egypt. It was formerly in the church of
St. John the Baptist, on the banks of the Jordan,
whence it was transported to Rome. In another
chapel of the same church is an « Ecce Homo,» a bust
of our Lord crowned with thorns. It is very expressive. The eyes of this statue moved in the year 1796.
The miracle was witnessed by great numbers.

Saturday.—I assisted to-day at the opening of the
forty-hours' devotion in the church of St. John and
St. Paul, two noble Roman soldiers who suffered
martyrdom under the impious Julian the apostate.
The temple is built over the place where they
suffered, on a rising ground a little beyond the
Coliseum ; the spot where their heads were struck
off is surrounded by an iron railing in the body of
the church. This is where the Passionists live. The
body of St. Paul, their founder, is still preserved
under one of the altars ; it is as fresh as during the
saint's lifetime. I saw it as it lay dressed out in the
habit of the order.

Sunday.—I assisted at three sermons to-day. The
first was in the little church of St. John the Baptist.
The preacher was Mgr. De Charbonnel, formerly of
Toronto. He opened a retreat for the Zouaves pre-

paratory to their going home. Next I went to St. Andrea della Valle to hear M. Combalot, a fine old French priest, who, though 80 years of age, preached with all the fire of youth. A laughable incident took place in church during the sermon. You may know already that there are no pews in the churches in Rome, nor, indeed, in any place that I have seen except in Canada. There are chairs standing against the walls of one of the chapels ; and any one who wishes to sit down may take one, and go to the chapel or altar where he wishes to pray. In the case of a sermon or grand-mass, those chairs are placed around the pulpit or in front of the altar at which the mass is said. One of the bishops who assisted at the sermon yesterday was seated on a little rickety chair right opposite the pulpit. He was a tall, stout man, weighing, I should say, about 200 pounds, at least. Having leaned a little back, the treacherous affair gave way, and down came poor Monseigneur on the broad of his back, right to the marble pavement ; and there he lay for a few se- conds, trying to disengage himself from the ruins! Of course, there was a crowd of priests around him in a moment, very anxiously inquiring if his lordship was hurt, but yet quite unable to repress a smile at his ludicrous position. The poor man's only wound was that of his feelings ; and I assure you he was very much abashed, and blushed like a young maiden of 16. I pitied him sincerly ; and don't you think he was to be pitied ? *C'était une grandeur déchue.*

I next went to St. Louis-des-Français to hear M. l'abbé Bugeaud, the vicar-general of Mgr. Dupan- loup, and the author of the two beautiful works, *La vie de Ste. Chantal* et celle de *Ste. Monique.* I had the pleasure of becoming slightly acquainted with M. l'abbé Darras, the author of the *History of the Church.*

Monday.—I said mass this morning, dear C., in presence of a Crucifix which spoke to St. Philip Neri. I asked that it might to you and me and all mankind, winning us all by sweet words of mercy to repentance for our sins. To-day being the feast of St. Thomas Aquinas, there was a grand ceremony in the church of the Dominicans, called the Minerva. There were twenty cardinals seated around the altar with their rich purple robes, fur capes, and crimson *calottes ;* at their feet were forty prelates, and in the church about 60 more. Among them I distinguished Cardinal Bonaparte, and I took a good look at him, so that, if he ever becomes Pope, I can say that « I saw the Holy Father,» without returning to Rome.

In the evening there was an exposition of relics in the church called « St. Peter in Chains.» Here are kept the identical chains with which the Prince of the Apostles was bound in prison. They were suspended over the high altar, exposed to the veneration of the faithful. Here also is the famous statue of Moses, by Michael Angelo. It is considered a master-piece of sculpture. I saw here the ashes of the Machabees. After passing down the Capitol on our way home, we turned to the right a little below its base, and found ourselves, after a few moments, at the door of the church of St. Mark. On the walls outside the portico are several inscriptions which have been extracted from the Catacombs and encrusted in the masonry. The Latin is not always choice ; sometimes it is even barbarous ; but the sentiments are beautiful in their Christian simplicity and resignation. Some of them run thus : « *Here sleepeth Stephen* for a short time.» « Caius left us at the Lord's command, but we shall see him again.» Another, the most touching, might be thus translated into French : « Adieu ! au revoir dans le ciel.» It was in this church that St. Dominic raised a dead child to life. The mother had come to one of the

saint's sermons, and on returning home she found
her little son dead. She immediately carried him
to the church, and, placing him in the arms of St.
Dominic, *insisted* on his being restored to life. God
rewarded her faith, through the holy man's intercession, and she went away rejoicing.

On the Piazza, a few yards from the church, a
bust of Minerva leans against the wall. It is *seven*
feet high, and must have ence been beautiful. But,
alas for th echarm of beauty !—they pass like a shadow. The poor goddess has her nose broken off;
there is an ugly cut in her chin, and her left eye
looks as if she had been at a prize-fight, and came
off second best. She once had her day, and, not
knowing how to profit of it wisely, she has been set
aside like many another *belle*. And to complete her
degradation, she who once held the scales of Justice is now condemned to hold an unsightly *pole*,
on which the Romans, who once knelt at her feet,
now unconcernedly dry and bleach their linen. *Sic
transit gloria mundi !*

Tuesday, 8th.—No letters as yet from Canada, the
mails not having arrived. To-day I visited the « Exposition of Objects of Christian Art,» opened by the
Pope two weeks ago. The *grounds* occupy a large
part of the ruins of the Baths of Diocletian. I endeavoured, the other day, to give you some idea of
the size of the Baths of Caracalla ; that of Diocletian
was still larger. It contained 1000 bathing-rooms,
with libraries, schools, forums, gardens, fountains ;
in a word, it was the most magnificent work of Rome
at a time when magnificence had outstripped all
limits.

In one part of it, and preserving its former structure as much as possible, is the church of « St. Mary
of the Angels.» The columns that support the cupola
are those which were employed in the baths, immense tapering monoliths that rise to the height of

80 feet. A thought very naturally came to my mind while I was here. I will give you the benefit of it, such as it is. The baths of Caracalla have been left to themselves, and the mark of decay is sinking deeper into them day after day. The baths of Diocletian, on the contrary, having been converted into a church and monastery, have, as it were, arisen from their ruins, and are to-day as beautiful in marble and gold as when they were first finished. Is not this something like what happens in society? Society being a thing of human formation, its glory being the work of man, is naturally subject to the common fate ; no matter how great the power,—no matter how finely it is propped up by the policy of its rulers and the numbers of its subjects,—it diminishes with time, falls into decrepitude, and disappears. But if religion sustain it, it leans on the arm of the Most High ; its hope is in heaven ; its strength comes from God ; and time, instead of destroying it, only gives it renewed vigour.

But I am forgetting the *Exposition*, or, if you wish, the *Exhibition*. Everything that belongs to church service is here exposed.

There are statues of the Blessed Virgin, in marble, composition, and bronze ; one among others is touching—it is the representation of the « Mother most admirable,» with, oh ! such a sweet countenance !—one would almost say that the artist had a vision of our Lady. There are crucifixes of every size, model, and material ; statues of the saints ; those of St. Sabastián are the most expressive. Then come altars of the most exquisite workmanship and design ; tabernacles of Gothic and Greek architecture, resplendent with gold, silver, and precious stones ; bells, large and small,—chimes with such loving tones that you would think the angels were singing in the clouds. These, with a most valuable and interesting picture-gallery and chancels of stained glass, complete the outer gallery, and comprise the joint works of all the Catholic countries of Europe.

You then enter the middle galleries, a lengthy suite of tastefully-arranged apartments, where the eye is dazzled by the accumulated splendour: vestments of all descriptions and choir-habiliments; chasubles, manuples, stoles, albs, surplices, dalmatics, copes, birettas, mitres, tiaras, purple and black soutanes,—and all these according to the different rites, whether Latin, Greek, Armenian, or others; chalices, patens, ciboriums, ostensories, and altarfronts.

It is hardly possible to conceive anything richer. The chalices and ostensories are beyond description. I saw one of the latter, of the Gothic order, which stood eight feet high. It was a perfect temple. The twelve Apostles stand around the Host on the uppart part. In a lower story are the four great Prophets, who stand around the B. Virgin. The base is of solid gold. There were beautiful missals and breviaries of all kinds. One of the missals was a work of the monks of the 13th century, and its illuminated pages are almost as fresh and as brilliant as when it came forth from the hands of the recluse. How they must have prayed while performing their task, those dear old saints!—you can see the mark of love and prayer on almost every letter. As I stood before this monument of ages flown, my mind wandered back to the time it was made. I fancied I could see the holy monk in his cell. It was one of those secluded monasteries, the ruins of which meet the eye of the traveller in Germany. The cell was poor to austerity—a little bed in one corner, a wooden chair, and on the table stood the paints of divers colours. Nothing relieved the blank walls, save, perhaps, a crucifix and a statue of the B. Virgin, towards which the old man now and then raised

his eyes in supplication, or to offer up his labour.
And the rays of the setting sun, as they glanced
through the high turret windows, played among
the father's grey hairs, and seemed to cast a halo of
glory around his revered head. And as the picture
came out before me, I thought to myself how much
happier was the monk, in his apparent obscurity,
than many who, during his time, were surrounded
by worldly honour and fame. His name was not
attached to his work ; no monument would per-
petuate his memory ; his only vision of the future
was a life of constant obedience ; and then the little
wooden cross in the cemetery, when he would lay
him down to rest among his brethren, awaiting the
final summons. But then, God was watching him,
and counting each letter that he illumined. He knew
that a higher reward than any the world can give
was awaiting his perseverance, and in this hope he
lived content. And this explained the happy smile
of inner joy that lit up his features. Each nation
has its own allotted quarter or region. There was
one that bore the inscription, «Ingleterra.» It was
quite empty. The exhibitors had not yet had time
to unpack their goods ; but the « empty case » of
England appeared to me to be suggestive. Poor
England !—there was a time when her name shone
brightly in the annals of the church,—when her
kings and queens merited a place among the cata-
logues of the saints,—when her learned doctors and
great writers were the glory and support of the
Church of Cod ; then her works were many, and her
deeds were deeds of justice and honour. But since the
blight of heresy blackened her soil, her beauty has
been sullied ; her voice is no longer heard in the
vineyard among the workers ; the book of her martyrology is closed ; no English saints glorify the
pages of her history, save and except the chosen
few whom her own homicidal hands slew in unholy

hatred to the just cause; and, therefore, «her case is empty.» But, no ! it is not so : a new and strong branch has grown up where the old trunk was cut down, and already appear rare and beautiful fruits and flowers. ´ Her Wisemans, her Mannings, her Spensers, her Fabers, and others, are wortly of their predecessors in the faith ; and in a few days, when «her case will be filled,» it will be seen that the fruits of her zeal and industry in church-work are worthy of a high place among the competition.

Wednesday, 9th.—This morning the carriage of Monseigneur Bourget (of Montreal) was waiting for another priest and myself at the early hour of 5½ o'clock A.M. We all went together to the church of St. Françoise Romaine to say mass. This being the feast of the saint, all the relics were exposed, and we gained a plenary indulgence by praying at the crypt. I have already given you a description of the church : you may remember that the marks of St. Peter's knees are preserved under iron bars at the side-altar. The body of St. Frances lies in state under the high altar in a subterranean chapel. She is dressed out in the costume of her order. The naked skull, with its grinning teeth, appears underneath the *gitimpe.* This is done expressly to shew the Roman ladies that beauty disappears after death, and that worldly pleasures are only of short duration. We breakfasted ·in the community-parlor, and received a picture from the superior.

After dinner, MM. C., P. and I went on an excursion to Mount Aventine, where there are many curiosities to be seen. We passed by the «Cercle Canadien,» to see if our letters had arrived ; and, to my great joy, I found awaiting me letters from Canada. I read them over and over going along the road, and was so absorbed in their ·perusal that I came well ´nigh running over a carriage and pair of horses. We went first to the Tiber to view the remains of the

bridge of Horatius Cocles. You have read in Roman
history that in the first days of the Republic a
Roman soldier sustained the attack of the advancing
enemy until the bridge was cut away by his countrymen, when he jumped into the Tiber and swam
across in safety. How we used to burn with martial
ardour as we translated the account from the Latin,
long, long ago, in class! Leaving the Tiber to our
right, we came to an ancient temple of the Vestals,
which is still in a good state of repair. We cross an
·open square on which a company of Zouaves are
drilling, and arrived at the church of St. Maria in
Cosmedin, which dates as far back as the 3rd century. St. Augustin taught here for some time. The
image of the B. Virgin, which is over the altar,
comes from Constantinople, and goes as far back as
the days of the Iconoclasts in the 8th century.
Underneath are catacombs, but the doors have been
closed since five ecclesiastics perished in them some
years ago.

At the church-door is a large round marble slab,
with a lion's head cut on it; the mouth is wide open.
It is called *La bocca della verità*. It was used as a
swearing-machine in the days of Paganism. The
witness or attestor placed his hand in the lion's
mouth and gave his evidence; he believed that if
he spoke falsely the mouth would close and leave
him handless. We next ascended Mount Aventine
to visit the convent of the Dominicans, called St.
Sabine. It was here that St. Pius the V. lived and
died. I saw the room from which his spirit ascended
to heaven, and the miraculous crucifix which was
his constant companion. In another part of the
monastery is the cell in which St. Dominic dwelt
for many years. In the garden we were shewn the
orange-tree which the saint planted with his own
hands.· While Père Lacordaire was here, a branch
sprung from the roots of the old tree, and is now

strong and vigorous. You know that the eloquent preacher, who was also a saint, introduced some necessary reforms into the order. From the convent-terrace you get a grand view of Rome and the surrounding hills. There is something heavenly in the calm. silence and peace that reign everywhere throughout the building.

At about five minutes' walk from St. Sabine is the church dedicated to St. Alexius. You remember his history. He lived in voluntary poverty at the door of his own father's house, under the staircase, for many years, without making himself known to his father or mother, who constantly mourned his departure. The staircase is still to be seen; the church has been restored by the piety and munificence of a religious society of laymen, aided by Pius the Ninth. It is handsome, but to my taste the ornaments are a little too gaudy. A convent of Theatine Fathers is attached to it. They received us well.

Thursday, 10th.—This morning I went to the Irish college and church; it is called St. Agatha in Suburra. I visited O'Connell's monument, containing his heart,—that noble heart that was filled with such pure patriotism and noble sentiments of true devotion. The liberator's bust is very well executed. I called on Dr. Kirby, the superior, a genial, kind-hearted man. He received me with open arms, and invited me to sing high-mass and dine on Sunday.

After dinner, Monsg. Laflèche, Monsg. Langevin, MM. C., G., P., and myself, visited the Castle of St. Angelo. It is strongly built and well'defended; but with the modern appliances of offensive warfare it would not long stand siege. The zouaves are in garrison here now. It was built by the Emperor Adrianus as a tomb for himself and family. It communicates with the Vatican by a subterranean passage.

Friday.—The same party visited this morning the

museum and astronomical apparatus of Père Secchi, in the Roman College : we were shewn through by Father Secchi himself, who has all the modesty of a real savant. The instrument which he himself invented for meteorological observations is a world's wonder. It gives the intensity of the winds, the state of the atmosphere, and indicates the changes that are about to take place. It received a large gold-medal at the Paris exhibition. We were then shewn through the cabinets of natural science ; and the professor made some very interesting experiments on *light* and *sound*, for our special benefit. We then went to the rooms of St. Louis de Gonzague and the Ven. Berchmans, which are now fitted up into handsome chapels. They contain many relics of different saints. Passing through the long corridor of the college, we came to the wing occupied by the fathers' cells, and it was with some emotion we read on the doors the names of some of the occupants : Père Perrone, P. Ballerini, Liberatore, Franzlin, Patrizi, etc. These are names that have filled the world with the renown of their science and learning,—names that posterity will extol and admire ; and yet the occupants were here in small, mean cells, surrounded by all the signs of strictest poverty and humility. Ah ! the enemies of Christ and His church may well fear the Jesuits ; for as long as they are thus humble in their riches, they will oppose an invincible barrier against the attacks of infidelity and irreligion.

Every Friday evening the devotions of the Stations of the Cross are performed in the Coliseum. I went thither this evening, and found vast crowds of every nationality and religion. At half-past four the procession entered the arena. Eight men, in the garb of penitents, came first, one of them bearing a large cross ; then came the preacher, a Capuchin monk ; and after him a number of ladies dressed in black,

belonging to some pious association. They recited
the beads in a singing tone along the road, and until
they came to the large cross which stands in the
middle of the arena. The procession then wended its
way to a platform on the left side of the building;
the audience stood all around, and the monk made a
very impressive sermon on the *flagellation of our
Lord*. At the end of the discourse the whole assembly
knelt, and we all repeated aloud an act of contrition. The stations then began; they are placed all
around the Coliseum, at the distance of 200 or 300
feet the one from the other. There were bishops
and priests; men, women, and children, rich and
poor: all were mixed together without distinction;
and the ceremony was all the more imposing for
the piety and recollection evinced by every one. I
prayed with the rest, and I can assure you that it
is impossible not to feel moved when you think
that you are kneeling on the very spot where so
many martyrs generously offered up their lives for
Christ. Eighteen hundred years ago, those vast cir-
cles that rise above us, majestic even in their ruins,
were filled with 100,000 spectators; the ground on
which we stood was vacant; a trumpet sounded,
and there was a hush of expectation on all sides.
Suddenly, at a sign from the emperor, a large iron
gate swung on its hinges, and a fierce lion sprang
forth from the cage, which you still see opposite
the place where the royal box looked down on the
arena. A short time after, another gate opened a
little to the right, where you see the tenth station,
and several persons were seen slowly advancing.
Their arms were stretched forth in prayer; their eyes
were raised to Heaven; they were the holy band of
Martyrs. Some were young; others were advanced in
years; there were young maidens and tender youths;
but you could trace no signs of fear on their coun-
tenances: on the contrary, in the sweet and placid

serenity that beamed forth, you could read the joy
that pervaded their souls. A cry arose from the
multitude: *Christiani ad bestias !*—«To the beasts with
the Christians !» It was the solemn condemnation of
Pagan Imperial Rome. The soldiers threw javelins
at the lion to excite him to fury. The beast lashed
his sides, and, perceiving his victims, he crouched
low for a spring, approached them with soft velvet
steps, and then with one mighty bound he was among
them. You could hear the cracking of bones ; you
could see the rich red blood as it spouted forth from
ugly wounds ; but no cry of anguish, no manifestation of pain. One by one they fell, and in a few
moments they were a heap of mangled flesh weltering in clotted gore. Others were then brought in,
and others still, until the brutal thirst for blood was
satisfied. The performance was at an end, and the
thousands issued out from the 24 huge gates to gain
their respective homes.

These oft-repeated scenes took place on the spot
where I was kneeling, and I, thank God—a descendant of those heroes,—I—a priest of the religion for
which they died,—was there to-day to thank the
Divine Saviour for having given them grace and
strength to fight the good fight, and bear witness to
the truth and might of the faith which they upheld
unto death. What if some of the old Pagan Emperors
could come forth from his forgotten grave, and,
seated on the ruins up yonder, could look down for
a moment on what was taking place ! The seats once
so crowded of the tiers of galleries are now vacant ;
the voices that so fiercely clamoured for the blood of
the Christians, and proclaimed, in tones of the most
abject sycophancy, that Cæsar was divine, are all
hushed and silent now. He would look around him
in vain for the smallest vestige of his power, once
universal. And from his solitude above he would
see the arena filled with hundreds, nay, thousands,

of those Christians he so much hated and derided. His thought would probably be to call for the tigers and lions to come forth from the vivarium where they were kept in his day ; but the vivarium is empty, and in ruins, too. He might summon his pretorian guards to rush on them and despatch them ; but the legionaries and pretorians have long since disappeared. Then, in rage, he could ask of the grave a refuge for his discomfiture, and sink into it with the cry of Julian the apostate expiring on the battlefield : «Nazaren, thou hast conquered !»

Saturday, 12th March.—This day five years, dear C., I said my first mass in the little interior chapel of the Ursulines (of Quebec). What a happy day it was ! Would to God that all my masses since had been as fervent! Last night I endeavoured to prepare in a fitting manner for the solemn anniversary. I went to confession to Father French, an Irish Jesuit residing in the Roman College, and afterwards said my breviary at the altar of St. Louis de Gonzague in the church of St. Ignatius. This morning I had the happiness of offering up Holy Mass in the crypt of St. Peter's; on the altar beneath which lie the remains of SS. Peter and Paul. I repassed in my memory the five years of priest-hood already passed, and, alas ! found no great consolation in the thought. Had I been faithful to all my promises made on the morning of the 12th March, 1865 ? No. Had I lived as a priest, closely copying the Divine model? No. Had I endeavoured to bring souls to God ? Had I worked faithfully and constantly at the great work of the extension of the church ? No. And yet I had been filled with graces ; I had had many warnings, many opportunities. It had been given to me to see with my own eyes the Holy Places, to walk in the footsteps of Jesus along the sorrowful way. I had prayed at the Holy Sepulchre and on Mount Olivet. I had been to

8

Bethlehem and Calvary. And now, as a new favour,
I was allowed to celebrate the beginning of a new
year in presence of the most holy relics of the two
·great priests of the Jews and Gentiles,—the immediate successors of Christ Himself. I clearly heard
our Saviour say to me, in the language of Holy
Writ : « What could I do that I have not done to
gain thy heart and win thy love ? » Yet I could not
answer firmly and fondly, with St. Peter : « Lord,
Thou knowest that I love Thee.» The past would
have given an emphatic denial to the assertion, if I
dared to make it. All, then, I could do was to deplore
the last years, to detest my past conduct, and renew
my promises of fidelity for the future. May God,
through the intercession of the glorious Apostles,
grant that they may not be in vain ! (¹) I prayed
for you, too, dear C., and for other friends in whose
welfare, both spiritual and temporal, I have a right
and a duty to feel interested. I invoked the blessing
of God on all the generous friends who had contributed to my coming here, and prayed that the
Church founded on Peter, by Christ, might triumph
over all our enemies. As I prayed I could hear the
voice of music and psalmody stealing softly through
the vaults of the tomb from the chapel above. It
seemed as if the angelic choir had caught my
prayer and were repeating it before the Throne
of God. And I felt comforted, for I remembered the
words of Christ : « Ask and you shall receive ; seek
and you shall find ; knock and it shall be opened
unto you.» (²)

(¹) These lines, for all those who know how worthy a priest
Mr. Doherty has constantly been, will be the best proof of his
great humility and sincere piety.

(²) Here ends the relation of Mr. Doherty's travels. The
following pieces we have selected from his papers, as most
interesting and worthy of publication.

A LETTER ON THE IRISH QUESTION,

ADDRESSED TO A NUN.

GRAND SEMINARY, 22nd April, 1864.

Dear Rev. Madam,

How uncouthly vulgar you must no doubt think me, to attempt writing to you on such unqualified paper ! But listen to my reasons : with a stretch of your wonted charity, they may win an excuse for what otherwise would seem unpardonable. I have just completed the lecture of the beautiful letter you sent me yesterday. I need not tell you how much I admired its high tone. The lady who wrote it is evidently of a powerful stamp of mind: Her mind is well stored with varied knowledge—indeed, without the least tinge of flattery. I am almost sure she has read a course of philosophy, so correct her views, so lucid her ideas. I can well imagine how such a mind must have ardently loved and embraced the dogma of our holy church, especially after having seen them, as it were, reduced to practice in so perfect a way by those among whom God's grace was pleased to place her. It would have been a miracle if such a person as she evidently is would pass some years in a convent without becoming a firm and steadfast Catholic. Without knowing it, I shall venture to say that she must have been very bigoted (pardon the expression) when she first entered the convent. She must have been also at first slightly defiant of the apparent kindness by which the zeal of the Rev. ladies surrounded her; but soon her lofty spirit must have pierced the mysty haze that domestic education had thrown around it; and as, one by one, the chains of prejudice, perhaps even fanaticism, fell from her limbs, like St. Peter, long ago, as he stood beside the angel when the scales were removed from his eyes,—like

as unto Tobias before parting with Raphael,—oh !
what a pure light, what a sweet atmosphere, must
have pervaded her soul ! What delight must have
filled her whole being when the magic wand, or,
to speak in a more Christian manner, the sweet
voice of God, whispered its loving accents, and told
her to be free, pronounced in her case the all-power-
ful *fiat lux*, and gave her the boon of faith ! Were
you, Rev. Madam, the confident of those first
motions of grace which touched her ? If so, how
you must have adoringly admired the ways and
workings of Providence !

What joy you must have felt at seeing the impressions produced by virtue on such a noble mind !
And then, how great must be the reward of those
who were instrumental in winning back to the true
faith so precious a pearl !

But, how fast does my pen run ! Surely I promised
you a reason for my want of etiquette ; and here I
am, dilating in a highly imaginative manner on what
I know nothing about, instead of fulfilling my promise. Well ! when I came to that part in which the
lady undertakes to answer your patriotic question,
« Are the Irish suffering, and what is the cause ? »
I redoubled my attention, and promised myself a real
treat ; for, thought I, the great intelligence of the
writer has, before this, looked on and examined the
sad picture before her eyes, and has, no doubt, found
out its real cause. Must I say it ? I was entirely
mistaken in my anticipation ; nay, though it was
most ungallant of me, I felt somewhat indignant at
seeing so important a question handled in so flip-
pant a manner. The lady gives for causes what
are in reality effects ; her conclusions are illogical,
and, in some places, it is evident enough that she
has been looking at poor Ireland through the big
end of the telescope. This, Rev. Madam, is harsh
language, an unsought-for disapprobation, and may,

perhaps, pain you. But allow me to say that my high esteem for your many qualities, especially the *Irish ones*, lead me to thus speak. You have, I am sure, placed a deal of confidence in the intellectual power of your former pupil, and you would be prone to take her opinion, even on these subjects, as standard.

On the other hand, you have, I know, an «enlarged view» of Ireland imprinted in your heart. You feel for its sufferings; you worship its glorious firmness in the faith; you love its good humour and pathos, its wit, its genius, its mountains, its lakes, and its beauteous vales,—aye, even its very faults. Is it not so?

Do I exaggerate one iota? If so, I am entirely at fault as to the estimation I have made of your character. Are you, then, not sensibly pained at having such an appreciation of Ireland's condition given by one whom you feel bound to believe both enlightened' and impartial? All that you thought about Ireland's unhappy state, about the dreadful persecutions, the unjust exactions, the tyrannical power, that have broken, as it were, her fair form, all is illusion. The whole fabric must, like Aladdin's wonderful palace, sink into the ground at one magic word; and hereafter you must begin to think: "Well! poor Ireland! she is certainly suffering; but, after all, it is her own fault,—or at least her rulers may have good reasons for thus fettering her."

Dear Rev. Madam, this thought struck me as I continued to read; and no sooner had I finished than I took the resolution of undeceiving you, and that as soon as possible. So I seized my pen, drew out a sheet of paper, the first come to hand; and here is the reason of the total want of politeness you must remark in the form of this—shall I call it

letter ?—and this is also why the language I employ
swells now and then into diatribe.

Permit me, then, to answer your question, « Do
the Irish suffer, and what is the cause?» and to
refute some of the lady's propositions. I flatter
myself that I shall be able to do so without much
difficulty,.for what I say comes under the head of
palpable truth : facts are stubborn things, and cannot
be inverted, while historical parallels and deductions
are equally headstrong.

Ireland suffers, and has suffered for many a long
year, both physically and morally, and that to such
an extent that it forms a subject of astonishment to
some that she has not sunk to a degree of moral
degradation even below that of the islanders of
Oceanica. When the Irish first came into contact
with the Normans, they were just recovering from
the effects of the prolonged stay of the Danes. You
know that during the wars that covered Europe with
ruins, when the Northern barbarians poured down
on the Roman Empire, Ireland remained intact, and
preserved brightly glowing and well-trimmed the
lamp of science and religion. It is an historical fact
that her shores became the refuge of learning, which,
like the sacred fire hidden during the captivity of
Babylon, was after a time to illumine, by its bright
rays, the dark night of barbarity that covered with
its sable wings the whole face of Europe. This, I
repeat, is history, nothing more. But in her turn she
was to feel the weight of the barbarian's strong arm,
and then commenced the series of those long sufferings which, through a mysterious dispensation of
Providence, have, with more or less intermission,
oppressed her ever since. The *rôle* of each nation is,
in my opinion, different : some are destined to be
glorious and great in a worldly point of view ; others
to be still greater and more glorious, according to
faith,

The former, like Assyria, Egypt, Greece, Rome, England, &c.,will be mighty in war, powerful in commerce ; their flags will float proudly over prostrate nations ; but, as the prophet Daniel says, «Their feet shall be of iron and of clay,» a feeble and fickle foundation, which, if struck by the little stone detached from the mountain, will cause the whole superstructure to crumble. Others there are that, like the people of God, like poor Poland, or suffering Ireland, must go down into Egypt and be persecuted by Pharaoh : . must cross the desert-sands of persecution and suffering ; must be carried away in captivity into a strange land, where they must hang up their harps and remain in mute desolation ; but who, nevertheless, are ever under the protection of the luminous cloud of faith ; whose virtues and trials ever ascend as a perfume before God's throne, and whose place is marked in golden letters among the most worthy portions of Christ's church-militant. Which is the more noble destiny of the two ? Oh ! if those who rail and mock at poor Ireland had but the eyes of faith, how they would fall down and kiss the hem of the garment she wears, all besprinkled as it is with the blood of her martyrs !—how they would envy her degradation !—how they would exalt her lowliness !

As far removed as is Lazarus from Dives, so far removed is Ireland's true and real glory from the paltry, wan, and sickly halo that worldly success has shed around the person of her rival. After many years of sufferings, the brave Brian Boru, like Alfred of England, collected his country's scattered forces on the plains of Clontarf, and before the nation's might the stranger fled in dismay. But, alas ! the land was covered with ruins, and, the sources of education having been taken away, the necessary effects of ignorance and its concomitant evils followed. You must not, then, be surprised if in the

twelfth century the Irish had not yet totally recovered from the bad effects caused by the barbarian
rule of the Danes. This is, however, certain : they
were not one whit less advanced in civilization than
the wild and boisterous Norman barons who came
clad in iron and steel to conquer the fair lands of
Ireland, as they had in the eleventh century conquered those of England.

« They came,» says the lying Hume, « to restore
peace and union, and at the request of the Pope.»
Regenerators, forsooth ! See how well Ireland was
repaid by Providence, according to them: In the fifth
and sixth centuries her sons had gone forth with
no other arms save the crucifix, with no other
buckles save that of a firm and efficient faith ; their
armour was their fortitude ; their sword the word of
God ; their steeds were the wings of heavenly zeal ;
and here, six centuries afterwards, when the Irish
fell into barbarity, apostles came to them in iron
helmets on barbed steeds, with heavy lances and
ponderous battle-axes, and the first act of regeneration is the foul massacre of an unsuspecting garrison !! Think you that such gospellers came on the
strength of a *Papal Bull*? Do you imagine that his
most Catholic Majesty Henry II. had great purity of
intention, though he had washed in penance the
stains which the murder of St. Thomas had left on
his hands ? But this is not the question.

The Irish were more chivalrous and less easily
subdued than their Saxon neighbours. William the
Conqueror, notwithstanding what Sir Walter Scott
says, found little difficulty in establishing his sway
throughout England. Not so in Ireland ; and so the
lords of the Pale had for many a year a hot time of
it, and many a time did the assembled clans push
their depredatory excursions as far as the very gates
of Dublin. There was, therefore, constant war.
Religious hate fanned the flame of national dislike,

and, even in the time of Elizabeth, the wily patriot Hugh O'Neil came nigh freeing Ireland for ever. At length, when transportations of colonies, butcheries on a wholesale system, hamlet-burning, and, finally, the unsuccessful issue of the war for the Stuarts, closed by the treaty of Limerick, Ireland was prostrate and fettered at the feet of her foe. You know the series of enactments that followed. You have heard of the penal code, so I need not detail it to you. Then just let me ask you one question : What makes a people what it is ? Is it not education — I mean education in the widest sense of the word ? Take any given people, no matter how barbarous ; give them missionaries to teach them the faith ; teach them industry and the fine arts ; give them a model government ; and, be they Laplanders, Patagonians, or South-Sea islanders, you will make of them, in the course of time, a noble, polished, enterprising, and highly civilized nation. Is not this true ? Look to the history of the western nations of Europe : you see the verification of the fact. On the contrary, take the French, the English, or any other people : deprive them of their means of employment: you will have necessarily a set of idlers, cut-throats, and robbers, for all these crimes are the offspring of idleness. Take away their manufactures, their inven tions ; forbid them to be rich ; oblige them to live in squalid wretchedness by setting a price on all their goods ; deprive them, moreover, of knowledge by banishing their pastors, their learned men ; and if any of them, perchance, do become learned, forbid them any honorable employ, such as judgeships, members of parliament,—nay, the very liberal professions,— and you will necessarily reduce them to ignorance. Then, when you have thus debased them, give them over to starvation ; send in among them hale, hearty, sleek and sanctimonious proselytisers, with fat soup and Protestant Bibles; open schools to teach corrupt morals. Nay, more : if they do not prefer their animal comforts to their wretched condition ; if they are stubborn in resisting the devil and you, then turn them out of their hovels and let them die in the ditches, by the hill-side, on the public roads, or beneath the ruins of their mud-wall cottages. Do all this, I say, to the French, the English, or any other people; and if in fifty or a hundred years you shall not have reduced them to an exceedingly low par in the scale of society, then, indeed, reasoning *a pari*, or, in other terms, experience, is a myth. How unreasonable, then, it is to say : «Oh! the Irish are idle vagrants; they are not industrious;. they are not over-given to cleanliness: therefore, it is small blame to their rulers to keep them down.»

Rather say : What ! after so many centuries' suffering, deprivations, bad moral training,—nature, the while, being almost left to her own resources, —they are yet so good, so generous, so apt for training ! How noble the spirit must have been that could not be broken by human efforts the most multiplied and persevering! It is with nations as it is with individuals, by whom they are composed. This is an admitted fact. Well, then, take a child ; place him in a corrupt society ; neglect his moral training; teach him vice : will that child be good, docile, obedient? No, surely. And whom must you blame for his fault ? Not the child, but his guardian. Apply this simile to Ireland's case, and you will at once see how many bad reasonings are made by those who judge of what they see without seeking out the cause. The lady says that the Irish do not suffer to-day; she must then be sadly ignorant of what passes within the British senate-chamber. Has she read Peel's late admission ? . Has she read an article which appeared in the *Times* some months ago ? Has she heard the cry coming from the west ?

Surely its wail must have struck on her ear, since it awakened a sympathetic echo from Australia to the shores of America. Has she heard of Bishop Plunket? Has she read the burning letters of poor Father Lavalle ? « But, in the great cities they are not suffering.» Why, then, do they contemplate a *rise* similar to that of the Young Irelanders ? Why does the Fenian Brotherhood exist? In the first place, even granting that their happiness be real, I could still say : Do not be surprised at our ingratitude. You reap what you have sown. You sowed the seeds of moral degradation by your endeavours to deprive us of our faith ; and if those whom you corrupted arise against you, whom can you blame? The Fenian Brotherhood is a bad association, I believe; but its members act in accordance with what you have taught them : they reduce your lessons to practice. You taught them to act on the *law of the strongest :* most certainly they will do so if they can. She says that machinery is the cause of the misery. This is, in some sort, anti-social.

There are more machines in England than in Ireland, and we do not hear any outcry. There are machines in France, in Germany, in Italy, in the United States : why are not the laborers crying out ? Why are they not starving ? The same cause always produces the same effect. If machinery produce famine and laziness in Ireland, why not in France or in England ? No ! no ! you must go deeper than the surface ; causes are like hidden springs : they are far removed from the superficial gaze. « The Irish are not actually suffering from persecution.» Very true. But tell me : If you were standing under an immense tree, which suddenly tumbled down on you ; and if, on its fall, it were impeded by some branches *not too strong*, would you quietly maintain your position, and say : « Oh ! the danger is past ; I need not stir » ? Not a bit of it, nor the lady either ;

both she and you would quietly, but quickly, remove, lest the branches might give way. This is the case with Ireland. The arm of persecution is stopped by the force of circumstances; but the penal laws have not been repealed. We all remember the « Ecclesiastical Titles Bill »; and we know that, if certain *props* were removed, the arm would again fall; for it is ever uplifted, and its force would be as crushing as ever.

Therefore, the Irish suffer, as you may see from British statistics, and the cause of their sufferings is *misrule*. So, dear Reverend Madam, keep alive all your fine Irish susceptibilities and sympathies for the dreadful fate of fatherland. Do not believe those who flippantly tell you that the greatest sufferings of Ireland are like the equator, imaginary...

AN EXCURSION TO LA TRAPPE. [1]

I paid a visit to the Trappist Fathers during the last week of August. The voyage was to me a very interesting one, so that I hope, dear Revd. Madam, you will not be displeased if I allow myself to enter into some of its details.

The Revd. M. P., parish priest of Frampton, being down on a trip to St. Joachim, [2] invited me to spend the last fortnight at his place, and promised, as an inducement, that we should visit *La Trappe*, if I consented. The latter inducement, though great, was unnecessary; for the amiable qualities of the good *curé* were, of themselves, sufficient prospect of

[1] This is an extract of a letter addressed to one of the revd. ladies of the Ursuline Convent of Quebec.

[2] The place where the Seminary has its summer residence.

a pleasant time. And, indeed, the prospective was
in complete accordance with the reality, for I never
spent anywhere such a pleasant fortnight. However,
as I must not trespass too long on your patience, I
shall say nothing of how we passed the interim. between Friday and Monday, the day on which it was
agreed we should start.

We were few in number—the curé, myself, and
two others,—the one a student in the Seminary; the
other, named Victor, a wild lad, full of fun and mischief. He lives with the curé, and is the terror of
the environs for his pranks, but still a universal favorite. Early on Sunday evening we began to pack
up. You may think the preparation somewhat too
much before-hand ; but do not say so to the curé's
ancient aunt, much less to the *vieille 'ménagère*, An-
nette,—else you would run the risk of being looked
on and treated as a personal enemy of both. The two
said personages live in the presbytery, where they
reign with divided supremacy. Annette holds
absolute sway over the kitchen, pantry, dairy, and
out-houses ; while Mademoiselle extends her benign
rule over the dining-room, bed-rooms, and drawing-
room, and, indeed, might be looked on as having a
kind of feudal supremacy over the whole establishment. I must except the curé's little *sanctum*, or
office ; there we hold a republican government, and
could retire to smoke, romp, or play, as we wished.

I have said that theirs was a divided supremacy.
On one point, however, they hold absolutely the
same doctrine, that is, in their love, veneration, and,
if I might say so, their worship of *M. le Curé*. *Mademoiselle* is in constant fidgets lest he might want
anything ; and as for Annette, to say that any one
was better, or presume that any one could be higher
than M. le Curé, would be nothing less in her eyes
than a heinous sin. «*Monseigneur*,» (she will say, with
a slight toss of her head,) «*ben oui, Monseigneur, mais*

éé n'est pas M. le Curé. Mon Dieu, je le connais depuis qu'il était haut comme ça;» and as she says this, she stoops to shew with her hand from the ground a height so extravagantly small that baby Tom Thumb might be ashamed of it. The poor *curé* shrugs his shoulders, and generally lets them have their own way in everything, except when they go too far; then there is usually a rebellion, in which, I can assure you, he is not always the conqueror.

On the present occasion a regular intestine strife took place; and the curé may thank us for having even partially succeeded in carrying the day. *Mademoiselle* and Annette, as soon as they heard of our projected voyage, held a confabulation, and worked each other into a high state of excitement as to the perils which must surround us during a voyage of five days through the woods. No danger imaginable from wet feet and colds, to the likelihood of starving to death, or been torn by wild beasts, escaped their tremulous surmises. Accordingly, they set about packing-up all sorts of articles proper to ward off dangers imminent. If we had listened to them, we would have taken provisions enough to carry a caravan across the Sahara; and what with blankets, buffalo skins, etc., etc., we would have had at least cargo for a schooner. *Mademoiselle* would open fire by dilating on some impossible hardships, and then would propose a preservative in the shape of a woollen scarf or fur-coat. The *curé* would ridicule the idea of wearing the one or the other in August.

Annette would then come in with reserved fire to support *Mademoiselle*, when Victor would route her by some sarcastic observation which would draw down upon him the combined ire of the two. It was a rich scene all through; and it was only at half-past nine P.M. that we were let off with four large portmanteaux chock-full,—not, however,

without several dark hints being thrown out as to
the pro-bability of our being frozen or starved, and
a mumbled wish on the part of Annette that « the
ne'er-do-well Victor » might get his merits one way
or other.

Next morning we rose betimes, and, after the
usual devotions, we began the demolition of a whole
army of sandwiches and rolls. Annette's coffee was
good, and we praised it outrageously to put her in
good humor. Then, donning our top-coats, and lighting our cigars, we all packed ourselves and baggage
into the *curé's* cosey little wagon, and started. We
had scarcely been gone five minutes when we heard
a faint scream, and, looking around, we descried
Annette in the distance in full sail after us, and
under press of canvas, the strings of her high-
crowned cap flying against the wind like a ship's
pennants. « What now ? » said the *curé ;* « can there
have come a sick-call to stop our voyage ? » Annette,
on seeing us pull up, had stopped also, and was
beckoning violently. The *curé* requested Victor to
go back and see what was the matter, which he did,
though somewhat reluctantly, prophesying, as he
left, that it must be « some extravagance of old
Annettes'.» The scene which followed was highly
amusing. We could see Victor, as he came up to
Annette, receive something from her, which he
immediatly flung at her head, and ran back. It was
nothing less than the *curé's* night-cap that she had
found, and feared he might want. Victor was highly
indignant at having had his journey for nothing,
and evidently so was Annette ; for, as far as we could
see her, she stood in the middle of the road, alternately shaking her fist and the night-cap at us ; to
which the juvenile answered, notwithstanding the
remonstrances of *M. le curé*, by ironical bows and
waiving of caps. This was our first adventure ; the
second was not so laughable.

After six miles' travelling through the bush we came to the Etchemin, a *bridgeless* river with a bad crossing, and slightly swollen by the preceding rains. We had no alternative ; so we persuaded «Cæsar» to plunge in, after some difficulty, the stream being pretty rapid. The *curé* and myself were in the front seat, half-standing´; the boys, behind, were clinging to the seats like grim-death. Not a word escaped our lips. Suddenly, whether from dizziness or fright, the horse deviated slightly, and ran the front wheel on a rock. The *curé* immediately threw me the reins and jumped from the vehicle ; the boys disappeared, from the jerk, over the back seat, and in an instant I was the only living soul on board.

Such splashing ! such hopping from rock to rock ! such exclamations ! I managed to keep a tight hold on the reins till the rest got to the shore ; then, throwing the whole of my weight (you know how immense it is) on the uplifted side, *Cæsar* and I started and arrived safe. No sooner did he get on *terra firma* than he dashed up the steep pathway, grazing the *curé*, who, leaping aside to avoid being struck by the wheel, missed his footing, and rolled down the embankment, the horse still rushing on like a meteor till he reached the brow of the hill, where he stopped of his own accord.

Then, for the first time, I looked back ; and, oh ! such a sight ! How Annette would have enjoyed her revenge, if she could have seen us !— the *curé*, slightly bruised and bespattered with mud ! the boys wet and cold ! I assure you they presented a woeful spectacle as they toiled up the steep ascent. However, we all took our mishap gaily : a change of stockings, a little refreshment, a new cigar, and we were again *en route*, laughing heartily over our adventure. The rest of the journey was performed without anything remarkable.

At 5½ p.m. we arrived at Lake Etchemin, which lies almost midway between Frampton and La Trappe, being about at six leagues' distance from each. We lost no time in getting supper, as we were almost famished ; then, after enjoying a delightful sail on the lake, we retired early to rest, as we wished to start early next morning.

The next morning, Tuesday, we renewed our journey ; and, indeed, I never remember to have experienced more lonesome travelling. A thick fog had settled down on the landscape, accompanied by a drizzling rain. Our route lay through a thick forest ; the new roads were horrible, and the tiring sameness of trees, rocks, and patches of clearance, most monotonous. We had determined not to be overcome by difficulties ; and, accordingly, during the first half of the way, we managed to while away the time pleasantly enough with songs, jokes, stories, &c. But, one by one, we became tired, and, after rallying several times, we sank into a kind of lethargy, from which we were roused after six long hours by the tinkling of the convent-bell, calling the monks to vespers.

The convent is a wooden structure of humble appearance, long and low. There is a good clearance around it of about fifty acres, with a fine crop of wheat, potatoes, &c., running out on all sides to the borders of the deep, deep forest. There are also out-houses, and a new building destined for the reception of strangers, but which is not yet completed. On the whole, it is striking to come suddenly on those marks of cultivation, after having been so long in the wild woods ; and the effect is not at all lessened by the sight of the sturdy brothers in their brown cassocks and skull-caps, as they hurry from different points to the monastery at the sound of the bell.

The Superior received us at the door with true

French politeness, and ushered us into the little parlor, poorly furnished, but perfectly neat and tidy.

The *curé* requested at once to be allowed to follow the exercises which were just then commencing, and, moreover, informed the Superior, much to my discomfiture, that I was a premature reprobate, who, at the call of grace, had come to pass the rest of my life in penance at La Trappe.

Father François smiled, and said that I was heartily welcome, but that, before beginning my austerities, it would be well to give me a last glimpse of the world, in the shape of some refreshment. « Then, » said the *curé*, « if that be the way you treat your penitents, I must say that we are all more or less guilty, and desire to perform the same penance. » Accordingly, we partook of a frugal but hearty meal, during which the Superior served us, entertaining us all the while with the details of the rules and regulations, and giving us some amusing anecdotes of Trappists in general, and of himself in particular. He had formerly been a French soldier, and had evidently seen much life. The rules of the house are pretty nearly as follows :

The monks retire to rest at 7 o'clock P.M., and rise at two, except on feast-days, when they get up at midnight. They recite matins, make meditation, and hear mass from two to six o'clock. The lay brothers then go to the fields, where they work in silence until twelve. The priests divide the hours until twelve between their masses, little hours, and house-work, with a spiritual lecture.

At twelve, all the community proceed to the refectory, where they all partake of their first and only repast for the day. Even this is, I assure you, very frugal, and, owing to their present poverty, sometimes very spare. They can neither eat meat, nor eggs, nor butter, nor milk, nor cheese. Vegetables and bread alone compose their food ; however, I believe there is some allowance made here, in the shape of milk and cheese, on account of the want of a sufficient quantity of vegetables. But this the Superior informed us would soon be done away with. After dinner there is a spiritual lecture ; then the brothers go again to the fields till 6. P.M., and the priests again divide their time between the recitation of the Penitential·Psalms, part of the breviary, lecture, and housework. Then comes the recitation of complices, the singing of the *Salve Regina*, the *Angelus*, and at 7 all retire to rest. There is some necessary alteration in the rule during winter. I assure you that the recitation of the office is something very impressive.

Imagine a lovely chapel·in the backwoods, poorly ornamented, but on which reigns a scrupulous neatness. A dim light from the altar-lamp allows you to but half-distinguish the immense folio volumes, containing, in antiquated print, the office of St. Bernard, and which repose on a long *lutrin* running up the middle of the choir. On either side stand the monks ; near the altar are the Fathers, robed in white, their features completely hidden by the large hood or cowl ; below them are the lay brothers with their flowing beard, wrapped in their ample brown cassocks. The solemn, measured tones of those holy men ; the stentorian voices of the lay brothers ; the death-like silence which reigns for some time after each psalm ; the *Salve Regina*, chanted in a solemn, simple strain, entirely different from ours ; the *Angelus*, during which all lie prostrate,—and all this taking place in the wild woods, far away from the habitations of men ! Oh ! it is beautiful, solemn, and impressive, and makes one love and venerate the grand old faith which inspires such self-abnegation, or, rather, such true heroism.

I asked the Superior, after the office, to pass the night on a Trappist bed. He at first laughingly refused ; seeing that I desired it, he caused one to be transported into the little alcove where I was to pass the night. It is a low, narrow box, about three feet wide, standing on four short feet. The tick is stuffed with *shavings;* there is but one covering, and a pillow of straw. Nevertheless, I must say that I slept soundly, and rose refreshed at two, when the *curé* and I assisted at the morning exercise of matins and meditation. The *curé* said mass at 6 o'clock. I had the happiness of receiving Holy Communion. At seven we partook of a hearty breakfast, and at 8½ A.M. started again for home.

The *curé* made a very handsome offering to the Superior. His answer was singular : « It is a great deal too much, but it is against our rules to refuse donations.» We were obliged to sleep at the lake again on Wednesday night, and arrived at the presbytery on Thursday evening, safe and sound, to the immense satisfaction of *Mademoiselle* and Annette, who, in her joy at our safe return, forgot her spite, and welcomed us all right heartily......

A PROPOS OF A PIE.

QUEBEC SEMINARY, 26th October, 186...

Dear......

I have just terminated the rather uncanonical process of despatching an apple-pie, and can fully testify to the genial sensations superinduced by such a feat.

« Mon Dieu, » dites-vous, « quel acte d'immortification ! Et il s'en vante encore ! »

Don't scold ; I don't like it. There are many reasons why I should eat the pie aforesaid ; and as, for the time being, I have nothing else to do, I may as well give you some of them to calm your ireful scruples.

The first, and, perhaps, principal one, is : « Why should n't I eat it ? » There it stands, or, rather, stood ; who'll eat it if I don't ? I am the only permanent resident in my little room, excepting a half-a-dozen fat mice ; but I have long since found out that these eccentric characters thrive better on tallow candles.

And, talking of thriving, how in the world do the little creatures manage to entertain their corpulency ? There is nothing here, or in the environs, but hardwood bedsteads, woollen coverlets, and small crockery ; and yet, there is not one of them but could grace an alderman's chair, or be considered fit to fill a mandarin's office among the celestials.

I first thought, when I came here, that they had better immigrate to the kitchen, and gave them sundry hints to that effect, in the shape of mouse-traps and rat-exterminators. This, I know, was betraying the interests of the community, besides giving bad counsel. But I thought it hard to see the dear little things starve.

They did not, however, leave the premises, and, some how or other, managed to live,—though not at my expense, as I thought.

The idea then came to me that they had taken a liking to me, and that their visits were disinterested and purely *de cérémonie.* My heart softened accordingly. I destroyed my traps, and allowed them to roam about at their pleasure, and, indeed, often went so far as to imagine that my heart beat responsively to the pattering of their little feet.

One day, I took it into my head to overhaul my winter gear and divers other articles. My snow-shoes were the first to be examined,—when—*oh ! murther! ate out of a face !* My *caribou* shoes ? Gone ! The only decent pair of chamois mittens I possessed ? In ribbons ! Here was a case for a jury. And were it only this !—but, as my fears were awakened, I resolved to make a thorough search, and it was only then that I discovered the extent of my loss. A well-bound note-book, containing all my treasured lore in Scripture,—the result of last year's notes and reading,—gnawed maliciously and feloniously, and evidently serving as a bed, behind the shelf, for the wicked troops of marauders. A large dictionary of Latin synonyms, a copy of Cowper's poems, Théry's essay on literature, and Demosthenes, were all more or less *chewed.* Evidently they had been for some time going through an indiscriminate and disordered course of reading.

You may be sure that my bad temper was in nowise cured by this discovery. I think I remember saying something very harsh, what the inimitable French would term *des gros mots.* I almost can assure you that......but, good gracious !—what have I been doing all this time ? Entertaining you with nothing less than a mouse-story ! Fie on my wanderings ! I crave pardon, and instantly shall retrace my steps.

I said, just now, that myself and the mice (botheïation to them) were the only *habitués* of my room ; there is, to be sure, the *dortoirier*, a sleepy-looking individual who does up the rooms every morning, and in comparison with whom Pharaoh's lean kine would most certainly have been considered as fat cattle. He, as I say, might, perhaps......but, there I go again......Flighty, eh?

My second reason for demolishing the pie is that, being a descendant of Eve, who was lured from Paradise by a rosy apple, it is no wonder that I should be, now and then, lured from the dogmatical depths of a «Treatise on Faith» to explore the more savoury profundities of a pie-dish. Then, again, my taste is decidedly in favour of the sweet orthodoxy of the Blessed Liguori, who, as you are aware, was raised up to combat the errors of the rigid heresiarch Jansenius. And, finally ....good-bye !..... There goes the bell !

À WORD ABOUT IRELAND AND THE IRISH. [1]

There is, perhaps, no subject which has been more universally treated than that of Ireland and the Irish. The attention of writers of almost every nationality, and of every shade of opinion, has been directed towards the history of our country; and whatever may have been the bias of their genius, all have found in it ample matter for study and a fruitful theme for disquisition.

The chequered events of her annals furnish historians with a rich and varied narrative; the philosopher can here grapple with religious and social questions of the most vital importance; the numerous monumental relics of by-gone days open a wide field for antiquarian research; whilst—not to speak of her music, so exquisitely tender, and which, gently stealing through the aisles of time, fills the soul with melancholy and reverence,—her literature, holding equal claims to excellence with that of any other nation, fully repays the critic for the study he bestows on it. But besides the innate beauties and the deep fertility of the subject, there are other reasons which have no less powerfully contributed to bring it under notice. The name of Ireland has, through the labours of hersons, become, in a measure, identified with the foundation and development of western civilization. Irishmen have materially aided in raising some of the most splendid monuments that attest the progress of ages; their memories are embalmed in the annals of every nation of Europe, and—the glory of the children redounding on the parent—the fame of Erin's sons

---

[1] A lecture delivered by the Revd. Mr. Doherty, at the Music Hall, Feb. 12th, 1869, in reply to the Rev. Dr. Irvine, of Montreal.

became the measure of her own renown. Her past and present were considered matters of interest and of affectionate inquiry; for when the historian recorded the deeds of the Irish benefactors of his nation, he felt it as a labour of love to revert to the land that bore them.

I am not one of those who claim for the Irish or Celts a marked superiority over other races. I rather think that such an assumption, from its absurd pretensions, is calculated to bring discredit on them; but I do not go beyond the limits of historical truth when I assert that the nations of Europe owe Ireland a debt of gratitude, deep and lasting, for the benefits she has conferred on them; and the highest meed of praise for the glorious example she has set them of fortitude, of unflinching firmness under oppression, and for teaching them lessons of the noblest courage that ever steeled the heart of man—that of giving testimony unto death for the convictions of the soul.

A rapid survey of the history of our country will shew the truth of this assertion. It is known that at that period which is set down by historians as the opening of the middle ages, the northern barbarians, coming forth from the depths of their forests, poured down with irresistible fury on Southern Europe. Their fierce hordes, under different names, appeared almost simultaneously in every country, and their passage was everywhere marked by ruin and desolation. Whole countries were depopulated; flourishing cities were destroyed; and if the Church had not succeeded in bending beneath the yoke of religion those savage conquerors, the light of civilization would have been lost in impenetrable gloom. But, true to her mission, she withstood the shock of barbarity, as she had resisted the strength of paganism. Her Popes and Bishops confronted the savage warriors, and filled them with admiration by the

9

lustre of their virtues; her missionaries went forth
amongst them; they softened the rudeness of their
manners; they opened their eyes to the light of
faith, and founded in their midst a new religious
society, stronger and more healthy than the one
which it had superseded. Now, in this work of
regeneration the Irish missionary holds a pre-em-
inent rank. The conversion of Ireland by St. Patrick
had already borne fruits a hundredfold; the Island
was studded with monasteries and pious retreats of
learning; wisdom and sanctity, with the blessings
of holy peace, reigned triumphant throughout the
land, precisely at the time when the torrent of
invasion was sweeping over the plains of Europe,
destroying all that opposed it, like burning lava
from a volcano. The horrid din of war was re-
echoed back on the Irish shore; the cries of afflic-
tion came from across the seas; with generous
resolve, the soldiers of Christ went forth to the
rescue of their brethren, and then did Hope lift her
eyes to Heaven in blissful expectancy. The tempest-
cloud was dark, but behind it the light was rising,
for in the wake of the barbarian followed the Irish
monks. Into the thickest danger they plunged
with all the true zeal of Apostles, and with something of the characteristic impetuosity of their race.
The struggle was long and bloody; many of those
heroic soldiers fell in holy martyrdom; but God it
was who inspired their coming, and He blessed
their efforts. The storm at length spent its fury;
and when the gloom was changed into the calm
light of peace, the Saxon, the German, and the Frank
might be seen kneeling in reverence before the
shrine of some Irish saint whom they had loved
on earth as their apostle, and whom they now
revered in Heaven as their protector. And so great
was the number of those holy men,—so wide-spread
became the renown of Ireland as the retreat of

learning and sanctity,—that admiring nations gave
her the title of the « Isle of Saints.» But the brightest day darkens into night. The most glorious
period of Irish history was already fast drawing to
a close. « We must now,» says Mr. McGee, « turn
away our eyes from the contemplation of those days
in which was achieved for Ireland the title of the
land of Saints and Doctors. Another era opens
before us, and we can already discern the long ships
of the north, their monstrous beaks turned towards
the holy isle, their sides hung with glittering
shields, and their benches thronged with fair-haired
warriors, chanting, as they advance, the fierce war-
songs of their race. Instead of the monk's familiar
voice on the river-banks, we are to hear the shouts
of strange warriors from a far-off country; and for
matin-hymn and vesper-song we are to be beset,
through a long and stormy period, with sounds of
strife and terror and deadly conflict.»

The terrible Vikings landed on the peaceful
shores of Erin; and so terrible was their onset, so
numerous their hosts, that they well nigh succeeded
in over-running the whole Island. Fierce and fre-
quent were the battles that were fought; but the
ever-succeeding wave bore down all resistance:
cities were destroyed; monasteries were pillaged;
churches were burned down, and literary records
dispersed to the winds. As the tempest-laboring
ship reels before some mountainous wave, and appears, for a moment, as if about to sink beneath the
deluge of waters, so Ireland appeared for a time
as if about to lose forever her political existence, so
fiercely did the iron storm of war sweep over her;
when suddenly, rallying for a desperate and supreme effort, her warriors assembled under the
command of Brian Boroihme. On the plains of
Clontarf, with one mighty blow, they struck the
invader to the earth, and stood once more free and

unenthralled beneath the glorious folds of the Sunburst.

At that moment Ireland was free, but the land was filled with ruins. The lamp of learning burned dimly ; the generations of pious students had disappeared ; and the people, from constant contact with the Danes, had caught something of their barbarity ; in a word, the entire social edifice had to be rebuilt. But this undertaking should necessarily be the work of ages. A nation does not lose its civilization in a day; neither can its loss be repaired in a short time. Historians who speak of Ireland during the century and a-half that intervened between the victory of Clontarf and the Norman invasion, sometimes lose sight of this. They quote the censures which St. Bernard passed on the Irish during that period.; but they do not take into account the causes which produced the evils he alludes to, nor the efforts which were being made towards their removal. If they did so honestly,—if they studied with fairness that part of our history, they would become convinced that no work of regeneration was ever pursued more steadily. The people of God were not more arduous in rebuilding the walls of the Holy City, after their return from the captivity of Babylon, than were the Irish in restoring the faded beauties of the land, and in raising it to the high moral and intellectual level which it had previously attained ; and their generous efforts were on the point of being crowned with success, when they were called away from their labors to defend their hearths and homes against the incursions of a new enemy.

The Norman invasion of Ireland, which took place in the second half of the twelfth century, was, in point of fact, the greatest misfortune that could have fallen on that country ; and its permanent continuation, by the English nation, one of the most flagrant outrages that has ever been perpetrated against the rights of a people.

It sprang from crime and falsehood ; it was carried out in bloodshed and persecution; and it was sealed by the Union of 1800 in treachery, hypocrisy, and infamy. Its first effects were to deprive a free and unoffending people of the lawful ownership of their lands ; its second effort was to deprive them of their religious and intellectual life, by making it criminal for them to drink at the sacred fountain of learning, or worship God according to the dictates of their own conscience ; and its final fruits were to drive them from their homes in countless numbers, and disperse them over the face of God's earth, where, with bleeding hearts and wasted forms, they had to incorporate themselves into different nationalities, and toil on in the upward road to fame and respect, amid the difficulties of foreign manners, customs, laws, and language. They had to shut out all hope of ever seeing the land they loved : its green mountains would never rise before them, nor the waving corn-fields ever greet their gaze. The sunny hillocks where they played in the happy buoyancy of youth ; the cottage where their father taught them first to pray to Jesus and invoke Mary, morning and night ; the churchyard where the poor mother rests, or any of those things that endear home to the heart, could never be restored to them. They might, indeed, assemble in foreign lands and listen to the story of Ireland, or drink in the music of her songs ; but this was only the pang of memory, not the bliss of reality.

"And, oh ! to hear the sweet old strains of Irish music rise,
Like gushing memories of home beneath far foreign skies,
Beneath the spreading calabash, beneath the trellissed vine,
The bright Italian myrtle, or dark Canadian pine !
Oh ! do not those familiar tones, now sad, and now so gay,
Speak out your very, very hearts,—poor exiles far away ?

*، But yet, how many sleep afar, all heedless of these strains,
Tired wanderers who sought repose through Europe's battle-
   plains ? '
In strong, fierce, headlong fight, they fell as ships go down in
   storms ;
They fell ! and human whirlwinds swept across their shattered
   forms.
No shrouds but glory wrapt them round; nor prayer nor tear
   had they,
Save the wandering winds and the heavy clouds, poor exiles far
   away !"

What I have said of English rule in Ireland may
appear harsh, but it certainly is not exaggerated;
and, did time allow me, I could adduce a thousand
authentic documents in confirmation of my verdict.
I could cite the very work of amelioration which
has been begun to-day,—a work of tardy justice to
our land, which must end in no half-measures.
The British Parliament, in declaring the disestab-
lishment of the State-church a measure of justice,
imply that its existence for three centuries has been
a wrong and an injustice ; and when, as it is to be
hoped, that same legislature will have abolished
the existing laws relating to the tenure of lands by
the bulk of the people, it will be admitted that
heretofore the system was wrongful and oppressive.

But a lengthy consideration of these matters
would lead me beyond the scope of my present
lecture, which is to rectify certain erroneous statements concerning Ireland and the Irish. Indeed, I
may have already wandered too far from it in these
introductory remarks ; but my desire to prove the
claim Ireland has on the respect and gratitude of
Europe, will, I trust, be considered a sufficient
apology for my having done so.

I shall now enter into my subject ; but at the
very outset I hasten to repeat what I have already
said in public : I act in no spirit of aggressiveness.
Doctor Irvine made, through the press, statements
derogatory to historical truth : I shall, through the

same medium, rectify his errors; and I must say that some of those errors are so glaring, that they would be unpardonable if traced to anything beyond irreflection,—so much so, that when I attempted to analyze the lecture, I almost regretted that I had undertaken its refutation ; for I felt loth to attack a work which bore no evidence of careful preparation. Still, my promise was given ; and to fulfil it, I am before you this evening.

Hence, my present disagreement with the reverend lecturer is purely on historical grounds ; beyond these, I disclaim any. With regard to the division of the subject, my course is necessarily shaped after his own : I shall take up his statements one by one, and shew you why I object to them ; and lest it might be thought that I misquote him, I shall in every case read to you the passage that I wish to bring under your notice.

The first point denotes, I fear, a very lamentable confusion of ideas concerning Roman history.

The Doctor says :—« While Imperial Rome was planting her iron heel on the necks of the other nations,—whilst her greatest military chief was actually conducting his steel-clad warriors over the fertile plains of Britain, Ireland was the retreat of the learned, the cradle of art and science, and the home of the peaceful and pious student, who fled from continental Europe to find an asylum on her hospitable and happy shores; and when the Augustan age at last arrived, strange to say, learning had attained such a pre-eminence in Ireland as to secure for her the enviable title of the ' Isle of Saints,' by which name, for centuries, she was known in the annals of Roman history. »

Now, this, you will admit, is very unguarded, and justifies the remark I have made concerning the lecture,—namely, that it bears no marks of careful study.

Still, even on that supposition, I cannot wholly exonerate Dr. Irvine from blame ; for there are in history certain facts so generally known that the simplest student would blush to ignore them.

When the Rev. Doctor speaks of the great military chief who led his warriors over the plains of Britain, he evidently alludes to Julius Cæsar ; he, therefore, asserts that « pious students,» or, if you will, « Christian students,» were then to be found in Ireland. Now, you will remember that Julius Cæsar lived and died before the birth of Christ ; he fell assassinated at the foot of Pompey's statue on the Ides of March, B. C. 44. How, then, could those pious professors of Christianity have flourished in Ireland before the founder of Christianity came into the world in a visible manner ?

Nor must it be said that I distort the Doctor's words by saying that « pious student » is here synonymous with « Christian student ;» for, even if their meaning were not obvious, the next sentence determines their signification. «When the Augustan age arrived,» he says, « strange to say, Ireland had secured the enviable title of the ' Isle of Saints.'» But the arrival of the Augustan age cannot be fixed at a later period than the lifetime of Cæsar's adopted son, Octavius. Therefore, if Ireland was known at that time as the ' Isle of Saints, the saints whose learning and piety won for her that name must, of a necessity, have been the « pious students » who, according to the Doctor, flourished there whilst Cæsar was in Britain.

In truth, these are very unfortunate assertions ; and though the phrases are well turned,—though they have a certain ring of modern oratory,—yet, from the statements they contain, there might be drawn conclusions very damaging to the Doctor's reputation as a historian.

The next point exhibits the same disregard for

historical *data*. He says: « Nor had the sun of
Ireland's literary and intellectual glory set at a still
later period ; for when Alfred the Great founded the
University of Oxford, he turned his eye to continental Europe in search of men competent to fill
with efficiency the various chairs of science and
philosophy in that institution ; and the only man
found in all Europe fit to occupy the chair of pure
science was an Irishman, who is known in the
records of that great seat of learning to this day by
the name of Joannes Mathematicus Hibernicus. »

For peace sake, I will allow that this Hibernian
mathematician enjoyed the honors conferred on
him by Alfred, and that his memory is still cherished
and revered by the Oxonians. Yet, though Oxford
still persists in giving him the highly, classical
appellation of Joannes Mathematicus Hibernicus,
I would humbly submit that he is known, if I am
not mistaken, in history, under the name of Joannes
Scotus Erigena, or even plain, honest John Scott.

But that he was the only man of his time to. be
found in all Europe fit to fill a chair of pure science
is an assertion, the truth of which I cannot admit
without some further and better substantiated proof.

l can perfectly understand that the Rev. Doctor
Irvine, being an Irishman, wishes to atttach a note
of excellence to éverything Irish ; but we must
never let the love of country get the better of our
love for truth. This might be pardoned in the
fanciful language of poetry, but it cannot be adapted
to sober prose, especially in the regions of history.

At the time of Alfred the Great there were in
many countries flourishing institutions where a
relish for study and learning was carefully preserved. On consultation the Doctor will find, for
instance, that in those days there were renowned
schools of learning in Italy, France, and Germany,
at Paris, Rome, and Paderborn. There were also

high and noble names that shed a lustre on every branch of knowledge. The Doctor may even have read the learned treatises of Lupus, Abbot of Ferrières; he must, too, know something of Agobardus, of Radbertus, of St. Ado of Anastasius, of Hinemar and others; nor can he ignore that Leo was considered the greatest mathematician of his day.

These men are well known to students; their works have come down to us; it is, therefore, empty boasting to say that Joannes was the only man found fit to enjoy the confidence of Alfred or the emoluments to be reaped from the possession of a chair of pure science.

Now comes another very singular passage in relation to the early history of Ireland. It runs thus :

« The history of Christianity for seven centuries subsequent to the mission of the Patron Saint is mingled with a vast amount of legend. Indeed, to such an extent is this the case, that some have regarded this as the fabulous period of Irish history. We read so much of the extravagant in the numberless lives of St. Patrick, as at times to question whether he was a real or imaginary man. »

It is true that the Doctor does not assume on his own shoulders the whole responsibility of this statement ; but I do not think I mis-interpret · him when I say that his evident leaning towards it almost amounts to approbation.

It is, nevertheless, a very serious charge, though happily it is utterly devoid of foundation. It is a base attempt to throw rudely over the brightest period of Ireland's life the dark mantle of fable, and surround with impenetrable mist the purest and holiest glories that ever a nation might boast of. What ! through the long lapse of seven centuries has there been no one found to record the deeds that illustrate our annals ? Has no historian's pen clearly and authentically traced through the course of ages the various phases of Irish history? We call the fabulous periods of a history those times in which events are clouded in the twilight of uncertainty,—those pre-historic ages, of which, as in the first stage of infancy, the people is scarce conscious of its existence; But to extend this with regard to Ireland to the comparatively recent date of 1172, is the deepest insult that could be thrown upon us.

When such statements are made by Cambrensis, or a few others who, like the *servum pecus* mentioned by Horace, follow blindly, if not maliciously, in his wake, we are not surprised; but, honestly, when men like Doctor Irvine give publicity to them, and partially concur in them, there is much to wonder at.

With regard to St. Patrick, I cannot, for the life of me, see how some very highly legendary accounts of his life can at all diminish our certainty of his existence. If such were the case, there is many a man to-day living whose flesh-and-blood reality we would be entirely justified in doubting.

We have the life of St. Patrick: the Doctor must have read it, and he knows that it bears as many marks of authencity about it as that of any other great man of his time. The date of his coming to Ireland, his works, his writings, are all established upon the firmest basis of authority; and the extravagant legends which sneering malice, rather than a spirit of veneration, has connected with his life, can neither affect the reality, nor lead us, as the Doctor assures us, « at times to question whether he was a real or imaginary being.»

Next we have a passage in which are bound up so many errors of various kinds, that the task of refuting all of them, though comparatively easy, would be extremely wearisome. I shall read it :

"It appears to be admitted that about 700 years after St. Patrick founded Christianity in Ireland, Henry II. of England, with the sanction of Pope Adrian IV., who was a native of Wales, and known by the English name of Nicholas Breakspeare, invaded the island with the view of bringing its inhabitants under the jurisdiction of the Romish See. In compliance with the Pontifical decree, and acting under the directions of a special Bull for the purpose, Henry mustered his legions, and, crossing the Irish Channel, he found the Island divided into five petty monarchies.   *   *   *   One fact, which greatly facilitated the conquest of Ireland by King Henry II. deserves special attention. At this time Dermot McMurrogh was King of Leinster, and, being a man of indomitable passions, he carried away the wife of Roderic Oroirc, one of the petty princes of the Island, which so aroused the indignation of many of the people, that they resolved to avenge the disgraceful deed by the murder of the royal seducer. To escape the merited vengeance, Dermot fled to Wales, where he soon attracted the notice of King Henry, and was, of course, reported to the Welsh Pontiff at Rome as one most likely to serve the interests of the Pope and the British monarch in the contemplated invasion of Ireland. Nor did the project prove abortive ; for, by the aid of this royal refugee, Robert Fitzstephen and Maurice Fitzgerald brought 30 knights, 60 squires, and 300 archers, all skilled in the art of savage war, before whose fearless assault the ramparts of Wexford fell ; and though this invasion was met and bravely resisted by Roderic O'Connor, at the head of thirty thousand men, who had heretofore stood upon the walls of Dublin, yet was it impossible to protect the country from the grasp of the determined invader. Ireland's capital fell beneath the sword of England's monarch ; and the moment that the victor's flag was

planted on the walls of Dublin, an edict was issued
demanding a penny each from every family in the
Island, in support of the Romish See, which tax
has ever since been known by the name of Peter's
Pence ! Historians of different political and religious
belief are not agreed as to the part which the then
Bishop of Rome took in the matter of the invasion
of Ireland at this time. Most of our British historians
hold that the whole matter was planned by Pope
Adrian, with a view of bringing Ireland under the
jurisdiction of the Romish See.»

Let us now see to what extent the Doctor is
right. It is, indeed, true that Henry the Second
invaded Ireland: the Doctor need not have used here,
through excusive scrupulousness, the dubitative
form, « *it appears to be admitted.* » It is equally true
that intimately connected with the causes of the
invasion was the heinous crime of the arch-traitor
McMurrogh ; but when Doctor Irvine flippantly
asserts that the ruffian was, *of course*, reported to
Pope Adrian as an instrument likely to serve his
purpose, and thus insinuates that he became an instrument in the hands of the Pope, wherewith to
work out his designs, he asserts that for which he
can offer no further proof than his own word, and
which shews an ungenerous desire to malign the
character of the Pontiff, and engender hatred
towards the exercise of Papal authority.

The name of Pope Adrian IV. stands out in clear
preëminence among those of the successors of St.
Peter. Historians who have studied his reign and
weighed his acts in the balance of just criticism,
agree in extolling his integrity as a sovereign and
his sanctity as a Christian. I defy Doctor Irvine to
adduce, not only direct proof of his connivance with
McMurrogh, but to shew that one single act of his
life was sullied by baseness or darkened by intrigue.
He may, indeed, on the hypothesis that he really

granted the Bull to Henry, have been deceived by
the wily artifices and canting hypocrisy of the
Norman prince ; but that he profited of his position'
to unjustly aggrandize the power of a king to
whose race he did not belong, is a heavy accusation
which my reverend friend must substantiate, or
stand convicted of false malignity. As to the au-
thenticity of the Bull, I decline pronouncing any
judgment. In the *Bullarium* it is given with the
express annotation that it is taken from Cambrensis,
which fact alone would render its genuineness
extremely doubtful. But, in any case, its conditions
were not fulfilled by Henry nor any of his successors ; and, therefore, supposing it to be really authentic, its authority is annulled.

This may, perhaps, be the proper place to remark
the term used by Doctor Irvine when speaking of
the seat of Pontifical authority. He invariably calls
it the *Romish See.* Now, this is not its historical
appellation ; it is rather a partizan term, and smacks
of bigotry. Of course, I do not hereby accuse the
Doctor of narrow-mindedness; but most undoubtedly
the term *Romish* is not a component of courteous
language : it is more abusive in its import than
gentlemanly.

But we now come to the account of the invasion.
My learned friend mentions the arrival of Fitzstephen and Fitzgerald with 60 squires, 30 knights,
and 300 archers. These, he tells us, being skilled
in the art of savage warfare, took Wexford by storm,
and that, notwithstanding their being met by 30,000
men, under Roderick O'Connor, the country came
into their possession. Ireland's capital fell before the
sword of England's monarch, who immediately imposed a new and heretofore unheard-of tax, called
Peter's Pence.

Now, this is fearfully garbled, and, indeed, a most
inaccurate account of the first invasion. Any one

unacquainted with Irish history would most naturally infer from it that the subjugation of the
whole Island was the work of a few hundred men.
I may be told that in a lecture of an hour's length
it is impossible to enter into minor details. I admit
this ; but I hold that the Doctor could have given,
in the same space, a more truthful account of the
war, and which, besides being true, would be infinitely more honorable to the country which he
calls the land of his birth.

Would it not, for instance, have been as easy to tell
us that, in 1169, 1,000 men laid siege to Wexford,
and that the city capitulated on honorable terms ?—•
that in 1170, notwithstanding a treaty signed between Roderick and McMurrogh, and by which
the latter promised to bring no more Normans into
the country, Strongbow was welcomed by the
King of Leinster ?—that 500 prisoners were massacred near Waterford, and that the allied forces,
amounting probably to 12,000 men, marched on
Dublin ?—that the city, being unprotected, (there
being then in it only a Danish garrison under As-
tulph,) consented to capitulate ?—that while the articles were in the act of being signed, the enemy
treacherously burst in on the affrighted inhabitants
and put them to the sword ?—finally, that in 1171
Henry came, for the first time, to Ireland, with a
large force, and received the submission of several
Irish chieftains ? It would have been thus seen
that the followers of FitzMaurice did not achieve
the conquest of the Island. Moreover, we see no
account of their being met by 30,000 men ; we have
no account of the levying of the Peter's Pence,
which, by-the-bye, had been long before known
and levied in England ; nor can it be said that Ireland's capital fell before the sword of England's
monarch ; for, in the first place, Dublin was then
the capital of Ireland, as it is now ; and secondly,

it was not the sword of England's monarch that
subdued it, since Strongbow acted in direct opposition to the mandates of Henry. As to the whole
result of this first period of the Norman invasion,
you will allow me to read a passage from Mr.
McGee, in which it is summed up :
Vol. I., folio 194 :—« From Dermid's return until
his retreat to Cong, seventeen years had passed
away. Seventeen campaigns, more or less energetic
and systematic, the Normans had fought. Munster
was still, in 1185—when John Lackland made his
memorable exit and entrance on the scene—almost
wholly in the hands of the ancient clans. Connaught
was as yet without a single Norman garrison.
Hugh de Lacy, returning to the government of
Dublin, in 1179, on Fitz-Aldelm's recall, was more
than half *Hibernicized* by marriage with one of
Roderick's daughters, and the Norman tide stood
still in Meath. Several strong fortresses were, indeed,
erected in Desmond and Leinster, by John Lackland
and by de Courcy, in his newly-won northern
territory. Ardfinan, Lismore, Leighlin, Carlow,
Castledermot, Leix, Delvin, Kilkay, Maynooth, and
Trim, were fortified ; but, considering who the
Anglo-Normans were, and what they had done
elsewhere, even these very considerable successes
may be correctly accounted for without overcharg-
ing the memory of Roderick with folly and
incapacity. »

We must now turn to the consideration of the
inferences which the rev. lecturer has, with the
keenest perception, drawn from a very unpreten-
tious passage in the first volume of the late Mr.
McGee's popular History of Ireland,—inferences
which militate as strongly against all the known
rules of logical deduction as they do against the
expressed opinions of the author in question. And,
indeed, were Mr. McGee still amongst us, I am of

opinion that the Doctor would not have undertaken thus to explain his meaning, through a salutary fear of drawing on himself one of those severe castigations which the late member for Montreal West knew so well how to administer.

The passage in Mr. McGee's work runs thus (vol. I., pages 179 and 180) :—« After spending a right merry Christmas with Norman and Milesian guests in abundance at Dublin, Henry proceeded to that work of religious reformation under plea of which he had obtained the Bull of Pope Adrian, seventeen years before, declaring such an expedition, undertaken with such motives, lawful and praiseworthy. Early in the new year, by his desire, a Synod was held at Cashel, where many salutary decrees were enacted. These related to the proper solemnization of marriage ; the catechising of children before the doors of churches ; the administration of baptism in baptismal or parish churches ; the abolition of *Erenachs* or lay trustees of church-property, and the imposition of tithes, both of corn and cattle. By most English writers this Synod is treated as a National Council, and inferences are thence drawn of Henry's admitted power over the clergy of the nation.»

After transcribing these lines, the rev. lecturer passes a well-merited encomium on the accuracy of language and appropriateness of expression which distinguished the author, and then goes on to say that :

«On this account the quotation from his excellent history which we have copied justifies the following conclusions :—*First*, That St. Patrick could not have held his commission to plant Christianity in Ireland from Rome.»

You see, then, that Dr. Irvine has quoted Mr. McGee, and drawn an inference from the quotation. You will, therefore, I trust, allow me the advantage of quoting Mr. McGee also, and of drawing *my* inference. I quote from the same volume, pages 11 and 12 :

« If the year of his captivity was 405 or 406, and that of his escape and manumission seven years later (412 or 413), twenty years would intervene between his departure out of the land of his bondage and his return to it clothed with the character and authority of a Christian Bishop. This interval, longer or shorter, he spent in qualifiying himself for Holy Orders or discharging priestly duties at Tours, at Lerins, and finally at Rome. But always by night and day he was haunted by the thought of the Pagan nation in which he had spent his long years of servitude, whose language he had acquired, and the character of whose people he so thoroughly understood. The natural retrospections were heightened and deepened by supernatural revelations of the will of Providence towards the Irish, and himself as their apostle. At one time, an angel presented him, in his sleep, a scroll bearing the superscription : 'The voice of the Irish; ' at another, he seemed to hear in a dream all the unborn children of that nation crying to him for help and holy baptism. When, therefore, Pope Celestine commissioned him for this enterprise, ' to the ends of the earth, ' he found him not only ready, but anxious to undertake it. »

Hence, I, too, knowing Mr. McGee to be a careful writer, feel justified in concluding that St. Patrick *did really* hold his commission from Rome to plant Christianity in Ireland. I, moreover, conclude that if the Rev. Doctor be right in *his* inference, Mr. McGee must be a very careless writer, since he contradicts in page 180 what he had previously said in pages 11 and 12; but the Doctor said that Mr. McGee *is* very *careful* in his writings; therefore, Doctor, you are very *careless* in *your* conclusions.

In relation to the connexion between the Irish
Church and the Church of Rome, there are incon-
trovertible proofs of its existence from the days of
St. Patrick to the present time. I should be tempted
to give them here, but I feel that it is foreign to my
purpose ; however, in order that it may not be said
that I shirked from the point, I hereby promise to
furnish them at any time the Doctor may think fit
to call for them. For the present, I shall merely
read you a letter written by St. Columbanus to the
Pope in the seventh. century :

Haverty's, folio 424 :—« Saint Columbanus told
the Pope ' that although dwelling at the extremity
' of the world, all the Irish were disciples of SS.
' Peter and Paul, receiving no other than the,
' evangelical and apostolical doctrine ; that no
' heretic, or Jew, or schismatic, was to be found
' among them, but that they still clung to the
' Catholic faith as it was first delivered to them by
' his (the Pope's) predecessors,—that is, the successors
' of the holy apostles ; that the Irish were attached to
' the chair of St. Peter, and ·that although Rome·
' was great and renowned, it was only on account
' of that chair it was so with them. Through the
' two apostles of Christ, ' he added, ' you are almost
' celestial, and Rome is the head of all churches, as
' well as of the world. '»

For the present, I shall, therefore, content myself
with citing one more passage from Mr. McGee, so
as to fully exonerate him from the charge which
his *soi-disant* friend attempted to establish against
him :

Vol. I., folio 16 :—« The fifth century was drawing
to a close, and the days of Patrick were numbered.
Pharamond and the Franks had sway on the
Netherlands ; Hengist and the Saxons on South
Britain ; Clovis had led his countrymen across the
Rhine into Gaul ; the Vandals had established

themselves in Spain and North Africa; the Ostro-
goths were supreme in Italy. The empire of bar-
barism had succeeded to the empire of Polytheism;
dense darkness covered the semi-Christian countries
of the old Roman empire, but happily daylight still
lingered in the West. Patrick, in good season, had
done his work. And as sometimes God seems to
bring round His ends, contrary to the natural order
of things, so the spiritual sun of Europe was now
destined to arise in the West, and return on its
light-bearing errand towards the East, dispelling, in
its path, Saxon, Frankish, and German darkness,
until at length it reflected back on Rome herself
the light derived from Rome. »

It is clear that, in Mr. McGee's idea, there was a
connexion between the Roman and Irish Church.

We now have to deal with the second conclusion
taken from the passage quoted. It is nothing short
of a huge, weighty rock, which, with unerring aim,
the Doctor shies from his logical catapult at the
bulworks of Rome ; or it might also be likened to
the skilful thrust of a two-edged sword, which,
severing the tie that unites Ireland and Rome,
wounds both at the same time. I shall read you
the passage :

Secondly : « The annexation of Ireland to England
is the work of the Bishop of Rome. But if the
Bishop of Rome be infaillible, then all the acts must
be infaillibly right ; therefore, the union of Ireland
to England is infallibly right, and to seek a repeal,
either by political or military efforts, is infallibly
wrong. And, on this account, it seems that the
repeal agitation under the late gifted Mr. O'Connell
and the more odious and disgraceful ruffianism of
the Fenians, are as utterly antagonistic to the canon
law of the Romish Church as to the constitution of
Imperial Britain.»

This, if I might use a homely phrase, is decidedly
« a good hit.»

«You Catholics,» says the Doctor, «believe that all
the Pope's acts are infallibly right.
«Now, the annexation of Ireland to England is an
act of the Pope.
«Therefore, it is infallibly right, according to you.»
This is crushing! The Catholic Church, the
College of Cardinals, and a number of bishops, will
never recover from this blow. As for the Pope, if
he comes to hear of it, he will be covered with
confusion. I shall leave the syllogism of the Doctor
in all its compact solidity, and propose, as in the
case of his inference, a syllogism of my own.

Any man attempting to speak on what he is
entirely ignorant of commits an act of absurdity.

Now, the Doctor evidently knows nothing about
the Pope's infallibility; and yet he speaks on it,
and draws inferences from it, and makes them up
into huge balls, and fires them at his enemy.

Therefore, the Doctor, in doing all this, has been,
I am sorry to say, very foolish and very absurd.

Probo minorem. That he knows nothing about
the privilege of infallibility is very evident; for if
it were otherwise, he could not, surely, be ignorant
of the fact that this privilege, according to the
teaching of our Church, only attaches itself to acts
performed, as is said, *ex cathedra.*

What is the meaning of the term *ex cathedra?*
The Pope is said to speak *ex cathedra* when presiding over a council, or on his own authority, but
professedly acting as the visible head of the Church
and the Vicar of Christ, addressing himself to all
the faithful, in the name of the Blessed Apostles
Peter and Paul, formally invoked, or in equivalent
terms he solemnly decrees a definition of faith or
morals.

In such cases the acts of the Pope are said to be
infallible, and his decisions are accepted as the
decisions of the Holy Ghost. Whether Catholics

be right or wong in this belief, is not now the
question. I only wish to circumscribe the limits of
the privileges of infallibility; and from what I have
said, it is evident that this Bull of Adrian IV., being
only an act of temporal jurisdiction, is not, in the
most distant manner, connected with the infallibility of the Pope. Dr. Irvine should have known
this ; he should have distinguished between dog-
matic and disciplinary Bulls,—between acts of
spiritual and temporal authority, before he attempted
to fasten on the Vicar of Christ, *as such*, the responsibility of the annexation of Ireland to England
and the evils which it has caused to our country.

The next conclusion drawn from Mr. McGee's
words is very remarkable :

Thirdly : «The method of solemnizing marriage in
the Irish Church, as instituted by St. Patrick, and
observed by his successors for 700 years, could not
have been the Romish method. Why should the
Synod of Cashel introduce a new marriage-law into
the country, harmonizing it with the canons of the
Church of Rome, if St. Patrick had already done
so ? Every one, in the least degree familiar with the
marriage-law in Ireland since the famous Synod of
Cashel, knows that marriage is regarded as a *sacramental* vow,—that marriage is, in fact, a sacrament.
The inference, then, is, that from the time of St.
Patrick until the time of Henry II. a marriage was
not regarded as a sacrament by the Irish Church ;
therefore, the patron saint of Ireland must have held
views of the ordinance of marriage very different
from those enjoined and promulgated by the Synod
of Cashel.»

The Doctor says : «The method of solemnizing
marriage»—that is, the ritual or ceremonial observances—«in the Irish Church, as instituted by St.
Patrick, and observed by his successors for 700
years, could not have been the Roman method.»

Now, just one question : How does the Doctor know that this ceremonial was observed faithfully for 700 years? He told us, a short time ago, that this was the fabulous part of Irish history, and now he is able to trace, all through that time, the ceremonies of marriage, and assert that they were the very same in 1172 as they had been all through to the days of St. Patrick. But, if there are records so accurate on this one point, there must be also records on points of more general interest ; and if so, how can that period be the fabulous period of Irish history? But to proceed : « Why should the Synod of Cashel introduce a new marriage-law into the country, harmonizing it with the canon-law of the Church of Rome, if St. Patrick had already done so ?»

Bear in mind that this law, of which the Doctor is speaking, relates to ceremonial observances, according to his own words. But now he is going to make a leap :—« Every one in the least degree familiar with the marriage-law in Ireland since the famous Synod of Cashel, knows that marriage is regarded as a *sacramental* vow,—that it is, indeed, a *sacrament*.» Here he is crouching for a spring : « The inference, then, is, that from the time of St. Patrick until the time of Henry II. marriage was not regarded as a sacrament by the Irish Church.» There he's off. From the *ceremonies* of marriage he has leaped headlong into the *matter* of the sacrament itself, when, after a short struggle, he rises in triumph to the surface, bearing his *inference* aloft : « The Synod of Cashel made a change in the ceremonies of marriage ; therefore, marriage was not regarded as a sacrament for 700 years in Ireland !»

Really, ladies and gentlemen, the Doctor, besides being an enthusiast, is about the most reckless person, with regard to his logical reputation, that it has been my privilege ever to have met with.

I will now lay before you the true state of the question. The first canon or enactment orders that marriages shall not be contracted within the prohibited degrees. This, as you see, relates to discipline, and has no relation to dogma whatever. If abuses had crept in, by the intermarrying of persons too closely connected by relationship, the Synod was performing a duty in prohibiting it; and in doing so they made no alteration or innovation concerning marriage as a sacrament.

This is clear. But, even on the supposition that they had declared the law concerning the dogma of the sacrament, would it follow necessarily that they had introduced a change? Might it not be a reaffirmance of a law already known? I find the following passage in Mr. McGee's history. Speaking of the state of things in Ireland previous to the Norman invasion, he says:

Vol. I., folio, 139 :—«The attention of Rome was thoroughly aroused, and immediately after the appearance of the Life of Saint Malachy, Pope Eugenius III.—himself a monk of Clairvaulx—despatched Cardinal Papiron, with legantine powers, to correct abuses and establish a stricter discipline. After a tour of great part of the Island, the legate, with whom was associated Gilla-Criost, or Christianus, Bishop of Lismore, called the great Synod of Kells, early in the year after his arrival (March, 1152), at which simony, usury, concubinage, and other abuses, were formally condemned, and tythes were first decreed to be paid to the secular clergy.»

Now, if we follow Doctor Irvine's method of reasoning, we must come to the conclusion that, from the fact that enactments were made against those vices, they were not regarded as such from the time of St. Patrick until the year 1152.

The next conclusion is as follows:

Fourthly: «The method of catechizing children,

it seems, was different, from the days of St. Patrick
to the Synod of Cashel, from what it has been since.
As it appears that the Synod of Cashel enjoined
that children should be catechized at the door of the
Parish Church, the inference is that prior to that
time they were catechized in some other place.» * *

«Hence, again, we reach the inference that St.
Patrick must have established in Ireland a faith
which was not Romish, but essentially different in
its ordinances from that of Rome.»

Here, at last, is a fair conclusion. And how forcibly
it impresses itself on our minds I How strongly the
Doctor has brought it forth, notwithstanding the
depth of cogitation and the long study which it
must have cost him !

The children were to be catechized at the door of
the Parish Church ; hence, prior to that time they
must have been catechized somewhere else! Does
it not remind you forcibly of the deep observation
made in the story we used to repeat in childhood ?

"There was an old woman who lived on the hill,
And if she's not gone, she's living there still."

After the important discovery just mentioned,
the Doctor proceeds to inquire where that « other
place» could possibly be located. He declares that
charity will not allow him for a moment to suppose
that the children were catechized in the church,—
though, indeed, I cannot understand why he should
be so scrupulous in this case. Presently, remem-
bering that the « Old Culdees » of Scotland used to
cathechize in the family circle, he thinks it is most
reasonable to suppose that the Irish followed the
same method ; therefore, he says, St. Patrick *must*
have established a faith in Ireland which *essentially*
differed in its ordinances from the Romish faith.

One word about those . « Old Culdees.» Mr. Mc-
Gee says :

10

Vol. I., folio 24 :—« The growth of Iona was as the growth of the grain of mustard-seed mentioned in the Gospel, even during the life of its founder. Formed by his teaching and example, there went out from it apostles to Iceland, to the Orkneys, to Northumbria, to Man, and to South Britain. A hundred monasteries in Ireland looked to that exiled saint as their patriarch. His rule of monastic life, adopted either from the far East, from the recluses of the Thebaid, or from his great contemporary, Saint Benedict, was sought for by chiefs, bards, and converted Druids. Clients, seeking direction from his wisdom, or protection through his power, were constantly arriving and departing from his sacred isle. His days were divided between manual labor and the study and transcribing of the sacred Scriptures. He and his disciples, says the Venerable Bede, in whose age Iona still flourished, ' neither thought of nor loved anything in *this* world. ' Some writers have represented Columbkill's *Culdees* (which in English means simply ' Servants of God ') as a married clergy. So far is this from the truth, that we now know no woman was allowed to land on the Island, nor even a cow to be kept there ; for, said the holy Bishop, ' wherever there is a cow, there will be a woman ; and wherever there is a woman, there will be mischief.' »

Let the inference go by. I will certainly not insult your common-sense by refuting it. If, from the fact that an enactment was made relating to the *place* in which children were to be catechized, it can be justly inferred that *religion* was thereby changed, I must confess that I know nothing about the rules of logic or the requirements of faith. But this enactment was of a totally different import from that which the Doctor has given it, as may be seen by consulting the canons decreed by the Synod of Cashel, contained in the *Collection of Councils*.

The next conclusion has reference to the *Eirenachs.* These are the Doctor's words :

« *Fifthly :* It seems that the Synod of Cashel enact· ed a law abolishing *Eirenachs,* or lay trustees of church property. Such being the case, we are conducted to the conclusion that from the time of St. Patrick till the time of Pope Adrian IV. the Irish Church managed all her property by a lay trusteeship.   *   *   *   But as this was not a Romish practice, it follows that the Irish Church, during that period, be she what she may, could not have been Romish. »

The Doctor says that the Irish Church managed *all* her property by a lay trusteeship. This is an error, and I am quite at a loss to know how he could have fallen into it. It cannot be from his having read the Canons of the Synod, for the enact- ment alluded to runs thus :

«In the case of a murder by laymen and compo- sition with their enemies, clergymen who are the relations of such are not to pay part of the fine.» And further : « All ecclesiastical lands and property connected with them shall be exempt from the reactions of laymen. »

Now, does it not strike you that if the Doctor had just read over this enactment he would have un- derstood Mr. McGee's meaning, and have thus saved himself a deal of unnecessary trouble, whilst shun- ning a very palpable error ?

On the two final conclusions I will not dwell at any length ; for I do not—I cannot—think the Doctor was serious in delivering them.

He infers that the doctrine relating to baptism could not, by reason of another Canon of the Synod of Cashel, have been identical in the Irish and Roman churches.

Now, it is known that from the foundation of Christianity baptism has been regarded as a sacrament by Christians of every denomination. We know, too, that during the fifth and sixth centuries, and even up to the twelfth century, Irish missionaries were abroad on the continent as teachers of the Christian religion ; that they were received in Rome, and even commissioned by the Popes to preach and teach.

But if they differed from Rome concerning the very fundamental doctrine of baptism, can it be supposed, that Rome would have thus employed them ? Would they not have been treated as heretics ? We should have some accounts of this difference in dogma, as we have of the disciplinary difference concerning Easter and the tonsure. Yet, not one word has ever been heard on the point until Doctor Irvine thought proper to *infer* it. We must, therefore, look on this inference as having the same weight as his previous ones, and pass on to another subject,—merely referring him to the text of the Canon, from a slight study of which he will, no doubt, become convinced of his error.

He finally assures us that all the evils rising out of the tithe system in Ireland must be traced to the court of Rome, throwing, of course, on Mr. McGee's shoulders the greatest part of the responsibility of the assertion. This might be considered extremely childish, were it not evidently malignant.

A Synod of Catholic Bishops decree that their people shall pay tithes to their lawful and acknowledged pastors, and those on whom the law is imposed accept it as fair and equitable. But some time after, a new church is forcibly established in the midst of this same people, and though not received as an exponent of the true doctrine, the high hand of authority decrees that it must be supported by the people, that they must pay heavy tithes for the sustenance of its ministers.

The case comes under the cognizance of Doctor

Irvine, and he says :—« My friends, you are not satisfied with this new imposition ; yet, do not ask me to
pronounce judgment on it, for I will neither com-
mend nor condemn it. All I will say is, that the
fault—if fault there be—must be attributed to
Rome.» And with this very consoling observation
he lets the matter drop. Yet, I will venture to
assert that if the positions were reversed, the same
Reverend Doctor would not display such deep-
seated equanimity.

I have now terminated this part of my subject,
and am very happy at having done so, for I am free
to confess that the Doctor's inferences are sometimes very trying on the temper. It is quite a
meritorious act of patience to read them through
without being somewhat ruffled.

There is a story told of an Irishman who requested
an Italian organ-grinder to play « The Boyne Water.»
The artist consented, and, having set his keys, began
to wind out the notes of that very popular ditty ;
but he had hardly got through the first bar, when
Michael rushed at him, and, with a fierce gesture,
ordered him to stop instantly, if he set any value
on a whole head. « But, my God, said the Italian,
in extreme terror, did you not ask me to play this
tune ? » «I did,» replied the other, « but it was only
to see how much of it I could stand. »

I might almost say as much in the present instance, and I fear I could not have stood the Doctor's
logic much longer.

Seriously, it is to be deplored that Dr. Irvine
should have thus attempted to torture the phrases
and disfigure the meaning of a man whose voice is
silent—in the silence of the tomb. It is to be
deplored that, calling Mr. McGee his friend, he should
have thus laid at the door of his memory conclusions against which that friend would have been
the first to protest. Ah ! Mr. McGee was often told

by those who were true to him in the dark days of
misfortune that a smiling face and a flattering
tongue were no indications of heartfelt amity. We
have here a sad proof of it.

The revd. lecturer says : «Mr. McGee was an
accurate writer. Mr. McGee weighed all his conclusions, and Mr. McGee was my friend. But
knowing and feeling this, I do not hesitate publicly
to advance that from his writings may be fairly
drawn the following conclusions :—«The Church of
Rome was the guilty cause of the annexation of
Ireland to England. The early Church of Ireland
had no connexion with the Roman Church.» But
is this friendship? Could there be anything more
damaging to Mr. McGee than this? If the Doctor
had boldly-said that the facts and appreciations
covered by his celebrated *inferences* were taken
from White, as I think they are, or from some other
ejusdem generis, though I should differ with him in
his opinion, I would not blame him for following
them ; but when he endeavors to connect the name
of Mr. McGee with them, I say that he not only
misinterprets the historian, but maligns the man.
One man took away his life in the still hour of
night; but you, Doctor Irvine, in the light of day,
attempt to blast his fair name and blacken his
reputation in the eyes of his fellow-countrymen and
co-religionists.

Oh! frienship, how many crimes have been committed in thy name, since Judas first imprinted the
false kiss on our Saviour's cheek !

After closing his remarks relating to Mr. McGee's
work, Doctor Irvine, under the title of *Revolu-
tionary*, turns to that period of Irish history which
is connected with the downfall of the Stuarts and
the sanguinary wars that it entailed on our country.
With his strictures on that dynasty, and his very
ungracious allusion to the Scottish nation, I have

nothing to do; I shall, therefore, pass it over, and merely signalize for comment the following passage :

« It has been truly said that England needed some foreign aid to sustain her ; the wasted resources of the empire required the husbanding skill of some foreign and sagacious economist to check royal extravagance ; and all the qualities requisite to meet the emergency were found in William, Prince of Orange, the man who led the 'Prentice Boys' to shut the gates of Derry against a tempest of iron and lead, and before whose noble daring James fled from the Foyle to the Boyne, where he was overtaken by the man of ' immortal memory,' and after a single engagement bigotry and tyranny were cloven down, and the glorious Constitution of 1668 ratified, which secured civil and religious liberty to every subject of the British empire. It is worthy of special notice that whilst William drove the Stuarts from the throne of England, he never sought to denude the Irish Celt of his civil and religious liberty. »

Now, there is something so inaccurate in these statements, that it becomes a question whether Doctor Irvine has ever taken the trouble of reading this part of Irish history.

Bigotry and tyranny cloven down by the Williamites, forsooth ! The rights of the Irishman secured by the campaign which ended at Limerick ! But, in the name of history, what can the Doctor mean ?

The rights of liberty were *promised* to the Irish people by the treaty sworn to at Limerick ; but Limerick is called « the city of the broken treaty. » The ink was scarce dry on the parchment when it was torn to shreds and trampled under foot by the brutal ascendancy. Bigotry and tyranny were cloven down, you say. No, sir ! freedom and equal justice and disinterested loyalty were cloven down, for these were the principles upheld by the Irish

Catholic army ; these were the words emblazoned
on their banner, and it was that banner that went.
down in battle, though it sank not in disgrace.

" On our side is virtue and Erin;
On theirs is the Saxon and guilt. "

Liberty secured ! Tyranny cloven down !
Listen to the words of Mr. McGee :
Vol. 2, fol. 601 :—« In 1695 Lord Capel opened
the second Irish Parliament, summoned by King
William, in a speech in which he assured his
delighted auditors that the King was intent upon a
firm settlement of Ireland upon a Protestant interest. Large supplies were at once voted to His
Majesty, and the House of Commons then proceeded
to the appointment of a committee to consider what
penal laws were already in force against the
Catholics,—not for the purpose of repealing them,
but in order to add to their number. The principal
penal laws then in existence were :
« 1. An act subjecting all who upheld the jurisdiction of the See of Rome to the penalties of a pre-
munire, and ordering the oath of supremacy to be a
qualification for office of every kind, for holy orders,
and for a degree in the university ;
« 2. An act for the uniformity of Common Prayer,
imposing a fine of a shilling on all who should
absent themselves from places of worship of the
Established Church on Sundays ;
« 3. An act allowing the Chancellor to name a
guardian to the child of a Catholic ;
« 4. An act to prevent Catholics from becoming
private tutors in families without license from the
ordinaries of their several parishes and taking the
oath of supremacy.
« To these the new Parliament added : 1. An act
to deprive Catholics of the means of educating their
children at home or abroad, and to render them

incapable of being guardians of their own or any other person's children ; 2. An act to disarm the Catholics ; and, 3. Another to banish all the Catholic priests and prelates. Having thus violated the treaty, they gravely brought in a bill ' to confirm ' the Articles of Limerick. ' ' The very title of the ' bill, ' says Dr. Cooke Taylor, ' contains evidence of ' its injustice. ' It is styled, ' A bill for the confir- ' mation of articles ' (not *the* articles) ' made at the ' surrender of Limerick. ' And the preamble shews that the little word *the* was not accidentally ' omitted. It runs thus : ' That the said articles, or *so* ' *much of them as may consist with the safety and* ' *welfare of your Majesty's subjects in these Kingdoms*, may be confirmed,' &c.»

And it must be borne in mind that those odious penal enactments cannot be classed among the acts of inconsiderate cruelty ·which sometimes sully the first flush of triumph. They were a return to the past ; they were a new, a stronger manifestation of that systematic, cold-blooded persecution which had previously reigned, and which was to increase in intensity as years rolled on, grinding down the people into hopeless impotence, or goading them on to rebellion, so that an excuse might be found for the imposition of more oppressive laws.

This would hardly be believed in our times, when, thank God, the recurrence of such things is an impossibility. It is, nevertheless, true that the people were sometimes excited to revolt, in order to justify a harsh or unjust measure which had been resolved on. . ..

I again quote from Mr. McGee :

Vol. 2, folio 696:—«It is no longer matter of assertion merely, but simple matter of fact, that the English and Irish ministers of George III. regarded the insurrectionary movement of the United Irish- men as at once a pretext and a means for effecting

a legislative union between the two countries. Lord
Camden, the Viceroy who succeeded Lord Fitz-
william in March, 1795, with Mr. Pelham as his Chief
Secretary, in a letter to his relative, the Hon. Robert
Stewart, afterwards Lord Castlereagh, announced
this policy, in unmistakeable terms, so early as
1793 ; and all the official correspondence published
of late years, concerning that period of British and
Irish history, establishes the fact beyond the possi-
bility of denial.

«Such being the design, it was neither the wish
nor the interest of the Government that the insur-
rection should be suppressed unless the Irish constitution could be extinguished with it. To that
end they proceeded in the coercive legislation described in a previous chapter ; to that end they armed
with irresponsible power the military officers and
the oligarchical magistracy ; with that view they
quartered those yeomanry regiments which were
known to be composed of Orangemen, on the wretched peasantry of the most Catholic counties, while
the corps in which Catholics or United Irishmen were
most numerous were sent over to England, in exchange for Scotch fencibles and Welsh cavalry. The
outrages committed by all these volunteer troops,
but above all by the Orange yeomanry of the country, were so monstrous that the gallant and humane
Sir John Moore exclaimed : ' If I were an Irishman
I would be a rebel ! ' »

I shall, for the present, say no more on this unpleasant subject, into which I have been drawn by
the unblushing assertions of my reverend friend,
save to remark that if, as he tells us, the sun of
liberty rose in 1688, it shed no effulgence over
unhappy Ireland ; its bloodstained orb was, to her
inhabitants, but an object of terror and dismay.

The Doctor now directs his attention to the educa-
tional and moral department, and with his usual love

for conclusions, though without the slightest effort to be urbane, states that the Protestant portion of the population is far superior, in learning and moral training, to the Catholics.

These are his words:—« In the Province of Ulster there are 3449 day-schools, and in Connaught there are only 1524 day-schools. In Ulster there are 2086 Sabbath-schools, with 230,000 pupils. In Connaught there are 130 Sabbath-schools, with 800 children, chiefly Presbyterian. Thus it appears that Ulster, with a territory and population very little larger than Connaught, has twenty times as many schools ! In Ulster there are 437 Episcopal Ministers, 567 Presbyterian Ministers, 115 Methodist, or 1119 in all, while there are 376 Roman Catholic clergymen. In Connaught, again, there are 153 Episcopal, 18 Methodist, seven Presbyterian, and 352 Roman Catholic clergymen ; that is, in Ulster the Roman Catholic clergy are to the Presbyterian as 376 to 567, while in Connaught the ratio is as 352 to 7. Yet there are two acres in Ulster under cultivation to one in Connaught, treble the amount of live-stock, six-times as many day-schools, and five hundred times less crime in the Northern province than we find in that of the South.»

Now, I have followed the rev. lecturer over the grounds of history with ready willingness, and I shall be happy to meet him there again, if circumstances should require it ; but when to struggle against him I must run the risk of wounding the feelings of my Protestant fellow-citizens, I experience no desire for the fight ; and if I answer his challenge, I protest that I do so with extreme repugnance. A sentiment of kindly feeling exists between the Protestants and Catholics of our good old city, and has manifested itself with genial warmth on many occasions ; religious differences are not allowed to mar the harmony of our social intercourse ; and may it ever be so!

I will not, therefore, in courtesy to many kind Protestant friends who have done me the honor of assisting here to-night, make any attempt to confute the Doctor on this point, further than to lay before you all a statement which may be found in « Chambers's Miscellany,» a Scottish publication, vol. v., in the article « Ireland » :

« The total population of Ireland in 1861 was 5,764.543 ; of whom 4,505,414 were Roman Catholics, say 78 per cent. of the whole, and 1,292,819 non-Catholics, say 22 per cent. of the whole. Taking the number of pupils attending the national schools, we find that 486,206 were Catholics, 64,686 Presbyterians, 34,717 Episcopalians, and 3402 belonging to various denominations.»

Hence, the total number of pupils was 589.012 ; and since the Catholic pupils numbered 486,206, we have an average of 82 Catholic children out of every hundred attending school, which exceeds the Catholic percentage of the whole population.

Again, comparing the Catholic population with the Catholic pupils, we have an average of about 10 per cent. ; and making a similar comparison with regard to non-Catholics, we have a little less than 8 per cent. going to school.

But, without establishing any comparison between the different parties, I think that the proportion of Catholic children attending school goes far to prove that they have no desire to remain in ignorance. There are schools in almost every parish ; the clergy are untiring in their exertions in the cause of education ; and if there be any locality unprovided, the cause may be traced to extreme poverty, for which it were ungenerous to upbraid them. As to the tillage of the land, I am not sufficiently acquainted with agricultural matters to give an enlightened opinion on it ; but I fancy that Catholic farmers are just as industrious and as intelligent as

Protestants of the same class ; moreover, in the case of Connaught, I have been told that it is in many places marshy, and that in general the soil is better adapted for pasture-lands than for cultivation. It is not, indeed, fair, on the whole, to compare Connaught with Ulster; for the population of the latter is double that of the former, whilst the positional advantages of Ulster are infinitely greater. I shall not detain you any longer on a subject with which a great many of you are better acquainted than I am ; but before concluding, I beg permission, to make a few remarks on a suggestive and important statement which the Doctor has merely glanced over. He says : « Strange to say, from 1848 to 1855, no less than £7,500,000 sterling was sent from the United States alone, to sustain in and carry out of Ireland the friends and relations of those who had already emigrated from its shores.» Now, this one fact is worth a whole column of statistics on education and moral training. The best and noblest education is the education of the heart ; one of the best proofs of good moral training in the child is the love he has for father and mother, for it rarely subsists without being accompanied by many kindred virtues.

But who were those who, in seven years, sent as many millions sterling home to Ireland? I do not hesitate to say it : they were, with very few exceptions, the Irish Catholic sons and daughters of Irish Catholic parents. And whence did they gather these immense sums ? They were the proceeds of honest industry ; they were hoardings from scanty salaries, and the fruits of many deprivations. But they were more than that : they were high testimonials of moral worth, both in parents and children ; they were the natural outpourings of that warm affection and unbounded generosity which had its root deep down in their noble Irish hearts. And because their acts give the lie to the defamers of Irish character ; because they have given us reason to be proud of them ; because they have done that which is just and meritorious in the sight of heaven, —I say, may the Almighty God pour down His choicest blessings on them, whether living or dead !

Ladies and gentlemen, I feel that I have already trespassed too far on your kind attention ; and as there are limits to all things here below, even to the exercise of the sweet virtue of patience, I am admonished that, were it but for my own sake, I must soon close this lecture, already too long, by half. I will, therefore, allow myself but one word in conclusion. ·

I repeat what I said at the outset : I am sorry for having been, in a measure, obliged to appear on this occasion; I am sorry that, being a Catholic priest, I felt called upon to publicly contradict a Protestant clergyman ; but as there is no championship at stake, I trust that both lectures will be viewed solely as a literary quarrel between two students of history.

The Revd. Dr. Irvine spoke on Ireland probably because he loves Ireland ; but I love Ireland, too ; and thinking that the Doctor treated the object of his affection in rather a rough manner, I thought I would just let him know that I was not pleased with him ; so the upshot of it all was a brace of very long lectures, and in my case, I fear, a very tiresome one. However, they are both sealed and delivered now, and there is an end to our quarelling, unless the Doctor vouchsafes a reply, in which event, I suppose, you will have to assist at two more.

But, be this as it may, I hope that no ill-feelings shall arise out of this action, and sincerely disavow any intention of offending. ·

If, before retiring, I might offer an advice, I

would say to those amongst you who lay claim to
Irish birth or parentage : love deeply and well that
dear old land beyond the seas; cherish her traditions;
sing the music of her songs ; read her history—the
true history of her by-gone glories and weighty
grievances ; and in relation to those grievances,
many of which have been removed, some of which
still remain, I would add that it is our duty and our
right to be outspoken and frank. We must not fear
to express a vehement desire to see our brethren in
Ireland in the full enjoyment of freedom, and the
land cleansed from the unsightly remains of a once
cruel and powerful oppression. The man who
would seek treason in that wish, or disloyalty in its
expression, is only worthy of the silence of disdain !

" Contempt on the minion who calls you disloyal !
Though fierce to your foes, to your friends you are true ;
And the tribute most high to a head that is royal,
Is love from a heart that loves liberty, too !"

APPENDIX.

On Thursday, 23rd May, 1872, all that was mortal of the gifted young divine, Rev. P. J. Doherty ; of the brain so full of lively wit and repartee ; of the tongue so eloquent and entrancing; of the hand that guided that pen so facile,—all were returned to mother-earth amidst those marks of respect which humanity delights in paying to the memory of departed friends. The funeral left the Presbytery of St. Roch's at half-past nine, attended by an immense concourse of citizens. The arrangements, under the control of Mr. Marcoux, were perfect; and the attention of Captains Voyer and Heigham, in detailing a number of policemen to preserve order, was the subject of commendation on all sides. Immediately following the body were the relatives and friends of the deceased, succeeded by the members of the St. Patrick's Institute, who wore crape on their arms, and who mustered in large numbers to pay their last tribute of respect and love to him who had presided over them as their President, and to whom they were so largely indebted for many evenings of amusing and, at the same time, instructive intercourse. Through the kindness of the Rev. Mr. Charest, the *Curé*, these gentlemen were provided with seats in front of the Sanctuary.

Arrived at St. Roch's Church, which, from floor to ceiling, was heavily draped in black, the body was met at the door by a large concourse of clergymen, presided over by the Rev. Mr. Charest, who intoned the *Miserere* and other psalms peculiar to

([1]) Written by one of his many friends.

the occasion ; after which it was removed to the
Sanctuary, and placed, as is usual in the case of
deceased clergymen, with the head towards the
Altar, attended by Rev. Dr. Louis H. Paquet, Rev.
Messrs. Neville, V. Legaré, Maguire, Lepage, and
Marceau, as pall-bearers. Solemn High Mass was
then celebrated by the Ven. Vicar-General ʿCazeau,
Rev. Messrs. Plamondon and Rev. Dr. B. Paquet
acting as Deacon and Sub-Deacon, respectively—the
chanters being Rev. Messrs. Roy, Sirois, Godbout,
and Audette, and Rev. Mr. Lessard master of
ceremonies. Amongst the clergymen present were
Rev. Messrs. Bolduc, Bonneau, Drolet (St. Michel),
Boucher, Hamelin, Lemieux, and Harkin. The
precarious state of the health of the Rev. Mr. McGauran, coupled with the inclement weather, prevented
his attendance. His Grace the Archbishop was
absent at St. Anne's on business. During the Mass,
voluntaries were sung by members of the choir.

At the conclusion of the Mass, the *Libera* was also
sung by the choir in parts ; but previous to this,
Father Cazeau adressed those present. He said, in
substance :

« Not long since the parishioners of St. Roch were
called upon to mourn the loss of one of their priests,
the Rev. Mr. Catellier, who had devoted the fifteen
years of his sacerdotal life tó their service. To-day
they were again called upon to weep over the tomb
of Patrick Doherty,—of one who, though only comparatively a short time amongst them, had left an
impression that he was sure would be ever precious
to them. A few years ago the deceased had been
enabled to visit Europe ; to go to Rome ; to throw
himself at the feet of the Holy Father; and, above all,
to tread those sacred spots which had witnessed the
life on earth of our Redeemer, and which had been
bedewed with His sacred blood. A native of Canada, he had also been able to visit the place so dear

to him, the land of his fathers, beautiful Erin, which had so faithfully and so heroically kept the faith. Assiduous in the discharge of his duties in the confessional, he abandoned it only when he could not help doing so; delicate in health, he could not be kept out of the pulpit, where his persuasive eloquence never failed to entrance his hearers and to produce abundant fruit. An Irishman, he loved his French fellow-Catholics as he did his own countrymen, and for many a long day will his loss be remembered by both. The corn was, however, ready for the sickle; and Providence, in His own inscrutable ways, had thought proper to call him away,—and it was not for us, mortals, to question the decree. He died in the glorious month of Mary, and there could be no doubt that he was now enjoying the reward of the faithful servant; but as even the just have cause to tremble, he would conclude by imploring the prayers of his hearers for their deceased friend. »

The very reverend gentleman, who, many times during his address, seemed to be deeply affected by his theme, then said he would like to say a few words to his Irish friends, whom he saw present in such vast numbers; he would wish to repeat in English what he had just said in French, were he not deterred by his want of sufficient knowledge of the former. He would, therefore, content himself by expressing his sympathy with the Irish people of Quebec in the great loss they had sustained, and of assuring them that in this, the hour of their grief, they had the deepest sympathy of their French co-religionists.

The funeral procession then reformed, and the body was conveyed to the chapel of the Ursuline Convent, where, after the *Libera* had been sung in a most touching manner by the good Sisters, Very Rev. Mr. Cazeau presiding, assisted by

Rev. Messrs. Beaudet and Audette as Deacon and
Sub-Deacon, it was interred on the Gospel side of
the Sanctuary. All the stores in St. Joseph street,
as well as many of those in the Upper Town where
the procession passed, were closed ; and the bell of
St. Patrick's, during its progress through Palace
street, rung out its solemn reminder to the faithful
of their duty towards the soul of him whom they
loved so well.

On the following Sunday, in St. Patrick's, the
Rev. Mr. Neville, acting in the absence of Father
McGauran, took occasion to ask the prayers of the
congregation for the repose of the soul of the
lamented deceased. The rev. gentleman was himself much affected, and among his large audience
there were many moved to tears. He spoke to the
following effect :

« The sad and melancholy duty has fallen to me of
requesting the favour of your prayers, during this
Holy Sacrifice, for the repose of the soul of the late
P. J. Doherty, whose unexpected and almost sudden
death has evoked the deepest sympathy and regret
from all classes of the community. While reminding you of this last tribute of Catholic piety to the
lamented deceased, I do but interpret the feeling
of the whole community in saying that the early
demise of one so young and so gifted in the priest-
hood, has proved a severe blow and most painful
disappointment to the Church of this Archdiocese.
This feeling is perfectly intelligible to you, gentlemen of St. Patrick's congregation, who have been
privileged, with many others, to appreciate and admire the brilliancy of his talent and the eloquent
force of his action, both as a Catholic preacher and
an eloquent lecturer. The record of his brief
though eventful career is better expressed in those
forcible words of Holy writ, so eminently appli-
cable to the deceased : ' I will raise me up a faithful

priest, who shall do according to my heart and soul.'—(Kings, ii. 35.) A faithful priest he was to the Church of God, ever careful in guarding the trust she reposed in him.

« We know how unremittingly he labored for the great purpose so dear to his heart and soul, to which he generously devoted the best energies of a debilitated and exhausted frame. During the whole period of his sacerdotal career, he was ever faithful to the solemn engagements of his ordination, whereby the newly-ordained Priest is pledged to 'believe what he reads, to teach what he believes, and to practice what he teaches.' God, in His inscrutable designs, chose to recall him early in the day from the field of his useful labours ; but the summons came not before he had realized the ideal of his priestly mission, and had edified the house of God by the fruitfulness of his preaching and the example of his piety.

« May Our Lord Jesus Christ receive his soul in mercy, and grant him, through the favour of His Blessed Mother, whom he so fondly loved, a happy repose in His Heavenly Kingdom. »

Requiescat in pace.   M. F. W.

CONTENTS.